"DRAMATIC . . . REALISTIC . . . TOUGH . . . VIOLENT"
Hartford Courant

"An insider's story . . . Torres has dealt at close hand with the police and criminals . . . Q & A is skillfully constructed . . . smoothly written. Mr. Torres flashes street talk, ethnic insult and squad-car banter as casually and insistently as his detectives flash their badges. The atmosphere of street, precinct and D.A.'s office are authentic . . . the plot is swift and Mr. Torres is a facile storyteller."
The New York Times Book Review

"Truly a first rate story"
Miami Herald

Q & A

EDWIN TORRES

AVON
PUBLISHERS OF BARD, CAMELOT AND DISCUS BOOKS

To my father, Edelmiro Torres,
for the red tricycle
on that Christmas of 1935

Photograph of the author by Anthony Lipski.

AVON BOOKS
A division of
The Hearst Corporation
959 Eighth Avenue
New York, New York 10019

Copyright © 1977 by Edwin Torres
Published by arrangement with The Dial Press.
Library of Congress Catalog Card Number: 77-73929
ISBN: 0-380-01862-4

First Avon Printing, April, 1978

AVON TRADEMARK REG. U.S. PAT. OFF. AND IN
OTHER COUNTRIES, MARCA REGISTRADA,
HECHO EN U.S.A.

Printed in Canada

1 The elevated railroad bed loomed over the tenements and the avenue below, its underpasses straddling the crosstown streets of Spanish Harlem like a Roman aqueduct. The last train to the suburbs would pass just after midnight. It was overdue.

The bare bulb in the underpass at 107th was out, its metal grille creaking in the winter gusts that howled through. Out of the tunnel's darkness came two men. They headed west, hunched against the biting wind, the huge man's gloved right hand clamped across the back of the short man's neck.

They crossed the street, then advanced, hugging the building line. At the second tenement they turned and descended a flight of concrete steps, the tall man tilting his head as the low ceiling scraped his gray fedora. At the bottom of the steps he released his grip and shoved the other forward into a courtyard boxed by a wooden fence and the side of the tenement.

The frail man rubbed his neck as he went on alone into the alleyway and stopped at a large metal door. He knocked. The door swung open, and loud mambo music blared into the alley. Then it closed behind him as he quickly entered.

Snow blew off the rooftops and drifted slowly down on the bundled figure waiting in the darkness, his enormous frame barely visible in the shadow of the stairwell. The yard grew quiet.

The metal door opened again in a rush of loud voices and music. The small man emerged, bunched in his trenchcoat. A coatless man in a gaudy sport jacket appeared, momentarily framed in the light of the doorway as he stepped into the alley.

"She's over here," the small man said softly, glancing over his shoulder at Tony Roman. "She don't wanna come in."

The door banged shut. Roman hesitated, then with drunken, faltering gait he followed the small man toward the stairwell.

"Where is she?" Roman shouted. "Where's Julio's ol' lady? For Christ's sake, Roger, I sent them money already, carajo!"

Roman stopped and squinted into the blackness, his body swaying. The small man was gone.

"Roger? Roger, ya fuckin' faggot, where'd ya go?"

Only the wind sounded in the alley. Tony Roman, uneasy, pulled at the lapels of his jacket. Then *setup, setup* raced through his brain, even as a squeaky voice by the stairwell said, "Hello Tony."

The first bullet bore cleanly on a straight line through Roman's left cheekbone just below the eye. It elevated him to full height, with his right knee coming up as his body pivoted to the left, like a halfback evading a tackler. The second bullet crashed into his brain in an upward trajectory above the right ear, shattering a large portion of his skull. Poised on his left foot, this second impact jerked him—as if by piano wires—onto an empty garbage can. Rolling to his side, Roman twitched in a brief spasm; then his body curled inward and was still.

The door smashed open, and a crowd surged out into the alley. Lights flicked on in the apartments overhead and in the adjacent buildings. Windows grated open. "Qué pasa? Qué pasa?" someone shouted down.

The huge man in the black coat was squatting alongside the body of Tony Roman, the spread of his wide back obstructing the crumpled form. More people spilled into the alley.

"He killed Tony. Blew his head off."

He rose to his feet, a revolver in his gloved right hand, a police shield in his left.

"Brennan, lieutenant of police! Everybody stand where you are!"

Without shifting his gaze from the group, he pointed his shield upward at a man in an undershirt peering out of a first-floor window.

"Tú, call policía, call ambulancia. Comprende?"

"Sí, señor."

The men in the alley huddled together, whispering in Spanish, the doorway behind them jammed with wide-eyed faces.

"Nobody moves. You're all witnesses. See that pistol in his hand? See it? He tried to kill me. So nobody's going nowhere, except downtown. Especially you, Mauricio, this is your club." With his gun hand he motioned at a man wearing a black dinner jacket.

"Not me. I didn't see nothing, Lieutenant. I swear to my mother, I'm closed up. Right, guys?"

There was shouting and cursing; some of the men seemed to be restraining the others. Brennan was unperturbed. He knew crowds; he knew real trouble from smokestacking. The worst was over.

"Everybody quiet down. We wait for help. Maybe he ain't hurt too bad," Brennan said, changing to a soft, almost solicitous tone, but the darkness did not conceal the suggestion of a smile on his face.

Police sirens wailed in the distance. The outbursts subsided as the reality of "downtown" set in. Who needs that? The commotion ceased abruptly, the men assuming casual poses. They looked away from the gunman and the corpse, dispersing into little clusters and lighting up cigarettes, factory workers taking a break.

2 "Reilly? Is this Assistant District Attorney Aloysius Reilly?"

The words filtered out of the receiver into Reilly's ear. It was 3:00 A.M. He was on his back, enshrouded in a gauzy mist. Reilly's mind rallied enough for him to utter, "Yeah, yeah. Who's callin'?"

"This is Quinn. Quinn, chief of the Homicide Bureau, Office of the District Attorney, County of New York? You have *heard* of New York?"

The telephone lay on the pillow by Reilly's head, but the sounds seemed diffused in the darkness. Then, like an oncoming headlight, the name Quinn pierced the haze. Quinn, the boss! Jesus.

"Yes, sir. Yes, sir, this is me—he."

"Are you catching tonight, Reilly?"

"Uh—yes, yes, I am, sir."

"A little shaky there; settle down. All right, I've sent a squad car to pick you up. I've already alerted the duty stenographer; he's on his way. Take note of the time. It is now five minutes after three. You should be here by four A.M."

"What precinct is that, sir?"

"No precinct, Reilly. My office, sixth floor, the Homicide Bureau."

"Yes, sir, right away."

"Do you want to know what this is about?"

"Ah—"

"The Anthony Roman shooting. It's on the radio. If you move quickly, you can wrap the case up tonight. I will see you at four." The phone clicked, and Reilly hung up.

Jesus H. Christ. First night catching homicides and he had to land Tony Roman.

•

Reilly stumbled into the police car double-parked in front of his apartment building. A venetian blind rattled at a ground-floor window.

"I'm new in this building," he said sliding into the backseat. "By morning the super will want to know why the police locked me up last night."

The two uniformed men laughed.

"One fifty-five Leonard Street, boys. West Side Highway is good."

It was almost four when they arrived in front of the Criminal Court Building complex. Reilly took the elevator to the sixth floor. He walked the length of a long corridor to the Homicide Bureau office, the marble walls and floor reflecting his quick strides, then turned into a shorter hallway lined with office doors. Another right at the end brought Reilly into the office of the chief, a rectangular room, running north to south along Baxter Street. The motif, consistent with the perennial budget crisis, bespoke bare and untrammeled austerity.

Peter Quinn, chief of the Homicide Bureau, New York County District Attorney's Office, sat in a heavy leather chair behind a large oak desk. The only objects on the desk were a 1968 Clevenger-Gilbert and an open folder, which Quinn was examining intently. Credentials emblazoned the walls: Phi Beta Kappa, law review, numerous certifications of his admission to other jurisdictions. Reilly was impressed. He stood inside the doorway, almost at attention, waiting. Quinn still seemed to be absorbed. The night air gusted against the frosted windows. Just as Reilly parted his lips, Quinn glanced up and fastened on him.

Quinn's facial planes and complexion were of a Celtic mold familiar to Reilly. Arched black brows half encircled eyes that penetrated with the intensity of an El Greco inquisitor. The darkness of his hair and jowls stood out against the whiteness of his skin. Black Irish, thought Reilly; armada galleons run aground in the Irish Sea. Well, at least, the boss is one of mine.

"Close the door behind you, and sit down, please."

Irish as Paddy's pig, thought Reilly, disabused of his fantasy by Quinn's faint Boston accent.

Quinn rose and came halfway around the desk, his right hand extended. Reilly gauged him to be about five feet ten, a hundred and sixty pounds. Nicely turned out in a gray pinstripe suit, even at four in the morning.

"Thank you, Mr. Quinn."

They sat down across the desk from one another. Quinn tilted back in his chair and brought his fingertips together lightly in the form of a cage.

"Aloysius?"

"Aloysius Xavier, Mr. Quinn, but my friends call me Al."

"Background, Reilly, tell me about it."

"Oh, well—eh—let's see. I was raised in Queens—Elmhurst. Catholic schools, minor league baseball. I did seven years in the Twenty-third Precinct in Harlem. My father was a police officer, Frank Reilly, killed in the Three-Two—"

"What law school?"

"Brooklyn Law."

"You failed the bar the first time?"

"Yes, Chief, I couldn't get any time off for a bar review course."

Quinn leaned forward abruptly, his palms joined flat, his manicured fingers pressed against his chin.

"I do not believe in second chances, Reilly. This is an elite office. However, I understand the tragic circumstances of your father's death may have been weighed by the district attorney in evaluating your application for appointment as an assistant district attorney."

Reilly stiffened.

"Do not misunderstand. You have an ally in me. It was I, in fact, who persuaded the district attorney to place you in the Homicide Bureau. And it is I who see in you the makings of an able prosecutor."

"Thank you, sir."

"I told the district attorney, we have our fill here of Ivy League types. We need men who have served in the streets, who can appeal to the common sense of our average juror. That's why you are in my bureau."

"Thank you, sir."

"You will occupy the office next to mine, and you will function directly under my supervision. You will not take any action or make any decisions without first discussing them with me. You need seasoning. Is that understood, Reilly?"

"Yes, sir."

Quinn swiveled back, folded his hands in his lap, and smiled for the first time.

"Relax, Reilly. Tell me about the Twenty-third Precinct. You were there '61 through '67?"

"Yes, sir, on the street, radio motor patrol."

"Tell me, have you heard my name up there?"

"Eh, yes, that you were the chief of the Homicide Bureau. As a matter of fact, I saw you in the house one night."

"I mean on the street, Reilly."

"On the street? No. No, can't say that I did."

"Sometimes one wonders if the man in the street, in the ghetto, even knows of our efforts in his behalf. No matter."

"Everybody in law enforcement respects this office, Chief," Reilly said, suddenly animated.

Quinn swung his chair around, facing the window.

"I'm assigning you your first case. Deceased, one Anthony Roman."

"Yes, sir."

"Classic case of justifiable homicide. Roman, a notorious thug, attempted to ambush Lieutenant Brennan. You know Brennan?" Reilly nodded as Quinn continued. "The police commissioner's people have conducted a thorough investigation, and Brennan has been absolved. You will advise Brennan of his rights and proceed to take a statement from him. Do not go too rapidly. The duty stenographer is Lubin, and he is crotchety at this hour of the morning. One word of caution—and this applies at all times while you are an assistant in the Homicide Bureau—when you take a statement from a prospective defendant or a witness, make certain everything said and everything that happens is recorded by the stenographer. We had an incident here where an officer lost his head and struck a defendant while the statement was being taken. The assistant attorney failed to note this on the record. You can imagine the furor when this fact was brought out during the trial. Put it on the record; protect yourself at all times, Reilly."

"At all times, sir." Reilly nodded.

"They are all outside in the waiting room. Tell them to come in here, please."

•

Reilly walked down the hallway. Brennan. How could he forget Guido Brennan. His second year attached to the Twenty-third Precinct in Harlem. He had come back to the squad room from a coffee run. Grimy green walls, plaster chips scattered over the desks and typewriters.

Reilly pushed open the gate on the wooden railing with his foot, a box full of coffee containers in his hands. A slight black man sat quietly in a chair by the detention cage. His pants were caked with blood, the cuffs drenched, as though he'd been wading. He was handcuffed, his hands folded neatly in his lap. He whistled a low tune, eyes straight ahead, while three shirt-sleeved detectives circled the chair, their index fingers in his face.

"What's the trouble, fellas?" said a voice from the side.

Brennan. He stood by the squad commander's door like an upright marble slab, immense, immobile.

"DOA, his roommate, multiple stab wounds. We can't find the weapon, Lieutenant."

He slid across the room as if he was on ball bearings, his gray eyes blank. Putting his huge hand on the prisoner's shoulder, he stood over the man, his feet spread. The black raised his head slowly, as if scanning a cliff.

Brennan said, "Where is it?" in a low, squeaky voice, and hunched forward, his hand on his knee.

"Motha fuck you, ain't tellin you shit. Who the

hell're *you!*" the prisoner shouted, sputtering saliva into Brennan's face.

Brennan snapped back, then forward, gun in hand. "Die, nigger!"

Three shots cracked between the prisoner's legs. Reilly froze. Shit-or-go-blind time. The squad commander came running out of his office.

"What in the hell are you doing? What's—?"

"The knife's over the wall," the black screamed, lurching back against the chair. "I throwed it over the wall, at 108th. He gonna kill me, officer, he gonna kill me."

"Guido, put that away, for Christ's sake. Don't do that in my house. Jesus."

"Don't get excited, Vince. The guy made a move for my gun, and I hadda fire a few warning shots. Right, guys?"

The detectives nodded, as did Reilly.

Brennan motioned over one of the detectives. "This is your prisoner, Nat. *You're* supposed to get that statement. Be a cop, Nat. They spit in your face, and you think it's rainin'."

The older detective lowered his head.

Brennan pointed to a young Hispanic sprawled on the floor of the detention cage. "Now, you see that guy in the lockup. That's *my* prisoner, mine. In a little while he's gonna need a fix, and he's gonna start bangin' his head against the door. No statement? No fix, no ambulance. I'm holding you responsible. Be back at five. C'mon Chappie, we'll be late for the racket. Vince, I'll make out a D.D.5 later. See ya."

The black detective followed Brennan out the front.

"Who?—" Reilly asked.

"Guido Brennan, lieutenant of Homicide."

"What kind of name is that?"

"Half Italian, half Irish. The bad halves."

"Tough guy, ey?"

"The worst. Always the first guy goin' through the door, the window, the skylight. He's got all the medals, okay. But he's a killer, Al. He don't hesitate, he don't look twice, and he enjoys it. He is not a well man."

"He got the statement."

"That was my prisoner. Brennan doesn't give you a chance to talk to people. He's not supposed to do that. One of these nights, he'll step on his cock. Don't be around."

•

Reilly turned the corner into the waiting room. Brennan was crouched in the middle of four men, his arm thrust forward, his thumb and index finger imitating a gun. They laughed. Brennan saw Reilly. He lowered his hand as he rose to full height and smiled broadly, his small, dull gray eyes disappearing into the creases of his flat-planed face.

"Lieutenant, I'm Al Reilly. The chief just assigned me to present your case to the grand jury."

"My pleasure, Mr. Reilly. Since I'm kinda the guest of honor, allow me the introductions. This is Inspector Flynn, Lieutenant Keeley from the PC's office, Detective Valentin of the Twenty-third squad. He's working the case with Detective Chapman, here, from Homicide."

Reilly shook hands with each of them, feeling both nervous and a little exhilarated at the deference being accorded by the department brass and the two line detectives.

"Gentlemen," he announced, "Mr. Quinn wants us all in his office to take the statement from Lieutenant Brennan."

"Mr. Reilly, Valentin tells me you used to work in the Two-Three."

"That's right, Lieutenant."

"About time they brought from up there"—Brennan pointed north—"down here."

The other four men nodded and mumbled accord.

"Thank you, Lieutenant. Is the stenographer here yet?"

The black detective said, "If you mean the little guy with the satchel, he's in the corner, fast asleep."

Stanley Lubin, the senior stenographer, sat in a chair, wrapped tightly in his overcoat, the collar pulled up to a hat covering his closed eyes. Lubin detested night work, but, an insomniac, he seemed able to sleep only on chairs and desks.

"Mr. Lubin," Reilly said. "Mr. Lubin."

"Wha—what?"

"Shall we?"

Reilly led the policemen to Quinn's office, with Lubin shambling behind, muttering to himself. Quinn stood behind his desk. When they had all filed in, he addressed the group.

"Gentlemen, I have assigned Mr. Reilly the presentation of this case to the grand jury. I have chosen to expedite matters so as to minimize neighborhood unrest and possible charges of cover-up. Unfortunately, we have all had experience with this phenomenon."

All nodded vigorous agreement, and Quinn continued, "And apropos of that I might add—Lubin, are you asleep again?"

"Eh—no, no, sir. I've got every word down," Lubin stammered, still wrapped in his hat and coat.

"Fool, you have not even taken your machine from its case yet," Quinn said, his face reddening.

"Sorry, sir. Right away," Lubin had rallied and was setting his stenotype machine atop its tripod stand.

"You will start taking Lieutenant Brennan's statement when Mr. Reilly so instructs. He has charge. I want a transcript of this statement on my desk by noon today. Understood, Lubin?"

"Yes, sir."

"Proceed with your question and answer, Mr. Reilly."

"Thank you, sir. Ready, Mr. Lubin?"

"Yes, sir."

"Lieutenant Brennan, my name is Aloysius Xavier Reilly, and I'm an assistant district attorney, Homicide Bureau, New York County. And we are at 155 Leonard Street, sixth floor, in the office of Mr. Peter Quinn, chief of the Homicide Bureau. Would all present please give their name, shield, and assignment to the stenographer before leaving. Thank you. Now, before we proceed any further, Lieutenant, you are acquainted with the requirements of the *Miranda* ruling, are you not?"

"Yes, Mr. Reilly. I've given them often enough in the last two years."

"Good. Still, I must advise you that you are under no obligation to make a statement but that if you choose to make a statement, that statement may be used against you and, further, that you have a right to seek the advice of counsel or have counsel present, and if you lack funds to hire counsel, you will be provided one free of charge. Is that clear, Lieutenant?"

"Perfectly, Mr. Reilly."

"Right. Now, Lieutenant Brennan, I'm going to ask you about the events of last night—I mean, this morning. What time was it?"

"It was around twelve thirty."

"Mr. Reilly, midnight would be this morning."

"Yes, Mr. Quinn, that's right. Approximately twelve thirty this morning, December 9, 1968, something happened; is that right, Lieutenant?"

"Correct, Mr. Reilly."

"Where did this something happen, Lieutenant?"

"At 81 East 107th Street, City and County of New York."

"Tell us in your own words what happened."

Quinn swiveled impatiently. "Reilly, in what other words could he tell what happened?"

"That's right, Mr. Quinn. Eh—Lieutenant, tell us what happened, please."

"Earlier this evening, before midnight, I was at the Twenty-third squad, situated on 104th Street between Lexington and Third Avenues. I was there in connection with the investigation of the homicide of one Julio Sierra, male Hispanic. Investigation had revealed that this deceased Sierra was a lifelong associate and friend of the deceased in the present case, Anthony Roman. And I was in receipt of information from a reliable informant that Sierra had cheated Roman out of a large sum of money in a narcotics transaction. Roman's yellow sheet indicated a long history of violence. Mr. Roman was considered a prime suspect in the gunshot murder of Mr. Sierra, the previous deceased.

"Okay, so a little after midnight, I get a phone call from a reliable informant telling me that the said Anthony Roman is in the after-hours establishment in the basement of 81 East 107th Street, City and County of New York. Realizing that the said Roman is wanted for possible connection with a homicide, I immediately looked for my partner, Chappie—Detective Horace Chapman, but unfortunately, he is previously tied up from another assignment."

The black detective, leaning against the wall behind Brennan, nodded.

"Seeing my duty, I immediately drive down to 107th Street and Park Avenue. I parked my car facing west— the street runs west—on the east side of the tunnel on Park Avenue. I then walked west to this building situated near the northwest corner of 107th Street. The door to the club was open. I heard music, a few people there. I saw the deceased, Anthony Roman, whom I know from previous encounters as Tony. I said, 'Tony, c'mere. I want to talk to you.' No fuss, no argument. I'm nonchalant; I don't expect nothing. He comes out in the alley with me, and I'm talking nice to him about Julio Sierra, when all of a sudden he pulls out this cannon, yelling, 'I'll kill you, you mother fucker,' or words to that effect.

"You know, in the heat of the moment you can't be exact about words, but near as I can remember, that's what he said. It was pitch-black. I don't mind saying I was very frightened. He's a known shooter. So, in fear of my life, I immediately retaliated and drew my gun and shot him twice.

"I could hardly see him, but God was with me, and both bullets hit him in the head. This I found out later, of course. Whereupon, the people from the after-hours joint—eh, club—came out and started screaming and accusing me of all kinds of things. I had to use necessary force to subdue them and hold them at bay until reinforcements came. The deceased was on the ground with a Colt .45 caliber automatic in his right hand. I understand it had a round in the chamber. Ballistics is checking now to see if it is the same gun that killed Julio Sierra, as it is known he was killed with a .45 caliber bullet in the base of his skull.

"That's about it, Mr. Reilly, except that I'm sick that a human life was lost, but it was him or me."

"Jeeze, Lieutenant, you certainly covered everything."

Lubin looked up from his machine. "You want that last remark of yours on this record, Mr. Reilly?"

"Uh—"

Quinn broke in before Reilly could answer. "That was a refreshingly spontaneous remark and should be included as a part of this record, Mr. Reilly. Lubin, just write down everything you hear, will you please?"

"I think we have a full statement, Lieutenant."

"I'll be happy to answer any questions, Mr. Reilly."

"Ah—we have no more questions to ask. Do we, Mr. Quinn?"

"That determination is yours to make, Reilly."

"Okay, end of statement. Thank you, Lieutenant Brennan. Thank you all."

Quinn gestured to Lubin and said, "Go home and get some rest. The responsibilities of high office are weighing heavily upon your shoulders, Lubin."

"Chief Quinn, I've spent most of my life in this business, taking Q and A's by the thousands. But I'm getting old, and these hours are rough on me. You know I got mugged going home."

"Yes, you were quite conspicuous last winter in your neck brace. Good night, Lubin."

Lubin drew his pouchy features into a scowl and shuffled in the direction of the door, the stenotype machine in his right hand. His whole frame seemed to veer crazily to the right, as if the machine was a suction tilting everything toward it.

Deputy Inspector Flynn started to light a cigar as he got up.

"Inspector, please"—Quinn held up his hand—"I'm

allergic. Gentlemen, it has been a long day. Thank you for your cooperation. Good night. Reilly, stay a few minutes, please."

Reilly escorted the group to the door, then returned to Quinn's desk.

"Reilly, you handled that very well."

"Thank you, sir, but it's a cut-and-dried situation."

"I'll concede that. Nonetheless, it's an excellent case for you to cut your eyeteeth on. All right, let's take stock. First, Detectives Valentin and Chapman. I know their reputations. Two excellent men. Valentin, a Puerto Rican with vast experience in Spanish Harlem, and Chapman, long a legend in the black community. I do not like my assistants going out in the field. You are a lawyer, not a cop. Accordingly, your vantage point is this office, under my supervision. Valentin and Chapman will be your arms and legs. Understood?"

"Yes, sir."

"Essentially, all you will need for your presentation to the grand jury will be a statement from Brennan's informant, whose identity you will shield from all eyes, a statement from those present at the club, the ballistics report, and the autopsy."

"I'll get on it first thing in the morning, Chief."

"You're entitled to have the day off, as you have been up all night."

"No, I'll be here in the morning."

"That *is* the spirit, Reilly. I am expecting great things of you. Do not let me down."

"I'll do my best, Chief."

Quinn leaned his head back, his hands resting on his chest, fingertips lightly tapping one another.

"Forceful personality, the lieutenant."

"I have seen him move, sir, like a cat."

"More like a tiger."

3 Reilly tapped the sheaf of papers into a neat rectangle and placed them on the edge of his desk, then turned his attention to the two detectives.

"Suppose we get on a first name basis. I'm Al."

"Right." Horace Chapman grinned. "I'm Chappie; this is Johnny. I'm the Homicide man; Johnny is the squad guy. We put time on this thing over the weekend and have it pretty much wrapped up. Guido will probably get another commendation for it. The gun found on the deceased was the same gun that iced Julio Sierra."

"No shit, you already checked it out?"

"Yeah, the PC's office had Ballistics move their ass on this one. The bullet in Sierra's head was almost intact. The rifling and the ridges match up perfect with Roman's .45. And Roman didn't pick up the shell which ejected near Sierra's body, so we got that, too. Matches up perfect with the firing pin on the .45."

"We're going to wrap up two homicides, boys," Reilly said, putting both feet up on his desk and clasping his hands behind his head, smiling expansively.

"Quite an introduction to the Homicide Bureau, Mr. Reilly," Valentin said in a respectful tone.

"Call me Al, Johnny. Listen, I spent all my time on

the force in your precinct. I rode with Mullins, with Stokes"—Reilly lowered his feet to the floor and swiveled his chair forward, picking the names off his fingers —"Sabartelli, Forenzi—all them guys."

"Mullins, huh?" Chapman said. "That fucking Jimmy Mullins did his whole stint in uniform."

"Some guys are happier that way," Valentin insisted. "Besides, it wasn't like when we came on, Chappie. In those days one big collar and you were in the Detective Bureau. But now they flop you for nothing, shoofly all over," Valentin said, pointing his thumb downward.

"Yeah, I had to do seven years standing up." Reilly was bitter. "Couldn't even get into plainclothes."

"You mean an Irish guy like you didn't have no rabbi? I don't believe it," Chapman said.

"Rabbi? All my bosses broke my balls, said I didn't have my mind on the job, what with law school and all. I didn't get any cooperation."

"I'm starting law school myself," said Chapman. "By the time I get my twenty in, I'll be a lawyer."

"Yeah, and my father was killed on the job, up in the Three-Two, Francis Xavier Reilly." Reilly's eyes went from Chapman to Valentin, then to the wall to his right.

"Frank Reilly. I heard of him." Chapman sat up from his slumped position. "They got his picture up on the wall in the Three-Two."

"It's a rotten job," Valentin added, shaking his head.

"Yeah, piece of shit," Chapman said with a heavy sigh.

The three of them fell silent. Then Reilly's chair squeaked as he propped his feet back up on the desk.

"Tell me about Guido Brennan, Chappie. I've been hearing stories about him for years."

"What can I tell you. The guy's unreal. Guido's bulletproof, knifeproof, a hundred proof—you name it.

You ought to see him use his hands. Years ago, up-town, you'd get some big bad ass terrorizing a bar; owner would talk to Guido. *What?* Where's this guy? You the main gorilla around here? You and me, into the alley. Don't worry about the gun or the badge; he's holding it for me. Never saw anyone go more than three minutes with him, even some of the ex-pug ringers the Eyetalians would set up. Out, baby, like a lamppost fell on 'em. He was the heavy champ at Lejeune, y' know. Good war record, too. Was with the First Marine Division in Korea. He was at the Reservoir. The DIs at Parris Island were still talking about him when I was down there."

"You guys go back a ways then, huh?"

"We met on the job." Chapman shrugged. "He liked the way I worked and took me under his wing. Plus the fact that I'd been in the marines."

"I'll tell you one about Brennan." Valentin raised his finger. "Two years ago, when I first came into the Two-Three, there was a cat named Curtis Hayworth, a bad spook."

"I always knew you was a racist, rice-'n'-beans, jive-ass Po' Rican," Chapman said, narrowing his eyes in a mock scowl.

"Fuck you, jungle bunny," Valentin countered, his tongue puffing his cheek out.

"You ain't nothin' but a nigger with straight hair," Chapman shot back.

"Dig who's talkin'. Wasn't but yesterday you was conkin' yo' head with a steam iron at your ol' lady's beauty parlor," Valentin said, pressing his hands against his hair.

"Hey, take it easy. What's going on?" Reilly interjected.

"Just running a lil' game of the dozens, Al. Don't

mean nothin'. Go ahead, John, tell him how it went down."

"This the same guy that chased the detective out of the joint in the Heights."

"Who was the cop?" asked Reilly.

"From the Two-Three," Chapman answered.

"Bullshit, you don't know that," Valentin said.

"What happened?"

"Story is that Curtis was at the bar, Cal's Corner, on Broadway. This cop in plain clothes recognized him and made like a half grab for him. Curtis woofed him. 'You got yours, and I got mine, so make your play. Only one of us gonna be lucky.' So the bull turned tail. Like, he's gonna live to fight another day."

"He dogged it," Reilly said, nodding. "I heard about it."

"Anyway, this Curtis was blowin' people up all over the neighborhood, mostly policy and dope guys that wouldn't ante up, but still—anyway, this night he iced Cool Breeze, a pimp on 110th Street off Fifth. You know, near the garage over there? Anyway, me and Nat Zucker—you know Nat, Chappie—me and Nat chase this Curtis to 111th Street near Madison. He's firing at us with a big fuckin' cannon, look like a machine gun pistol. *Brrracatacatak*. He's blowin' up store windows, cars, everybody. Me and Nat ain't crazy about the idea, but we finally holed him up in his pad at 111th Street, top floor. We get uniformed guys on the roof and on the street in case he comes down the fire escape, but he ain't movin'. Me and Nat park outside the door. Mind you, Nat Zucker's already got over twenty years on the job. Nat says, 'We're not doing anything crazy. We're waiting for the gas and the flak jackets.' Which is okay with me. What the hell. Anyway, Brennan comes runnin' up the stairs, with Chappie, here, behind him.

'Where is he?' says Brennan, 'What are you doin'? Out of the fuckin' way.' And he whips out a second piece from a leg holster. So now, a gun in each hand, he goes through the fuckin' door like he was Frankenstein or somebody. Bam, boom—a fuckin' war. Then Chappie runs in, with me and Nat behind. Ol' Curtis was already a former bad ass."

"Dead, huh?" Reilly's eyes were wide.

"Deadest mother fucker you ever saw," Chapman said, chuckling.

"Two guns, eh?"

"He best to have had them. Curtis was takin' *everybody* with him."

"Big balls," Valentin said, forming semicircles with his curled thumbs and index fingers.

Chapman nodded. "Smart, too. Knows the street. He'll make anybody. Who got the gun, who got the skag. If you're dirty, Guido will read you. Guido will tell you, 'See that skell in the dirty sneakers? He can't afford no gun, but he will tire-iron the first john that turns the corner.' Wap! Another john gone. Or like black leather jackets. He'll follow anyone wearin' one, especially in July in the park. 'Another Central Park commando,' he'd say, 'crawling around the bushes on his elbows lookin' to pounce on any couple makin' out.' Yeah, Guido used to say they ought to cornhole the chump, too, for bringing his girl in the park at two in the morning. He's a tough guy, but he's all right. Somethin' else about him—he's okay on race. He hates all groups, kicks everybody's ass, so that makes him a liberal. He has stepped between me and a bullet, and we ain't the same shade."

"Say *that* again," Valentin said, his expression blank.

"Fuck you, Puerto Rican." Chapman turned to glare at Valentin.

"He's half Irish, right?" Reilly asked.

"That's the half he hates. Seems his Irish old man was rough on him and his momma, who's Italian. Booze. That's why Guido doesn't drink. Don't ever make fun of his name, either. He gets very hairy about that."

"Oh, great." Reilly glanced at his watch. "Okay, give me the rundown on the witnesses," he said, taking out a pad of yellow paper from his top drawer.

Valentin flipped open a small notebook.

"Here's the list. Mostly knock-around guys, not too many people. It was early for an after-hours joint. You got Santo Rivera, Maxie Correa, Angel Delgado—"

"All these Puerto Ricans is saints and angels," Chapman said, affecting a tone of wonderment.

Valentin scowled. "Fuck you, night fighter. You got Edward DeJesus—don't break balls—Manuel Obregon, Luis Alvarado, Joseph Castillo, Mauricio Valdes, Roberto Texidor, also known as Bobby Tex." Valentin looked up. "Yeah, the one and only."

"Bobby Tex?" Reilly asked.

Valentin nodded. "That's not the only funny fish that come up in the net. You got two scungeel in there, too."

"Italians?" Reilly said.

"Yeah, you got Lorenzo Franconi, a/k/a Larry Pesh, and his bodyguard, Bruno Calabrese."

"Bobby Tex and Larry Pesh in a cheap bottle club together," Reilly said, stifling a yawn.

"Two balls in the side pocket." Chapman simulated a pool hall pose.

"Yeah, Larry Pesh is on Pleasant Avenue, but he got heavy hooks downtown. He's a regular mob guy, a boss. What's he doing in a PR dive like that?"

Chapman shrugged. "Bobby Tex is a PR."

Reilly shook his head. "Yes, but very heavy. Bobby Tex was already living in Sutton Place when I was still on the street in the Twenty-third Precinct."

"No question he's the heaviest hangin' Puerto Rican with the mob." Valentin grunted, looking put out. "Jesus, to think I used to see that guy playin' stickball in the street. Now he's livin' in Sutton Place, and me with my in-laws around my neck. I can't even move out of the fuckin' projects."

"That's the trouble with you PRs. You breed like rabbits, don't wanna work, and now you want the Welfare to put you in Sutton Place."

"Fuck you, darker-than-me. Anyway, this Bobby Tex became the main junk connection uptown, but he had to whack out a few tumbe artists—"

"What's that toom-bay?" Reilly asked.

"Beaters, cheaters, guys that take the junk on consignment and then glom the money. Yeah, he got leery after the second homicide, and he moved downtown. His number-one man, Tony Roman—the *late* Tony Roman—was runnin' everything for him, and Bobby Tex been tryin' to get into show biz and society crowds."

Chapman said, "Yeah, an uppity PR. I been hearin' about some of his parties. Had the whole cast of a Broadway show over to his duplex, including the band. Hear they had to bring the coke in a wheelbarrow. He's a real candy man, our boy Bobby Tex. He's got the best heads, the best threads—for now. He won't last. He'll pull some swindle on the wops, and they'll put a contract on him. These PRs ain't got no smarts."

Valentin looked indignant. "As a matter of fact, Bobby Tex is a very slick dude, good rap and is a handsome sombitch."

"He must have a lot of women," Reilly agreed.

"As a matter of fact, he got one steady old lady he don't go nowhere without. She was there at the club, too; got her name on the list. Una salvaje—a savage. Nancy, Nancy Bosch."

"That mother fucker!" Reilly slammed a drawer and shot to his feet, the chair rocking and squeaking on its springs.

Chapman and Valentin locked glances. Chapman held up his hand as if to deter Valentin, but Valentin said, "What was that, Mr. Reilly?"

There was no reply.

"That's what I thought he said," Chapman said.

Reilly stood rigid, his face reddening. He put his hands in his pockets and walked to the window. He stood there, his back to the two detectives. Chapman glowered at Valentin, who remained silent.

"You guys go to lunch. I'll see you at two o'clock. I have to make a few phone calls."

Chapman rose quickly. Valentin sat, looking puzzled, staring at Reilly's back. Chapman gripped Valentin by the elbow, motioning with his head. They left Reilly by the window, closing the door quietly behind them.

•

Four years. The summer of 1964. He and Mullins had parked in the shade of the trees on the west side of Fifth Avenue, near 106th Street, to kill what was left of the tour. Mullins was dozing behind the wheel; Reilly was outside the car, leaning against the fender. Two Latin girls came walking out of the park, wearing shorts and sneakers. They were giggling and laughing. The short one was round-faced, with curly light brown hair. Cute. The other one . . .

She was eighteen that summer.

"You girls should be more careful. This park can be dangerous for unescorted females."

He winced at his own clumsy overture, but the girls laughed and appeared friendly. They drew closer. He stared at her. Long, black, Oriental hair, down almost beyond the white T-shirt she wore. The sun, filtering through the swaying leaves, danced up and down the brown freckles on her nose, her eyes crinkling deeply as she laughed with her friend. He could see the dimples at the corners of her mouth and imperfect eyeteeth in the whiteness of a smile that played off the burnished color of her high cheekbones. It was just no contest. She had a special message for him. He would have traded his uniform, gun, and badge for a rib shirt and a top-floor fire-escape walk-up with her, right there. It was settled in his mind that rapidly.

The short one spoke first. "Are you going to give us a summons, officer?"

"I would, but I don't know your names."

"I'm Betty Boop," she said.

"I'm Alley Oop," said Reilly.

The three of them laughed, but the tall girl said nothing, just her teeth and eyes glistening in his face. There was a lull, an awkward nodding of heads; then the girls turned abruptly and started walking northward along the east wall of the park. Jesus, Mary, and Joseph. Wait a minute. Do something, say something, Reilly, you asshole. In midstride, ten paces away, she stopped, spun around, flipping her hair back, and walked back toward him. He met her halfway, removing his hat.

"I'm Nancy Bosch," she said.

"I'm Al Reilly, and I think I'm in love with you."

"Wha—you must be sunstroke. I think I'll call a cop."

"Lady, have them carry me across the street. I'm blood type A."

"Estas loco. Elsie says you bleach your hair."

They were both laughing. Reilly put his hand on her forearm. Baby-kitten smooth.

"Where do you want to go tonight? Where do you want to go? Monte Carlo, Cannes, name it," he said.

"Mais non, m'sieur. What is better than to summer in the barrio?"

The short one, Elsie, chimed in, annoyed, "Nancy, come on."

Nancy searched his face intently; then she said, "I live on 108th Street near Madison Avenue."

"Eight o'clock. Cohn's Drugstore."

She crossed the avenue diagonally with her friend. He stepped off the curb beyond the parked cars and watched as she walked north. Near the corner, she turned her head toward him. At that instant he felt a subtle undertow, a warm current, course through him that would be years in abating. He stuck both arms out and up, as if imploring some divinity. She laughed, stood on tiptoes, and waving, turned the corner. Her smile and the symmetry of her pretty legs etched itself into his memory, an image to be drawn upon like a snapshot you pull out from time to time. There were such girl-phantoms around, but always with someone else at the next table or holding another guy's hand. Nancy was of that tribe.

Reilly put his hat on and walked back to the squad car. He felt as if coils inside him were priming. A priest exiting down the hospital ramp smiled, and Reilly doffed his hat again. He slid into the front seat. Mullins's eyes were half-lidded, his mouth slightly open and emitting a light whistle. The pot of his belly pressed against the steering wheel.

A cooling breeze came up, and Reilly went into his own trance. Mullins's Saint Christopher statuette on the dashboard reminded him of his father. A widower for a long time, he'd had an eye for a pretty face. Maybe not for Nancy. She was Harlem, Puerto Rican. "C'mon, fuck it."

Mullins's eyes opened. "Fuck who? You hump, think I'm asleep?"

"Talking to myself, Jimmy."

Officer Mullins looked at his watch and started the motor up, yawning.

"Another day, another dollar. Let's head for the lockers. I'm goin' to the trotters tonight."

•

The sinking sun was level with the trees in the park when he saw her step out beyond the building and turn the corner. Reilly was a block away on 107th and Madison. He wanted to see her do this sidewalk.

Her long, tawny legs in white heels reached out under a simple white dress that swayed with her every stride. Even her hair seemed to undulate to the same cadence. She would have been a feast anywhere, but that evening she was a banquet all by herself, and she had to run the gauntlet. First the two butchers from the corner shop; one took his apron off and laid it on the sidewalk behind her as she passed. Then the guy from Sonny's Luncheonette came tumbling out to the sidewalk. She never hesitated, never flinched. Now the crew from the Mayorquina Bar stepped out, one guy sweeping the floor with a handkerchief. He could make out the Spanish for phenomenon, vampire, goddess, and various threats of suicide. Demonstrative they were, but there was an element of respect in the banter. They knew her; she had been raised in that neighborhood. Yet Reilly thought it was more in the way she carried herself. She was just a special person.

Abreast of the photo studio, she saw him. He was in sport clothes. She gave a little skip and broke into a big smile.

Whatever I've got to do, he thought, I'm going to do. Period.

The glare of the row of faces along the sidewalk remained fixed as they met. There seemed to be someone visible at every window overhead.

"Hello, Nancy."

"Hi ya, Big Al. How's your sunstroke?"

"I think I'm having a relapse."

Reilly staggered as if he was going to faint, and Nancy's shiny-eyed smile rewarded him for his joke.

They went down to the Village, Raffaela's, near Thompson Street. By the end of the meal, he wanted to go off someplace with her for the rest of his life. She spoke animatedly about her Regents scholarship, her first year at the CCNY uptown center, her projects in Spanish literature (her major). He asked many questions, but the wine and exhilaration welling up had him high. He ran the backs of his fingers lightly over her cheeks and through her hair, stroking the loose strands around her face as if they were strings from which sounds could be plucked. Finally, she held his hand against her cheek. He leaned over the table and kissed her.

"What am I going to do with you, Nancy?"

"You're going to take me home. I have a class in the morning."

"I'm enrolling in your school."

"We don't have a law school, Al."

"Mexican pottery, whatever. I'm going with you."

Not a day went by the rest of that summer and fall that they were not together. They were deep into one another. And he kicked it over. And now, four years later, she reemerges as the woman of this pimp-faced—

The phone on his desk rang, jangling Reilly out of his reverie.

"Reilly here."

"You ready for lunch, Al?" It was Leon Blumenfeld, chief of the Indictment Bureau.

"Oh, yeah, Leon, I'll see you in the lobby. Where we going?"

"Let's go to Forlini's."

"Okay, see you downstairs."

4 "Mario, tell Frank we can't wait. We'll eat right at the bar," said Leon Blumenfeld to a waiter as he and Reilly turned away from the door of the dining room. They propped themselves on stools at the short shoulder of the bar, backs to the window, facing the interior of the room. Blumenfeld adjusted his black plastic-framed glasses as he looked around the room.

"Ever see anything like it, Al. You got judges at one table, DAs at another, and next to both, a table of defendants."

"Everybody's got to eat, Leon."

"Not everybody." Blumenfeld motioned to the bartender. "Give me a double, Tulio. And give my gumba over here a drink. We'll eat later. Give him a Scotch and soda."

Blumenfeld continued casing the room, squinting behind his thick lenses.

"Son of a bitch! Look at that Richie Schoenbaum, over here, in the booth. With the alligator shoes and the silk suit. Five years ago, he showed up in the building with the pants from one suit and the jacket from another and patches on both. Lookit 'im. Fuckin' thief. You go in on a disorderly conduct with him; you come out with a murder conviction. He's making money, and I'm over here pullin' my pork."

"Leon, everybody knows these guys can't shine your shoes."

"I been in the office thirty years. I shoulda left long ago. Made some money. Molly deserves better."

Reilly remained quiet, stirring the ice in his drink. Blumenfeld emptied his glass.

"Al, they shoulda left you in my bureau. Now I got nobody to drink lunch with. Tulio, give us another one."

"What about a judgeship, Leon? You got the gray hair."

"Me?" Blumenfeld laughed. "I haven't been in a clubhouse since 1945. The only toga I'll ever wear will be made out of terry cloth, over my drawers when I'm up at Kutsher's Country Club."

"You're still the best boss I ever had. You got my vote."

"Have a drink, for Christ's sake, Al. I don't know what's got into the Irish. Don't wanna drink; don't even wanna beat up the sheeny boys the way they used to."

Blumenfeld's eyeglasses slid down the bridge of his broken nose as he chuckled. Reilly pressed his own nose flat with his fingers and said, "Nat Zucker told me you got that fighting for nickels and dimes under the Williamsburg Bridge."

"Yeah, I was a bad kid. I'd take a beating, but I'd give one, too. Bug, Meyer—I was around some of those guys. I was lucky; a good ol' lady straightened me out. That's the main thing, Al, a good ol' lady."

"I'll have that drink."

"You got it. Well, so how you doing so far, Al?"

"Great, Leon. I caught that Tony Roman shooting

with Guido Brennan. Took my first statement from him. Chief Quinn was pleased the way I handled it."

"A toss, huh?"

"Yeah, sure, this Tony Roman has three yellow sheets. Vicious bastard. I remember him from when I was in uniform around there."

"Two guns, huh?"

"Two-gun Guido. Better believe it. They could have used him at the O.K. Corral."

"No, I meant Tony."

"Tony Roman? Two guns?"

"That's what I hear."

"Oh, yeah? I'm checking everything out. Don't have all the reports in, but I'm checking everything out. Been busy as hell."

"How do you like your new boss?"

"Great, Leon, great. A brilliant man, class. I tell you, I feel very lucky to be working under Quinn. I heard of his trial techniques and his track record with juries even when I was in Brooklyn Law. I hope to learn my trade from him."

"He did you a big favor. Pulling you up to the Homicide Bureau, your only being here a few months."

"He likes the fact that I didn't come out of an ivory tower, that I've been on the streets."

"Guy's not even forty. Already he's a bureau chief. He's won all the big ones; the DA swears by him. Learn what you can from him, Al. He wrote the book on jury trial tactics."

"I'm looking forward."

"Maybe not. Rumors from the eighth floor say that the governor has tapped him for a big slot—special assistant, some shit. Reorganize criminal justice system of the state. Make it more fucked up."

"He's chief of the Homicide Bureau. Why would anyone want to quit a job like that?"

"Keep a secret, Al?"

"Sure, you know me, Leon."

"He's a prick."

"A what?"

Blumenfeld pivoted on his stool and stared at Reilly. "Prick, *p-r-i-c-k*. Everybody's forgotten, but I remember when he first came here. Fucked every chief he worked under. Soon as your back was turned, he'd be running to the DA with memos and charts and statistics. Every day some new shit, like a fuckin' whirlin' dervish. You couldn't go on vacation, for Christ's sake."

"You get guys like that, Leon. Ambition."

"Ambition? We all got ambition. Wadda ya think, I wanna stay here all my life? But there's a difference. He's a prick. Married money, a socialite. He won't have a drink with the other bureau chiefs. Thinks he's John Jacob Astor. The philanthropy this, the bundles for that, gonna save the opera house, gonna donate forty-eight piss pots to the Mount Sinai Hospital. Then he thinks he's Hamlet, like at the office party." Blumenfeld removed his eyeglasses and held them out at arms' length. " 'Is that an asshole I see before me? Come, let me clutch thee.' That's the time I almost punched him out."

"*Quinn?*"

"That's right. You wouldn't know about it. What the hell. Thinks he's Tom Dewey. Full of shit. He's a racist, elitist windbag. Snide remarks. I can tell, Al."

"Just my luck to wind up in the soup again," Reilly said.

The waiter, passing by, interjected, "You want minestrone or pastafagioli, Leon?"

Laughing loudly, Blumenfeld said, "No, Mario, just a figure of speech. Gimme the special salad. What do you want, Al?"

•

Reilly returned to his office after lunch and immediately called the Twenty-third squad.

"Hello, let me speak to Detective Valentin. . . . Hello, Johnny. Why didn't you tell me Tony Roman had two guns? Do I have to find out everything for myself?"

"Wait a minute, Al. We just started this thing. I got a lot of other cases. I'm getting all the reports together. Me and Chappie will have them for you in the morning. We're bringing all the witnesses also. Only thing, I can't find the stool."

"The stool?"

"Yeah. Brennan's stool pigeon. He's a federal stool, too."

"What's his name?"

"Don't wanna say that on the phone, Al."

"Okay, let's whack this out quick. I'll see you in the morning."

"Hasta lumbago."

"Fuck you," Reilly said.

5 There was a gentle knock on Reilly's door as he sat behind his desk nursing his morning coffee and reading the Brennan file. The door was pushed in, and the head of a tall, bald man appeared sideways through the narrow opening.

"May I come in, gentlemen?"

"Please," answered Reilly, glancing at Valentin and Chapman huddled in the corner.

The man strode in, arms outstretched as if to embrace Reilly. A middle-aged man with a barrel-shaped body mounted on lean shanks.

Skinny guy who took a long time to get fat, thought Reilly. The guy was a concerto in brown: striped brown shirt with a white collar, brown silk tie with a gold stickpin, a brown silk and mohair suit, beyond whose sleeves protruded large gold cuff links and a gold owl-eyed pinkie ring. Kikey, he thought, but with an open face and manner that doesn't appear to take itself too seriously.

He clasped Reilly's right hand between his palms and shook it lustily.

"Mr. Reilly? Preston Pearlstein. I am the attorney for Mr. Robert Texidor. He's waiting outside with his wife."

Reilly looked at Chapman and Valentin. "I thought you told me that Texidor was single."

"Well," Pearlstein added quickly, "I meant common-law wife. You know, living together."

"Counselor, common-law marriages were abrogated in New York in 1931. You should know the law," Reilly said.

"Oh, that's the way we're going to play the game? Listen, kid, I've forgotten more law than you and your whole staff will ever learn."

"Don't call me kid. I've seen you standing outside night court with a vaudeville hook, waiting for clients to go by."

"What? I'm going to report—" Pearlstein raised his voice, his head swiveling from Chapman to Valentin in confusion.

Chapman stood up to intervene. "Pearlie, take it easy, Pearlie! You brought your people down here in good faith. We know you do a hell of a job. This is a bullshit case. We'll just take a few statements, and then everybody goes home. You can tell your clients you saved them from an indictment. Nobody is going to get hurt here."

Pearlstein seemed mollified at this prospect. "All right, Chappie, you know me. I'm a nice guy, but I demand respect. After all, I've been a member of the bar for—"

"Of course, Pearlie, of course." Chapman motioned toward a chair.

"Well," said Pearlstein, "it's a waste of time, Mr. DA. Everybody says the same thing. They heard noise, came out. Tony Roman was on the ground, shot, and Lieutenant Brennan was standing there. They don't know who shot what or who. It's as simple as that. I don't know why you have to drag all these people down here."

"Yeah," Chapman said, raising his eyebrows, "but if we don't drag these people down here, how are you going to make a fee?"

Pearlstein laughed. "You got a point there. Okay, who first?"

The witnesses were interrogated in inverse order of rank, lightweights first: Rivera, Correa, Delgado, De-Jesus, Obregon, Alvarado, Castillo, Valdes. Reilly remembered some of their faces from the street. He sensed Pearlstein had conducted rehearsals; the chorus sang in unison.

"I saw dee same thing, like Mr. Pearlstein said, Mr. DA," said Mr. Luis Alvarado of the golden-toothed smile.

"What do you mean, like Mr. Pearlstein said? He wasn't there."

Alvarado was not discouraged. "I mean like Mauricio and the boys said. You got dees big guy, okay. Poleezmen. He standing outside from the club. Okay, den you got Tony on the floor, focked up. Wow, qué pasa aquí? Wha' happen, das what I gwanna know, wha' happen?"

"Did you see a gun, Mr. Alvarado?"

"Gun, wha' gun? I don't could see no gun."

"There were all kinds of guns there, Alvarado."

"You got me, boddy. I don't see no gun."

"Get out of here. Mr. Pearlstein, would you step outside a minute? We'll be ready for the last batch of your clients in a few minutes."

Pearlstein left the office for the waiting room, where the remaining four witnesses were lounging. Reilly turned to Chapman and Valentin.

"I'll question them one at a time. I'll yell and break their balls. You guys then tone me down."

"Nah, nah," Valentin cut in, "take my advice. We'll question them all together—Bobby Tex, his old lady, and the two donskis. I know Bobby Tex from the street. He can't take the needle, not in front of his old lady and a wal-yo boss. He's a terrible hothead. I seen him years ago split Spruille's skull apart with a cue stick."

"Spruille, war counselor of the Comanches?" Chapman asked.

"Yeah, this was before the Korean War. The Comanches came in the poolroom on 106th Street, bassin' at everybody. Bobby Tex put the lock on the door, and him and his boys busted skulls like they was melons. Them guys were screamin' for God. Some of them went through the plate glass window to get out."

"Bobby's clique was the Sinners?" Chapman asked.

"Yeah, meaner'n a barrel of alligators, too."

"But Spruille came back."

"Yeah, Chappie, next night, with a turban on his head. Pulled up in a taxi in front of the poolroom, shot the shit out of the place. But the cab driver jumped out and ran away, and Spruille ran out of bullets. That's when Tony Roman come out and emptied a pistol into the backseat where Spruille was."

"Didn't hit him once," Chapman smiled.

"Mother fucker was jumpin' up and down," Valentin said. "You know how them spooks can dance."

"Yeah, but we don't wear tuxedo with Keds."

"Seems like Tony Roman had a habit of being late." Reilly rubbed his eyes.

"Tony had plenty cojones for a tiny guy," Valentin said. "He was only around five-three or four."

"Why we gotta set fire to Bobby Tex's ass? We trying to make a case against Guido?" Chapman asked, only half in jest.

Reilly leaned back. "Of course not. Just a little heat. Maybe we can find out why Franconi—Pesh—was there, rile them up. Do your stuff, Johnny, right in the ol' Hershey locker. I'll play off you. I'll be Mr. Nice Guy."

There was a knock on the door.

"Yeah."

Attorney Pearlstein led the way in. "Mr. Reilly, these are my clients. Mr. Franconi, Mr. Calabrese, Mr. Texidor, Mrs.—eh, Miss Bosch." They sat in a semicircle in that order, left to right, facing Reilly's desk. Flanking them were Chapman and Valentin.

Nancy. A woman. I knew a girl; this is a woman. She's cut her hair. Sets her features off. Better. Four years. It's like I saw her yesterday turning that corner. My cross for four years. I've done my penance.

"Are we just going to sit here, Mr. Reilly?" Pearlstein asked.

"No, no, just a few questions, Counselor. I want to apologize to you for our little misunderstanding awhile ago. You know the responsibilities of this office. What with the rising homicide rate, we're working under tremendous pressure."

Pearlstein nodded. "I know, Al. I have the greatest respect in the world for this office. And I want you to know I have always maintained an outstanding relationship with this office, second to none. Why just the other day—"

"Uh—Mr. Pearlstein, Preston, can we start the questions now?"

"Okay, but I want to tell you right off that Larry here, Mr. Franconi, refuses to say anything, invoking

47

the privilege under the Fifth and Fourteenth amendments."

"Is that under the advice of counsel?"

"Well, not exactly," Pearlstein said.

"I can't believe that an advocate as respected as you are would advise your client to plead the Fifth knowing that he is not the target of the investigation and that he is in no jeopardy whatever. Do you want us to become suspicious of Mr. Larry 'Pesh' Franconi from Pleasant Avenue and points south? You want us to grant him immunity, then march him upstairs to Part Thirty and have him imprisoned for contempt? Then maybe get in touch with the Federal Bureau of Narcotics and the Internal Revenue Service? I'm not saying I would, Preston, but there are people who get excited about things like this."

Pearlstein stood up. "Wait a minute, Al. We can straighten this out."

"I have every confidence in you, Preston."

"Lemme take my clients outside for a minute."

"Of course, Preston. Take all the time you need."

Pearlstein and his four clients left the room.

"You're gonna be all right, Al," said Chapman admiringly. "You're gonna be *all* right. Couldn't have handled ol' Pearlie better m'self."

"Boy, am I gonna break balls," Valentin said, rubbing his hands.

Again there was a gentle knocking on the door as it opened. "Al, we got it all straightened out. Mr. Franconi will make a statement."

The witnesses filed back in and resumed their seats.

Larry Pesh, real name Lorenzo Franconi. The FBI file on Reilly's desk read him as a middle-echelon button. Fifty-two years of age, reputed to have been "made" in the early 1950s. Considered to be a major narcotics distributor, presently acting as a liaison between the more conservative downtown mob and the wild west Pleasant Avenue mob uptown.

Pesh was fat. Thick layers of flesh rode his shirt over pants worn beltless and hitched just above his crotch and flat rump. The shirt was white, open-necked, with short sleeves rolled up in even folds close to his shoulders. A small, pudgy left hand displayed a star sapphire ring as he wiped his neck with a large white handkerchief. He carried a suit jacket neatly folded over his hairy right arm. His lips were curled upward, but lollipop eyes, encased in heavy pouches, fixed his expression as that of a melancholic fish. The sweat beads on his forehead confirmed his discomfort. Reilly smiled to himself. Pesh, as in *pesce*, meaning fish.

"Me and my chauffeur, here, Bruno, was drivin' downtown on Park Avenue around midnight last Thursday." Larry Pesh Franconi spoke in a voice that grated up in his throat like pebbles in a driveway. "All of a sudden I gotta take a piss. I says to Bruno, 'Bruno, I gotta take a piss. Find me a joint.' My kidneys ain't too good, but I don't wanna get pinched for pissin' in public. Ha. Meanwhile, we sees this joint on 107th Street. We go in to the john, come out; there's this big guy wavin' a big rod around. Figured he was a cop the way he was barkin'. Some kid was stretched out on the ground. The cop said we stay. We stayed." He shrugged his shoulders and raised his hands, palms up, in a helpless gesture.

"I'm a little confused, Mr. Franconi. You were going south, downtown on Park Avenue, is that correct?"

"Right."

"Never been to the club before?"

"Right."

"Didn't know it was there?"

"Right."

"Mr. Franconi, the club at 81 East 107th is the width of two buildings, west from the corner of Park Avenue, below street level, with no sign or lights and at the end of a dark passageway that opens onto a blind courtyard. How could you, in a moving vehicle, spot such a place under those circumstances?"

"Wad is this, third degree? I'm down here on my own time. I got a poultry business. I got no time to be jerkin' around. Pearlstein, straighten this guy out, will ya? I ain't sayin' nuttin' else."

"Mr. Calabrese, would you care to add to Mr. Franconi's statement?" Reilly asked, scanning a report on Calabrese.

Bruno Calabrese, thirty-five years of age, ex-pug, ex-bouncer. Fringe mob associate. Promoted in the last few years through marriage. Presently employed as chauffeur, bodyguard, and gofer to Lorenzo "Pesh" Franconi. Extremely violent.

"I'm wid him," Calabrese said, his lips barely parting.

The corner of Reilly's right eye had Nancy in range throughout. She wore a blue suede pantsuit, a sable coat, which was thrown over the chair. She had not uttered a word since entering the room. Too far out, Reilly thought; she'll never come back.

"Al. Al, are you through with these two?" Pearlstein asked.

"Let them stay a few minutes while we finish with Mr. Texidor and Miss Bosch. Something might develop which, perhaps, will refresh their recollection." Reilly was irritated at Pearlstein's prodding.

"My recollection ain't gonna get no fresher," said Franconi. "I can tell you that right now. You ain't talkin' to no greaseball here. I know my rights." Franconi pointed his handkerchief at Reilly.

"Yeah. I'm wid him," Calabrese added.

"Shaddup. Who asked you?" Franconi said, waving the handkerchief at Calabrese in anger.

"Take it easy, Larry. The man's just doing his job," Texidor advised in a gently modulated voice.

Bobby Tex, born Roberto Texidor, thirty-eight years of age. Prime distributor of narcotics in Spanish Harlem and the South Bronx. Born in Puerto Rico, brought to New York as an infant. Has strong ties with Italian, black, and Cuban mobs. Handsome, a fastidious dresser. Immensely wealthy since the early 1960s. Maintains a $2,000 a month duplex apartment on Sutton Place with a paramour, one Nancy Bosch, age twenty-two. He affects an air of affability but is known to possess a volatile temperament.

Reilly knew the file by rote.

Texidor sat casually, cross-legged.

"Mr. Texidor, suppose you give us your version of the facts," Reilly said, emulating Texidor's soft posture.

"Be happy to, Mr. Reilly. I know Mauricio Valdes from the old days when I used to live in the barrio. So, last Thursday, my wife and I decided to give his club a play."

"Your wife, Bobby Tex?" Valentin interrupted.

"I'm talking to Mr. Reilly."

"Detective Valentin is assigned to this case, Mr. Texidor. Is there some question as to your marital status?"

"Well, actually we're like married, only we haven't gone to church or anything. But we've been together for years now. Right, mámi?"

"Yes, Bobby."

Reilly felt sick. "Continue, please."

"We got to the club around midnight—early—just to pay our respects and leave. I don't have to tell you that you can get a rough crowd in the later hours in these places. Hey, I remember you. You were in the Twenty-third Precinct, Mr. Reilly."

"Is that right?"

"You had a good reputation among the Latinos. Tough, but fair."

"What a crock. I can't stand it," Valentin half shouted, putting his hand on his forehead.

"Johnny, take it easy," Chapman admonished.

"I got my wife here, Mr. Reilly. I don't want no profanity here, please," Texidor said, his voice rising as he uncrossed his legs.

"All right, all right. I'm sorry." Valentin said.

"Please continue," Reilly said.

"We had a drink. Mauricio runs a clean place. All of a sudden we hear a commotion."

"Like shots?"

"I can't say that, but noise. I go outside, and there's this big gentleman with something in his hand. It was very dark. And this neighborhood guy was laid out. The big guy said nobody moves. More cops came. That was it."

"Do you know these two gentlemen from before?"

"What two?"

"These two. Mr. Franconi and Bruno Calabrese."

"Can't say I do, Mr. Reilly."

"You saw them when they came in the club, didn't you?"

"Can't say I did, Mr. Reilly."

"What a crock!" Valentin blurted out. "These two burly wops walk into the joint like two hitters on a contract, and you ain't gonna see them?"

The uproar was immediate.

"This is an *outrage*, making anti-Semitic remarks," Pearlstein yelled, doing his best to appear shocked.

"Pearlstein, I *order* you to press charges," Franconi shouted, pointing at everyone.

"I'm wid him," Calabrese added.

Reilly banged the desk with his fist. "Detective Valentin, control yourself. Gentlemen, please accept my apologies. He's been working under a terrible strain on this case. Okay, let's settle down and get this over with —please."

It took a few moments for the feathers to settle, everyone shifting positions in their seats and Pearlstein affecting a look of horror.

"This neighborhood guy that was laid out was Anthony Roman, right?" Reilly asked Texidor.

"Something like that."

"You knew him?"

"Sort of—from around the neighborhood."

Valentin suddenly rose again. "I can't stand this. Bobby Tex, with my own eyes I seen Tony Roman save your life when the Copiens caught you by the museum on 103d. Yo' ass was grass, but he saved you. I seen it myself, and now you got the nerve to deny him over his dead body, cobarde!"

"*Cobarde?*" Texidor, white with rage, leaped forward.

"Yeah, coward," Valentin spat back.

"Fuckin' Honey Dripper. You was a punk when you was on the street. Tryin' to hang out with the big guys. Used to get yo' ass stomped regular then. Now you a detective—de-fective is more like it. You couldn't find a Jew on the Concourse. You got a badge, a gun, and you still a punk," Texidor shouted, flecks of saliva flying from his mouth.

"Please, Bobby!" Pearlstein pleaded.

"Shut yo' ass!" Texidor hissed, his eyes wide.

"You're a used-to-be bad guy, Bobby Tex," Valentin snapped. "The baddest guy is me now, 'cause I'm the law. I'm in charge of this case, and I'm wrappin' it up. This is a clear case of self-defense, and I'm gonna get a medal for the lieutenant and maybe a promotion for me."

"Self-defense, eh? You fuckin' turkey. Lil' Tony Roman, hundred and twenty pounds, gonna carry *two* loaded guns, a .45 and a .38, while he's wearin' Dak pants with no belt? He had the fuckin' .38 on his right hip in a clip holster. Meanwhile he's got a .45 in his right hand? Everybody knows he never carried no cannon like that."

"Now *you* a fuckin' de-tective?" Valentin shouted back. The two men were leaning forward, their faces almost touching.

"Motherfuckin'-A right."

"Are you sayin' that Brennan whacked Tony out?"

"That's for me to know and you to find out, Defective Valentin," Texidor said, wagging his head, smug in the triumph of his logic.

The room grew very quiet. Texidor could hear the sound of his own breathing, the blood straining at his temples. He looked down, the floor was there, but he felt himself propelled outward, arms fluttering. He turned to his left, to Franconi, whose eyes were bulging as if he'd been fished with dynamite.

Texidor brought his hands down, took his seat again, and smiled. "Heh, Mr. Reilly. You know how it is when a couple of PRs from the old neighborhood get together." He shifted nervously. "We start jivin' and playin' the dozens. I'm sorry, Johnny. I wasn't tryin' to put no ticket on you. I'm just upset about all this violence. I told my wife, 'From now on, we're stayin' home.' That's just what I told her."

The air in the room became dense, congealed. Tex had not cut through, but he tried again. "Imagine me runnin' my mouth off in front of an educated guy like you, Mr. Reilly. That's a hot one."

"Don't worry about it. Everybody is an expert these days. Pretty soon they won't need lawyers."

"God forbid," said Pearlstein.

Even Franconi made an attempt to laugh. The best he could affect was a croak that wedged in his gullet. From long experience his ear was unerring in its ability to detect the sound of disaster. He could hear it, smell it, and now, even taste it. A hole had been rent in the bedsheet; the toenail was in.

" 'Ey, Mr. Reilly, gimme a break. I got chickens to pluck," Franconi said, affecting good cheer.

"Will all the witnesses wait in the waiting room for just five more minutes? I want to compare these statements," Reilly said.

Pearlstein and the witnesses left. Chapman closed the door. Reilly swiveled his chair around and faced the window, his back to the two detectives.

"What do you think, Johnny?" he asked.

"I think this is going to be the well-known mother fucker."

Chapman said, "C'mon, don't get dramatic. You gonna listen to this blowtop, Texidor? You know Roman was his man. He bound to bad-breath Guido. What do you expect?"

Valentin turned back toward Chapman. "You think I'm gonna hurt a cop, Chappie? But this thing scares me. This is my neighborhood we're talkin' about. I know these people. I grew up with them, and ain't no way Tony Roman could have washed Julio Sierra. I never bought them tickets. They were both from the original Sinners. I have seen these two cats back to back, rumblin' against five or six of the Dragons; a bottle and a knife is all they had. They go back twenty-five years. I don't care if Julio beat Tony out of twenty keys. He couldn't hurt him that bad. And Tony was nobody's fool. That's why he was underboss to Bobby Tex. And even if Tony zapped Julio, you think he's gonna leave a shell casing around that's gonna match up with a .45 he was still packin' as an extra piece? And now Tony Roman gets washed. It stinks, Chappie. It stinks."

"What are you talkin'? You know these junk mothers fall out all the time. Could have been a kilo; could have been too much coke in his snorter; could have been a broad. Don't go crazy. You ain't had a gold shield but two years; right away you're Sherlock Gonzales." Chapman was genuinely angry.

"You got the ball, Al." Valentin waved it all off. "I had my say." He resumed his seat.

"Calm down, you guys. Jesus. I have to think this out. What—what about this guy, this informant who told Brennan where Tony Roman was? Who is he?"

Valentin rolled his eyes. "That's Roger Montalvo. Federal stool, pusher, beater, shooter, and a fag. I don't talk to that rat fink without a surgical mask. The feds pay him five hundred a month to rat. Meanwhile he deals his own shit; then he sets people up; then he beats them or shoots them in the back. Then he takes it in the ass, like a superfag. If he gets into this case, he'll get us all indicted, guaranteed."

"Where is this Montalvo?"

"Lotta people would like to know," said Chapman. "We're looking for him."

"Chappie, suppose, just suppose Brennan comes up wrong. Are you ready for that?" Reilly asked.

"I'm a cop. I do my job."

Reilly chewed the end of his pencil. "I got an idea. Strike at the weakest link, Nancy Bosch." He paused, his gaze shifting from Chapman to Valentin, then back. "You guys go and tell them we want to speak to her alone. Of course, this fuckin' shyster will tag along. When the two of them are in the room, you guys come up with something like there's serious complications about Franconi—Pesh—something like that. Get him out of my room for a few minutes so I can talk to the girl alone. I think I can find some things out."

Chapman and Valentin glanced at one another.

"Eh, Al," Chapman cautioned, "I don't want to tell you your job, but it can get sticky talking to a female witness alone. Later on she can say you tried to get alongside her or something. Know what I mean?"

"Look, fellas, don't worry. I'm not going to unzipper my fly. Do it my way."

Chapman and Valentin rose and stepped out of Reilly's office. When the door was closed, they paused and looked at one another.

"I don't blame him, Chappie. What a doll. That's the main thing I don't like about bein' with the good guys. The bad guys get all the good pussy," Valentin said as they walked to the waiting room.

Within a few minutes they returned with Pearlstein and Nancy Bosch.

Reilly motioned toward a nearby chair. "Please sit down, Miss Bosch. Mr. Pearlstein, I'm very worried about something—"

"Wait a minute," Chapman interrupted. "This ain't right. Mr. Pearlstein has been a friend of mine for years. Can I speak to him in private?"

"Well—okay, sure."

"Step outside a minute, Pearlie. C'mon, Johnny," Chapman motioned Pearlstein and Valentin out with him. The door closed behind them.

She sat cross-legged, her fur coat open, her long fingers folded over a dark leather handbag, gloves casually on her lap. She wore no rings or nail polish, Reilly noted approvingly.

Reilly rose from his chair, came around, and sat on the edge of his desk, not two feet away from her. Arms crossed on his stomach, he leaned forward. She tightened her lips and lowered her head slightly. His eyes followed the delicate lines of her cheekbones across the oval shapes of her slightly Asiatic eyes. She would not look at him. Reilly felt his eyes go dry, hazy.

"There's no need for this, Nancy."

She stood up quickly, her eyes finally on his. "Oh, then I can leave."

Reilly put his hands out. "Please, give me a chance to talk, to explain." He got to his feet, "*Goddamn* it, Nancy, even a criminal gets a second chance."

"You're not acting like a district attorney, Mr. Reilly," Her icy voice matched her glare.

"I'm sorry, it's just that—God knows how I tried to locate you, and now to see you here with these people—"

"Stop right there. I know you Irish talk a lot of religion, but I, for one, have not been in a convent the past four years."

Reilly stepped back, bumping his desk, stunned. "You don't have to talk like that to me. All I wanted to know was what happened to you, what happened to the baby, what—"

"Mister Reilly. There was no baby. Just a very short interlude of East meets West, or maybe North meets South. We were kids, that's all. I have nothing against you. Now I'd like to have my lawyer present."

"Wait a minute. Jesus. Eh—what about your mom, your father?"

"You hypocrite. As if you gave a damn. He's dead. That was his last Christmas, in '64. He was already a dying man that day on the corner." She turned her face away.

Reilly took a deep gulp of air. "Can I tell you something?"

"No."

"Nancy, I'm human. I was caught by surprise. You should have told me about your father, about his being . . . dark."

Her eyes flared. "Was I supposed to introduce you by stages? Like Pápi, like my father was some kind of leper?"

"No, Nancy, I mean, maybe you had reservations about his color, too. Those were different times. We're all human, all make mistakes."

She shook her head violently. "You bastard! Is that what you thought? That I was hiding my father from you? I'll tell you what I thought, stupid me. Love me, love mine. Right? Wrong. Okay. But it's you and your kind; you don't look into people's eyes, only their skin or hair or whatever. That's *your* hang-up, *your* problem, not mine. I don't want to hear a fucking thing. I want my lawyer present."

Her shouting and trembling alarmed Reilly.

There was a loud knock on the door, then Chapman, Valentin, Pearlstein, and Texidor all barged in.

Chapman, flustered, said, "Al, Tex, here, is raising hell outside. I told him that this was just routine questioning."

Texidor brushed past Chapman. Slapping his left palm with the back of his right hand for emphasis, he shouted, "Bullshit! Listen, Reilly, I know you went out with my old lady when she was a kid. I seen you with her in the neighborhood myself. And she told me about it. But that's over. She's my old lady now, and you best not—"

"Bobby, calm yourself," said Pearlstein.

"What the fuck am I payin' you for, Pearlstein, to let this guy mess with my old lady?" Texidor pointed at Reilly. "You been told, Reilly."

"Stick your finger up your ass, you fuckin' scumbag, before I break—" Reilly's bared teeth shone white against his face. His ears and neck turned bright red. He lunged forward, but Chapman grabbed him by a wrist.

"You gonna hit me with your nightstick?" Tex yelled. "You're not a lawyer; you're a fuckin' cop!"

Chapman shoved in between them. "Whoa, Al, take it easy. Pearlie, take your guy outside. Johnny, show these people to the elevator. Pearlie, you wait for me, hear?"

•

Valentin and Pearlstein herded the witnesses out of the office and down the hallway to the elevator. Then Pearlstein went to the waiting room. Chapman appeared a few seconds later.

"Pearlie, Reilly is a good kid. If you mess him up, you're gonna blow your credit with me."

"What do I give a shit. I'm trying to make a fee. What do I care about their love life? Forget it."

Chapman patted Pearlstein on the shoulder. "'M' man."

•

Reilly was seated with both feet on the desk when Chapman and Valentin returned. A yellow legal pad rested in his lap, a pencil poised over it, as if he had been writing. Chapman could see the hand quiver.

His chin on his chest, Reilly said, "I'm sorry, fellas. I made a jackass of myself. I'm not a lawyer. Brass buttons, brown stick, can't catch your father's dick. That's what's going through my mind. These diplomas on the wall don't mean a fuckin' thing. God, what an ass I made of myself."

"I thought only PRs went to the blades over a broad." Valentin was animated, almost jubilant. "See, Chappie, you can't make generalizations about people. You did the right thing, Al. You shoulda kicked his ass. I always hated that mother fucker."

"You're supposed to be a peace officer, Johnny, not an agitator. Jeez!" Chapman said, shaking his head.

"If a man don't fight for his broad, he ain't shit."

"Tex was right." Reilly broke in, his voice almost a whisper. "I used to go out with Nancy."

"What happened?" Chapman asked.

"She put me down. Ethnic differences."

Valentin looked concerned. "Fuckin' shame, but nothin' new about that. I had the same trouble with a Jewish chick. She took me to meet her folks. Father said his daughter was not going out with no wop. He was a shrimpy guy with bunions poppin' through his shoes. This was a long time ago, when people thought

Puerto Ricans came from Portugal. Anyway, I said, 'I ain't no wop. I am a *Puertorriqueño* and proud of it.' The old Jew almost fainted. He said, 'You mean those little cockers playin' maracas in the subway?' I called him an old kike with bad feet. We got it on. He kicked my ass. Unbelievable. Turned out he was a pug during the thirties."

Reilly almost laughed. "What was his name, Irish Bobby Katz?"

"What else? But I got even. I married his daughter."

Chapman shot him a surprised look. "I didn't know your old lady was Jewish. What do your kids look like?"

"Good lookin', like me. But my mother don't like them."

"Why not?" Chapman asked.

" 'Cause they came out with kinky Jewish hair."

"You are a fuckin' nut," said Chapman, indignant, slouching back in his chair and folding his arms.

Valentin was not discouraged. "I can't see puttin' a person down just 'cause they ain't Puerto Rican. Everybody knows that love is color-blind. Look at me. I'll take Dorothy Dandridge over Beulah Bondi anytime."

"Hey, Dorothy Dandridge is my woman. Your woman is Carmen Miranda," Chapman said, sitting up in feigned indignation.

"Fuck you, Ne-gro. We got all the good men actors anyway."

"Who you got? Duncan Rinaldo?"

"Get outta here," Reilly broke in, "both of you. I have to study all these reports and see what the hell I'm doing. That's the trouble with me. It takes me three days to figure anything out. I used to envy these fuckers in school. Soak everything up from the instructor's mouth. Me, I had to go home and kick it around and shit. Used to bug me."

Valentin's face became serious. "Me, I never had that trouble. Right away I see things. I go to the movies with my old lady. Bang. Right away I tell her. John Wayne's songs ain't gonna sell, and he's gonna start drinking, and pretty soon he's gonna lose Betty Grable. But they'll put on a big show at Radio City and get together at the end. My old lady says, 'How do you do it?' I don't know. These things just come to me."

Chapman shook his head in disgust. "That's John Payne, you turkey. John Wayne never made no movie with Betty Grable. He's so smart, Al. He's got three high school equivalency diplomas from the University of Delehanty."

"Imagine. Me, the guy that can hear a roach walking on yogurt," Valentin said.

"Yeah, with galoshes. I heard about that arrest. I also hear you're the man that uses Preparation H for an earache and been bending over to hear ever since. I mean, that's what I hear." Chapman beamed at Valentin.

"No more. The doctor put earplugs in my asshole."

They regarded one another, their faces suddenly serious. Invariably, Chapman would lean his head back and stare down at the shorter Valentin through narrowed eyes. Valentin would puff his cheek out with his tongue, his eyes wide. Chapman would put his hand out, palm up. Valentin would slap down on it with his own hand, saying, "Gimme five, 'cause yo' alive." Only then would they have their laugh.

Reilly was getting used to it. He gestured toward Chapman and said, "One last thing. And don't take it the wrong way, but I'm going to have to discuss this Brennan thing with my bosses. I know how you feel about the guy. But he is to be told nothing about this investigation."

" 'Nuff said. We'll call you tomorrow. Or sooner, if we locate Roger Montalvo. Which ain't gonna be easy. A stool with a fixed address ain't a stool for long."

Chapman and Valentin left. Reilly stared at the case reports. Nancy with that viper. What happened to all the idealism, the salvation of the barrio, the rainbow people?

6 Horace Chapman was dozing in an armchair in front of his television set. His wife, Claudia, was reading on the sofa, having put their two children to bed upstairs.

The chimes rang at the front door.

Claudia Chapman answered the door and quickly stepped back, momentarily startled at the vastness of the black-coated figure filling the doorway. Brennan quickly removed the light gray fedora, his right hand in a skintight black leather glove. He bowed respectfully, then leaned forward. Claudia saw he was holding a bouquet of flowers at his side in his other hand.

"Hi, Guido. Come on in."

"Hiya, Claudia," he said, kissing her on the cheek. "How's the kids?"

"They're already asleep."

"Hardly get to see them since you guys went suburban on me. Hey, I brought these for you." He handed her the flowers.

"They're beautiful, Guido."

"Yeah. Beware of Irish-Italians bearing gifts," Chapman broke in.

"That's not funny, Horace," Claudia chided.

They went into the living room.

"You should have called, Gui. We'd have made something for you," Chapman said.

"Nah. That's okay. Listen, can I talk to you, Chappie?" Brennan's voice was as quiet as his manner was diffident.

Chapman looked at Claudia, who turned and left the room. "Sit down, man. Take your coat off."

Brennan settled into an armchair. "They're trying to hurt me, Chappie. They're trying real hard."

"You didn't do anything bad. Don't worry about it."

"It's going to be open season on cops, Chap. I see it coming. I've been a headbuster, I don't deny it. But you know what it's been like out there these past years. It's been a slaughterhouse in this city. Worse than fucking Korea. That's what the Ricans call Harlem—Korea. Shit, I don't have to justify myself to you. You've been there, too."

"Of course. This is just routine, anyway. It'll all be straightened out in a few days. Take your gloves off, at least. Relax."

"I don't like this guy Reilly, with his gee-whiz bullshit. He's a phony, night school commando trying to impress the bosses. Meanwhile he's riding in the car with Jimmy Mullins, the twin-armed bandit."

Chapman nodded. "With pillowcase pockets. You know that clown would actually play family court and even swear in people on the spot and declare divorce decrees, like he was a judge."

"Yeah, so where does Reilly get off? And this guy, Valentin. I don't like him either. A ball-breaker. No question about it. I checked him out, too. Narco man. Spent all his time undercover. Crazy bastard. Would sleep in abandoned buildings with the junkies for three, four days. Smoke reefers. Came up in the street with all these hard ons from the old Bobby Tex crew."

66

"The Sinners."

"I don't know. Whatever stupid thing they called themselves. Leave it to a cop and an ex-cop to try to fuck another cop. Valentin figures he'll make second grade over my ass. Well, I'm not going to stand around pulling my prick. I'm going to do something about it. And you have to help me, Chappie."

"Sure, Gui."

"I have to find Montalvo. Roger the fag, he knows that Tony Roman carried two guns and that Roman and Sierra had a beef. He's the one that called me. He can straighten everything out, Roger the pansy; but I have to talk to him first, before Reilly does, or he's liable to get all fucked up and hurt me. You read me?"

"I don't know where he is. I've never even seen the guy. Johnny Valentin has the line on him, knows him well. We're working on it."

"You got Johnny's home address?"

"Yeah, but I don't like to—"

"Ey, this is me, Guido, talking to you."

Chapman looked at Guido Brennan for a moment, then rose.

"Okay. Let me get my book."

Chapman walked to the hall closet and pulled the address book from his jacket pocket.

"Guido, why don't you take your coat off?"

"Nah, nah. I'm all right. Got the address?"

"Yeah, here. One ninety-three Nagle Avenue, Dyckman Projects."

"Got it. He's probably home, right?"

"Yeah. I figure. We had a long day. You wanna call him up? Here's the phone."

"No, I don't want to call him up. Give me a drink, fella. Gimme a belt of Scotch."

"Sure, Gui, sure. I'll join you. Haven't seen you take a drink for six, seven years."

Chapman took a bottle and two shot glasses from the cabinet under the TV set.

"Yeah, yeah," Brennan said as he downed two quick shots. "Chappie, this was strictly a social call. That's all."

"Sure, Guido."

"I'll talk to you. Say s' long to Claudia for me." He left, his steps soft on the footpath outside as he walked to his car.

Chapman sat staring at the telephone. "Fuck it," he said and went to bed.

●

Reilly lay in bed propped up on a pillow, a *Sports Illustrated* on his lap. His TV dinner was wedged uncomfortably against his stomach. He sank back into the pillow, remembering the fall semester of '64. Amazingly enough to Reilly, it was in that enclave of muddleheaded idealism, the City College campus, that their love had bloomed. He was on the campus with Nancy every day that he had off and the afternoons before night tours. He would sit with her in the cafeteria, their conversations ranging from Cervantes and Garcia Lorca to O'Casey and Yeats. She was preparing a paper on three Latin American poets: Darió, Martí, and DeDiego, and Reilly would accompany her to the library to help with the research. Everyone assumed Reilly was a matriculated student; she never told them different. So he was included in the incessant political discussions, at times distasteful to him. But Nancy was Al Reilly's only interest and obsession. He had a feeling of incompleteness when he was not with her. Even on street patrol, with all its distractions, there was a sense of absence that slackened only when he could focus on her.

He was not, by nature, active. Smiling, he remembered running after Nancy and her schedule. She was in college full time, worked at the public library on 110th Street, and attended dance classes at a studio on West 52d Street. This last activity afforded Reilly a favorite view of her in black tights. Under duress, he had agreed to respect her chaste vow to her mother, but it was a hardship, particularly since he was no longer sleeping with his beautician girl friend from Lefrak City. He knew that when he turned the key on Nancy, it was going to be beyond anything, everything.

She was, of course, an idealist—the only friction between them. She would denounce American colonialism in Puerto Rico and British imperialism in Ireland, to the amusement of Reilly, who would say, "What Puerto Rico needs is a Parnell." She envisioned solutions to the problems of mankind that Reilly, already a veteran of the Harlem streets, regarded as naïve. She even believed in Reilly.

"If they've burned you so badly on the street, why are you playing baseball with the Bodega Hispana in Central Park?"

"I'm not out to save them, Nancy. They just needed a long-ball hitter."

"And what about the Sanchez wedding last year? I saw that from my window. You cared. You wouldn't let that other crazy cop shoot Moncho. Al, admit it—you care."

"That was a crazy night. A wedding party, all working people. Maybe it was the alcohol. Maybe it was the subway and factory existence." Whatever, Reilly remembered at least ten of them, in baggy rented tuxedoes, out in the middle of the street, running back and forth, carving knives, kitchen knives, 007 blades, a machete with wedding cake still smeared on the handle. Blood—in the hallway, on the cars, on the sidewalk—buckets. Reilly had seen donnybrooks at Irish wakes, but this was a massacre. When they finally broke it up, two were dead, and six were wounded, the bride with a broken arm. Someone from the Detective Squad told Reilly later that Moncho, drunk, had said the bride could fool his brother, the groom, but she couldn't fool him. That's all he had said. Jesus.

Yet she believed in the barrio, in its people, and that some political messiah, some Vito Marcantonio, or Muñoz Marin, would arise from their midst and lead them out. Where? Yonkers? She was just a kid. Let her tilt at the windmills. The world will be on her soon enough. Like the time he picked her up at the library near Lexington Avenue. A young couple with their baby in a stroller were standing by the traffic light. They were junkies, nodding, fading.

They were both out of it, gone. With their eyes half closed, they pushed the stroller out into the street against the light. Reilly could hear the cars screeching all around them before he even turned to look. He held onto Nancy. She screamed. Somehow the couple and their baby had made it across. Reilly caught up with them down the block at the next curb. The man—toothless, tattooed, scabbed, only his hands on the stroller's handlebars seemed to be holding him up. The woman—a pretty face with a scar down the cheekbone, one arm linked through his, her left arm dangling a hand that was abscessed and puffed, the size of a boxing glove. The baby was not a year old.

"I'm a police officer. You crossed this infant against the light. You coulda got him killed."

He tilted his head away from Reilly, as if to get a better look out of one eye. It was blue. He said, "Aw, man," and pulled back.

Reilly grabbed him by his fatigue jacket. "Show me some identification," Reilly yelled.

They were on 110th Street. Reilly could see the local rib shirt brigade forming up along the curb, unmistakable glee on their faces. It was a clammy summer afternoon. Some of them had stickball bats. Crazy bastards.

"Aw, raise, man. My wallet's in the pawnshop. Walsh is my name. Irish, like you. This here m' old lady, Perla." He shifted his eye to Nancy. "She ain't Irish."

The woman raised her swollen hand and waved it in Reilly's face. She wore rubber thongs; one of the loops was broken and stood up in the air. Crusted toenails. Cracked-skin heels.

"Don't fuck with Kevin, officer. We goin' to the hospital with the baby," she said.

"Yeah, man, we ain't got no time for no jaywalkin' whatchamacallit—"

He took a position facing the gathering street crowd, hands on his hips now, his head swiveling up and down, pumping up his own bravado. The spectators nodded agreement. Yeah man!

I oughta break his fucking head. But Nancy's here. This junkie will show up in night court with a turban around his head and say I assaulted him, his wife, and his baby en route to the hospital. Maybe I have to shoot one of these scumbags on the street. This is a loser, fuck it.

"Okay, go ahead. Take the baby to the hospital. But be careful crossing the street, for God's sake."

The crowd groaned its disappointment.

Reilly took Nancy by the arm, and they walked ahead in silence.

Reilly read the dope fiend as a spoil of war, left by the Irish when they fled the East Nineties. These ethnic strays were still around, the parents unable or unwilling to get out in time; their kids got the full treatment. Down the drain they went, strained through the sewage system. They bob up once in a while, junkie Irish and Jews, dregs.

He started to say something to Nancy. There were tears streaming down her face. When they got into the underpass on Park Avenue, he took her in his arms, and she cried on his chest.

"That poor baby," she kept saying, her words echoing in the stone cylinder.

"Nancy, some people are beyond reach. Let's just look out for one another. That's enough for me."

She looked up at him. "The Puerto Ricans say, 'You cannot cover the sky with your hands.' "

He took her by the arm, and they started walking. He said, "That's what I meant."

She shook her head vigorously.

"That's not good enough for me, Al."

•

If Valentin was surprised, he didn't show it. "Come on in, Lieutenant. Sit down. Gimme your coat. Break out that bottle of Barrilito, Phyllis. This is a special occasion. Turn the TV off, will ya, babe."

"No, leave it on. I like to hear it," Brennan said.

They stepped farther into the small parlor, where Valentin motioned Brennan into an armchair as he sat down on the sofa.

"Okay. What can I do you for, Lieutenant?"

"First, I want to tell you I've heard you're doing a hell of a job in the Two-Three, Johnny, a hell of a job."

"Well, you know how it is, Lieutenant. You do your best."

"I don't mean just breaking heads. I mean using diplomacy, the old noodle."

"That's my approach, Lieutenant." Valentin pulled his lower right eyelid down with his finger. "We need more of that and less of this," he said, raising a fist.

"That's exactly what I've been telling some of these clowns of mine in the Homicide Squad. In fact, I hear you have a special technique that you're using now?"

"Well, between entre nous, a lot of the credit has to go to my private little cards."

"Little cards?"

"Yeah, like my own little index. Got every hoodlum in the city in there. Wise guys, made guys, knock-around guys, you name 'em. Got them by categories, got them by trade, by vocation. This guy's junk, this guy's pot, this guy robs, this guy shoots—everything."

"What about stools?"

"Oh, yeah, sure. They are what makes me shine as a detective. Somebody gets dumped, I grab a stool. 'Who did it?' 'So and so.' Another brilliant detective work for Johnny Valentin of the Two-Three. Right, Phyllis?"

"You bet. El exigente of the police department. Here's the rum." Phyllis Valentin placed a bottle of Barrilito rum on the coffee table between the two men, then a plastic bowl filled with ice and two glasses alongside.

"Thank you, ma'am. Can we talk, John?"

"Oh, sure. Phyllis, take a magazine to the boudoir. We got official police business here." He leaned forward to make the drinks. "Shoot, Lieutenant."

"I'm the wrong guy to say that to."

They both chuckled. Valentin stuck his hand out, and they slapped skin.

"Johnny, you got a card on Roger Montalvo?"

"Roger? He's on all the cards in all the categories, includin' takin' it up the ol' service entrance."

"Fag, eh?"

"What? Don't drop the soap on this dude. *Stoned* faggot."

"You guys got a line on him?"

"Not yet, Lieutenant, but I'll find him. I got the stool brigade out now lookin'. Takes a stool to find a stool, and they will."

"You'll take him to Reilly?"

"Sure. Where else?"

"You trust me, Johnny?"

"Sure, Lieutenant."

"I have to talk to him first, Johnny. You find him for me. Bobby Tex is trying to destroy me. I have to talk to Roger first, before Reilly."

"That's a rough tip."

"Johnny, you were a narco man, right?"

"Yeah."

"You worked with Whalen, Trask, and them guys?"

"Yeah," Valentin said, tilting his head as if to get a side view of Brennan.

Brennan reached over and turned the TV on louder. "Ten big ones."

"What?"

Brennan's eyes bore into him, but Valentin could not decipher their flat grayness.

"I didn't hear too good," Valentin said.

"You heard. Don't play boy scout with me, Honey Dripper. I know you were with Whalen and them guys."

"I'm clean, Lieutenant."

"Don't pull my prick, Valentin. I know everything that goes on—everything. While you guys are out there drinking and humping, I'm working. There's not one score goes down, Guido Brennan doesn't know about. You want particulars? Maria Robelo. Sound familiar? You made the first buy, right? Your team hit the apartment. She was squatting on the shopping bag. You were all leaving empty when Trask said, 'Hey, what's she sitting on?' Remember? Eighty big ones, split five ways."

"*Four*. I never went upstairs, Guido."

"Lieutenant to you, Valentin. Bullshit. You got yours. Don't play with me."

"Lieutenant, I swear, I'm clean."

"Bullshit. Pour me another drink. You think I'm going to go down by myself? I'll take the whole Narcotics Bureau with me—including you. I'll take the whole fucking department."

"Lieutenant, please, my wife—"

"I don't give a fuck. Don't look down, Valentin. Look me in the face. Are you in? For ten?"

Valentin dropped an ice cube in Brennan's glass. "Yes, Lieutenant."

"All right. The contract is closed. You got ten big ones—in cash—when you find me Roger Montalvo. We will fuck Reilly in the ass. He's probably a quiff, too."

"Okay, Lieutenant."

Brennan stood up. "You know me. You know where I've been, what I've done. You fuck me on this one, better you piss a kidney stone through your hard on. Comprende?"

"I understand, Lieutenant."

"Walk me to the door." Brennan locked his arm tightly around Valentin's shoulder, almost lifting him off the floor as they walked. "You have to show me your card index sometime. You'd be great in the Homicide Squad. You're doing a hell of a job. Good night, Johnny."

Valentin closed the door behind Brennan. He waited for the sound of the elevator door. Then he looked through the peephole. Shaking his head, he went to the kitchen and dialed the wall phone.

"Chappie? It's me."

"Yeah?"

"He was here."

"Here, too."

"I figured."

"Don't talk on the phone. I'll see you downtown tomorrow."

"I'm all shook-up, Chappie. Chappie, he's crazy."

"Go to bed." The connection clicked off.

Valentin went to the bedroom.

"Phyllis?"

She was asleep. He sat on the edge of the bed in the dark. *"Se jodío la bicicleta."*

7 Jason Carlyle Bradley, assistant district attorney, Supreme Court Bureau, was being feted at a farewell luncheon at Gassner's by members of the DA's staff. There were fifteen guests, including Peter Quinn, seated around a long, rectangular table in the back dining room.

Bradley was slender, in his early thirties, with sandy hair, a crooked face, and an easy elegance. Reilly took note of the natural-shouldered, finely woven tweed suit. The shoes, particularly, intrigued Reilly. They had obviously cost a hundred dollars or more and shone brightly, but were old and cracked. Also Bradley, like Quinn, never wore rings, cuff links, or tiepins. Yet no one would ever say that Bradley could not match clothes or was poor. To Reilly, that was style. Reilly caught sight of himself and his plaid Ripley suit in the large wall mirror. The shoulder pads were large and bumpy.

Quinn's voice rose above the clatter of the dishes and the buzz at the large table. "Gentlemen, fellow assistants of the district attorney's office of New York County. Our time is limited; my discourse shall be mercifully brief."

Someone clinked a glass with his spoon for quiet.

"Jason Bradley has labored in these forensic vineyards for the better part of a decade. We can ill spare a lawyer possessed of his singular qualities. He has given of himself unstintingly, striving mightily to prosecute miscreants in behalf of the good burghers of this county"—a smile came across Quinn's face—"and he has smitten his share of villains. Alas, recent decisional case law has, no doubt, resuscitated most of them. But that is not our doing, and it matters not that our lances be lost, broken, or split down the shaft. The fight must continue. Jason has stood his watch faithfully, zealously, indifferent to the lunacies of the appellate courts." Then, in a lower pitch: "He has earned his respite in the form of Caldwell, Wells, Sheinbloom, etcetera, and he will no doubt flourish. But"—there was brief applause—"but I venture the prediction that there will come a time when Jason, submerged in a sea of moneybags, will look back upon his stay with us as the finest hour of his legal career. May I have the gift now, Mr. Lubin—Lubin!"

The loud laughter succeeded in awakening Stanley Lubin, who handed Quinn his napkin, then the gift-wrapped watch. Everyone applauded.

Reilly felt a hand on his shoulder. It was Leon Blumenfeld. "Did you ever hear such bullshit, Al?"

Reilly shrugged. "Sounds good to me."

"Job must agree with you. Never seen you look better, all decked out. Come on over and say hello to Sir Lancelot—I mean Jack Bradley."

"I hear he's a good lawyer."

"Another prick, but he's into the money, so it don't hurt to be nice. He's got big connections."

"Whatever you say, Leon."

Blumenfeld led Reilly over to the head of the table,

where the guest of honor was seated. They pulled up chairs.

"Reilly, ol' buddy, say hello to Jack Bradley, one of the top trial lawyers ever to grace a courtroom in this or any other jurisdiction. Waiter. Waiter, bring us another round. Make it a double. None of us are on trial. What the hell," Blumenfeld said.

"Leon, when is the last time you tried a case?" Bradley asked, smiling, as he shook hands with Reilly.

"What do you think, Jack, that it's easy to present all those cases to the grand jury? If we don't indict them, you can't try them. And we have to sift out all the garbage. Just this week, we had a poor guy on fifteen thousand dollar bail on a forced-rape case. Listen to this, Al. Lost his job, lost his wife. Seems he was shacking up with his girl friend for a few days. They decide to run away. She goes to the bank to withdraw her savings. The guy is waiting outside. Her mother and father are in the bank. She gets all rattled and starts yelling, 'rape,' 'kidnap,' 'I been a prisoner in a Chinese bakery,' etcetera. Poor jerk is in the Tombs. One interview with the girl, I knew it was from hunger. A throwout. No indictment. Maybe the guy can still pick up the pieces of his life. I felt good about it," said Blumenfeld, emptying his glass.

"A black or a Puerto Rican?" asked Bradley.

"A Puer-o Rica," Blumenfeld gulped, as he sucked on an ice cube, then spit it back into the glass.

"These people are beyond help. I want to practice law away from this charnel house. I feel as if I've been lost in a jungle and am finally stumbling out," Bradley said with a heavy sigh.

Blumenfeld waved his hand in the air, saying, "Waiter, another round here. What the hell. Ol' Brad is leaving for the big money. We got to give him a big send-off. Oops, watch that drink there."

"You know, Leon, you should have made the move long ago. You've given your whole life to this office, and what will you have to show for it in the end? Nothing, not even the gratitude of the great unwashed. Prosecutor—it's a dirty word to them. I say they can take their city and stuff it," Bradley said, his eyes focused on the horn-rims perched precariously on the tip of Blumenfeld's flat nose.

"C'mon, Jack," Blumenfeld said, "it's not that bad. There are still plenty of good people here. This is a great town. It doesn't turn its back on anybody. It'll bounce back. We gotta stay and fight it out. Oops. There goes the glass again. Where's that fuckin' waiter?" Blumenfeld unfastened his bow tie and unbuttoned his collar.

"Take it easy. We have to go back to work," said Reilly.

"Don't worry about it, Al. Have another drink. What the hell kind of Irishman are ya? Have a drink. Meet young Reilly, here, Jack. Tough cop from uptown Harlem. Met him in the grand jury. Made plenty of good collars uptown. Al, you were in the middle of the Harlem riots, as I remember. He don't take no shit. Put in, what—a good seven years up there."

"What bureau are you in now?" Bradley asked.

"I'm in the Homicide Bureau."

"God, you'll be up to your neck in Puerto Ricans and Negroes again," Bradley said, raising his hands in feigned alarm.

"You were right, Leon," Reilly said, his voice suddenly flat.

"Right about what?"

"This guy Jack Bradley *is* a jerk."

"Did I say that?" Blumenfeld said, looking around.

"You sure did. And that he's got a paper asshole to boot."

"Is this some kind of routine?" Bradley said, looking confused. "I—"

"It's just that I don't go for your put-down of this office and Leon. This is a great office, and Leon is among the guys who made it so. And I'm proud to be part of it and maybe do some good. But let me tell you, there are some fine people uptown: all colors, all shades, all varieties. For every scumbag, you have at least ten decent people breaking their hump trying to see their way through. And carrying some load. Like the plumbing doesn't work in summer; the heating doesn't work in winter; the rats and roaches work extra shifts. If the broken stairs don't get you, the falling plaster will—I know I'm making a big impression on you."

"No. On the contrary, a very interesting sociological treatise," Bradley said, crossing his arms over his chest.

Undaunted, Reilly continued. "Despite all this, I've received a hundred kindnesses from these people, and even the most prejudiced cop will admit the same. Knowing my temper, if I had to live in that shit-house, I'd have been up on the roof in '67 throwing chimney bricks, too. Don't get me wrong. I've busted plenty of heads. But the vast majority are just trying to make it in a tough town. And you know what? I'm betting they're going to make it. So here's to the folks from uptown. How about it, Leon? Salud?"

"Tha'sh right, Al. Salud. Let's drink up."

"You're both drunk," Bradley said. He pushed his chair back, rose, and walked out of the room.

"Great speech. You're all right, Jack."

"Al."

"I mean Al. Hey, look who's here—Pearlie. Hey, Pearlstein, come over and have a drink with us."

"Hi, Leon. Al. Yeah, I could use a drink. Look at my eye." Pearlstein's left eye was swollen almost shut and was beginning to discolor.

"What happened to you? You didn't have that yesterday," Reilly said.

"No, it happened this morning. Right in the fucking courthouse. I got a statutory rape case. You won't believe this. The girl is underage but built like a brick shithouse, and there's no corroboration. Shit case. The judge in 1-A throws the case out. So I'm marching out with my arm around my client. A big win. You pick up a lot of clients like that. Anyway, we're going out through the door to the hallway, and there's a couple of guys standing there. All of a sudden, they pounce on us and start to pound the piss out of me. I threw a few punches, but what the hell, I ain't in shape. Turns out to be the brothers of the broad. Cops locked them up. They'll probably retain me. But the kicker is, while I was in the courtroom, I had this South American lady client waiting in the hallway for me. She saw the whole fight. You know what she said to me? She said, 'Does this happen often in American courts?' How do you like that shit?"

"Terrible. You got your life in your hands, Pearlie. Have a drink," said Blumenfeld.

"It's a shit profession. I shoulda been a medical man like my brother, Dr. Keith Pearlstein."

"Jeez, that's a nice name. They gave you guys nice names. What does he do?" Blumenfeld asked.

"Nothin'. Looks at pussy all day."

"Jeez, that's a nice profession. What does his wife say?"

"Nothin'. Why should she squawk? He's gettin' paid,

ain't he? Sure. All he needs is a little table with these metal hoops at the end. Makes a fortune."

"I'll be goddamn. How do you like that shit, Al?"

"We better get back," Reilly said, getting up.

"Okay. Pearlie, see you 'round the Legal Aid, ha!"

"Don't mention those cock suckers to me. Steal the bread right outta my kids' mouths." Pearlstein's good eye glistened with rage.

"You ain't got no kids, Pearlie."

"So what? I could adopt some."

"Got a point there."

"Sure."

"See ya."

•

It was 5:00 A.M. Chapman at the wheel, Valentin seated alongside. 116th Street and Third Avenue slid into view. They parked near the southwest corner. Valentin removed his revolver and clip holster from his waistband and handed them to Chapman.

Chapman leaned his back against the car door, his arm draped over the wheel. "You crazy?"

"No other way. They won't even let me in otherwise, let alone talk to me. Gotta be. Shouldn't take long," Valentin said as he got out the other side. He slammed the door shut, then motioned for Chapman to lower the window.

Chapman, leaning over, cranked down the window. "Yeah?"

"Watch out for muggers, Chappie. They got some bad Ne-groes around here," Valentin said and started walking toward the corner.

"Fuck you," Chapman said, laughing to himself.

Valentin walked east on 116th. The narrow, red-brick tenements were tightly packed. Their exhausted frames and cracked walls seemed compressed and sloped for mutual support. The wind had toppled garbage cans, the refuse littering the pavement and the wide street as newspapers and food-stained cardboard plates twirled in the strong gusts sweeping the block. Late-model Lincoln Continentals and Cadillacs were double-parked alongside broken-down Impalas mounted on milk crates.

"Cats must be having a big party," Valentin muttered to himself and stopped in front of a dilapidated building with a wooden door. The windowpanes were mostly missing or shattered. A huge skull was graffitied on the wall by the blanket-covered ground-floor window. He walked into the hall and up wooden steps edged with tin to the first-floor landing and paused outside the chewed-up wooden door of an apartment. A junkie could puff the door down. He continued on up to the second floor, turned right, and stopped in front of a metal door that would have compared favorably with the vault of a bank. "Now that's a fucking door." He knocked twice and immediately heard the snap of a latch, high up, which exposed a tiny metal screen.

"Yeah?"

"I'm a friend of Casto."

"Yeah?"

"Tell 'im Johnny from the old Renegades."

There was a pause of a few seconds; then Valentin heard the locks unsnapping and the sliding of heavy metal bolts. A short, thick-shouldered man wearing a dark suit and tinted glasses appeared, pushing the heavy door with both hands.

"You clean?"

"Clean," Valentin answered, raising his elbows up and

out as the man quickly ran his hands up and down Valentin's sides.

The metal door was slammed shut, and a second door, made of wood, opened, revealing a tuxedoed figure of medium height, like Valentin, but with light skin and eyes under a bushy Afro. He was smiling widely through a thick moustache.

"Casto, I thought it was Cesar Romero in that outfit."

Casto laughed, putting his arm around Valentin's shoulder. "Let's go to my office."

The two men walked into what had once been a large apartment. The walls separating the spacious rooms had been knocked down to make room for a long bar with two bartenders, tables, a large dance floor, and a bandstand against the back wall. Valentin took in a piano, vibraphone, conga, timbales, and several horns. Louie Candelario y sus Caballos, the sign read. Horse is right, Valentin smirked to himself as he walked alongside Casto, his head tucked in, a man minding his own business.

Casto's after-hours club was jammed with expensively attired men and women at the bar, the tables, on the dance floor. The band was playing loud salsa music, and the floor shook under the dancers' feet. The walls were decorated with a maroon carpet; the lighting in the dim room gave it a dark cast. But the bar was brightly lit and decorated with zebra-patterned stools.

Valentin felt a pang. Lookit them foxes, and I'm playin' cops 'n' robbers. Shit. As they turned away into the office, an enclosed cubicle to the right of the doorway, he noted a sign.

* * *

POSITIVELY NO GUNS ALLOWED
NO TWO PEOPLE IN TOILET
DO YOUR THING OUTSIDE

THE MANAGEMENT
(Casto and Nestor)

Valentin paused in front of it, moving his head up and down in appreciation. "Casto, leave it to you to run a clean joint."

"I don't fuck around. Learned my lesson."

"How much?"

"Federal pound. Forty-four months."

They stepped into the office—a desk, several chairs, and a large safe. They sat down, Casto behind the desk, Valentin by its side.

"Need somethin'?" Casto asked, putting his finger to his nose.

"Nah, c'mon, Casto."

"How about a drink instead?"

"Thanks, no, babe. I don't wanna take your time. I'm looking for a stool pigeon, Roger Montalvo."

Casto's smiling face drew inward until his lips disappeared behind his moustache. His yellow-flecked green eyes glinted as he stared hard at Valentin. Then he flicked his fingers down the satin lapel of his jacket.

"Why do you come to me? Think *I'm* a stool?"

"Casto, Casto, we go back twenty years. Think I don't know your reputation as a man? But Roger's the guy ratted you out to the feds. He's a material witness, and I gotta find him. That Tony Roman thing."

"Brennan, huh? Figures."

"You know Brennan?"

"Keep him away from here. He's sick."

"It was self-defense. Tony had a piece—two pieces."

Casto sat silent, staring into Valentin's eyes. Then, "You fuckin' cops are all alike. Self-defense, eh?" Casto was nodding his head up and down in mock accord. "Moon would get a kick out of that."

"Where is Moon?"

"Fort Lauderdale, in his motel, except when he comes up here to break my balls over the money."

"Casto, I don't wanna interfere in your private—"

Casto laughed. "Full of shit, Johnny. You know Mullins is my partner, and you *been* knowin' it."

"Fuckin' Jimmy Mullins. . . . You can't help me out about Roger?"

"Wadda I know from that faggot? I see 'im, I'll kill 'im."

A large, muscular black man in a mock turtleneck sweater and suede jacket barged into the office. Big, almost as big as Brennan, thought Valentin. The man, who towered over the still-seated Valentin, clamped coffee-colored eyes on him. His head was shaved bald, as was his smooth brown-skin face, with its keloid scar that jumped over his left eye and ran down close to his broad nose. His knuckles on his hips, he said, "You got warrant, man?"

"This is just a social call. Who—?" Valentin said, looking to his host.

"Nestor, this is Johnny. We were kids together. He's all right."

Nestor turned to face Casto, waving his banana-fingered hands in the air as if about to launch himself. "Casto, I surprise wiz you. You know we got beeg people comeeng ober here in a leetle while. So you got a cop ober here. Das crazy." Turning again to Valentin: "You, fockin' cop!" He looked intently at his wrist-watch, "I geeve you five minute; then I throw you down the stair, okay?"

Valentín jumped to his feet, setting his face to match Nestor's. Not having his gun tempered his outrage. He glared at him, the mental mother fucker.

"Basta, Nestor, basta." Casto waved the huge man back.

Nestor stamped out of the cubicle.

Casto chortled. "How you like my new manager, Johnny?"

"Ave Maria, where did you get that fuckin' gorilla?"

"Santo Domingo, compliments of Trujillo. He's got a bullet in his head, so he don't give a fuck. When he's around I don't have to be takin' guns off people, and next time some niggers show up with shotguns to stick up the joint, I'm sendin' him."

"He ain't gonna be around long, Casto."

"That's cool. He's in a hurry. He's always asking me if anybody's causing me any trouble. But in the meantime everybody's scared of him, and I can make some money." Looking at his watch, smiling, Castro said, "Better make it. Nestor don't tell time good."

"Mother fuck him," said Valentín, walking out with Casto.

As they wended their way through the noisy crowd, Valentín's eyes caught and registered images in rapid succession. European-looking cats, speaking Spanish with the "vos" instead of the "tu," Argentinians—junk; short, bristly haired Indian types, gotta be Peruvians or Ecuadorians—coke; if they're white, perfumed, talcum-powdered, with see-through socks, they're Cubano—they're into everything; with ties hanging open, afangul, wops are easy—they're everything, too; tall, skinny, "ey, mon" spooks, Jamaicans or Haitians—that's the pot connection. Sprinkle them all with Puerto Ricans, and it spells m-o-t-h-e-r. A regular cornucopion here.

This is the only pot in the country that's melting, he thought. The one with the thugs in it. Shit, I can make a room with one suck of my eyeballs. How the hell can the Narco Bureau get along without me?

•

Valentin walked back to Chapman and the car. Chapman leaned over and opened the passenger-side door for him.

"So?"

"So nothing."

They drove south on Lexington Avenue.

"That's Jimmy's place, Chappie."

"Jimmy who?"

"Jimmy Mullins—Moon."

"I know. None of your business."

"Lookin' good up there, Chappie."

"What?"

"Dynamite pussy up there. Oo-wa, oo-wa," Valentin said, rolling his eyeballs upward.

"Horny mother fucker. Next thing, you gonna have your hand on my knee."

"Aw, lay down, will ya? Let's go eat. We got business to discuss."

•

Chapman and Valentin sat at a small Formica table in the back of Sonny's Diner.

"Why didn't you tell me Brennan was comin' over last night? You want me to have a shit hemorrhage?"

"Don't be a panic merchant. We'll talk now. Better this way," said Chapman, his voice calm.

"Hóstia santísima. The car's going a hundred miles an hour, and the steering wheel come off in my hands, and I'm a panic merchant. Hey, Chappie, are you right on this thing? 'Cause if you ain't, I'll go straight to Reilly."

Chapman's chair scraped loudly on the tile floor as he half rose in anger. "Fuck you mean, *if* I'm right? Check out your own dirty drawers, Mr. Narco Man. You was ridin' with some cannonballin' mother fuckers for a while there, right? And that was heavy paper. Wasn't no hundred-dollar policy pads. So dig yo'self, Honey Dripper. You're drippin' arsenic."

"You ain't hangin' too tough yo'self, Detective Second Grade. You and the pimp clothes you wear. You been ridin' piggyback with the craziest mother fucker in the police department, Guido Brennan. You know what he offered me in my house? In my house, can you dig it? Ten thou, bro. Ten thousand dollars to get him Roger Montalvo. I don't have to ask the easy question, namely, what's he gonna do with Roger the faggot? But the hard question comes in two parts. What he been doin' that he got that kind of bread, and who's behind him?"

Chapman sat back down hard. "He laid that on you, John?"

"My balls ain't shrunk to beebees for nothin'."

Chapman slid his hands along his temples. "Guido has gone crazy."

"Been crazy. What I want to know is, who's gonna be crazy enough to lock him up? I seen him go myself that time on 111th Street. Better you take a benzine enema. Later."

"Can't be worryin' about that now," said Chapman. "We gotta go to Reilly."

"I don't know why I didn't stay with the Bickford

chain. They had big plans for me." Valentin looked skyward.

"We're gonna rat him out, right, Johnny?"

"What are we supposed to do? You gonna blow wife, kids, house, job, pension? You wanna blow it all? A man can ask you to stretch your neck, but not to snap it off. Ain't nobody got that right, Chappie."

"I owe him," Chapman said softly, rubbing his chin.

"Stop right there. If you and this dude been sellin' homicides, I don't wanna hear about nothin', please." Valentin cupped his hands over his ears.

"It ain't like that. But the man has bailed me out more than once."

Valentin waved both hands in front of him. "No way I'm gonna leave my balls on the ceiling 'cause you owe Brennan. I got a guy, Lanigan, when I first come on. We get a squeal that a nut job has got a knife. The mother is callin' for help. We get up there. Like usual, the mother is yellin', 'Don't hurt Junior.' Meanwhile, the knife is yea long, and Junior looks like Sonny Liston—only in pajamas. We start dancin' around the table, finally get the knife off him. But he's beatin' the shit out of me, so I had to give him a few whacks. This gets the moms mad. Next thing I know, the moms got the knife, and I'm backpedalin' out the way I came in. But I tripped on the table leg and fell on my ass. She'd have spiked me to the floor. Lanigan put a cap in her."

"She croak?" Chapman asked.

"No, but close. Lanigan went through all kinds of shit and hearings just 'cause he saved my life. I owe *him*, but only so much. But this? This is different, Chappie. Brennan's got to do this one by himself. Think of what's goin' down. You know he's on some kind of pad. That's for sure. You know he's gonna whack out Roger. What are we supposed to be, accessories to murder? Buddy-buddy ain't gonna work here. I'm sorry, Chappie. It's bugout time. No other way. Let's talk to Reilly."

"What a cock-suckin' mess."

8 The Homicide Bureau of the district attorney's office had just ended its weekly Friday meeting in the office of the chief of the bureau, the fifteen members having decided the degree of homicide in the new cases they would recommend to the grand jury. Decided also were recommendations of dismissals.

Quinn addressed the group. "Gentlemen, you have all met Aloysius X. Reilly, the newest member of the bureau. From my limited exposure thus far, I predict that he will be a valuable asset to this office, by all accounts the best district attorney's office in this country. It has been and, I pray, will continue to be the embodiment of everything a prosecutor's office should be. I trust that my tenure here has contributed in some small measure to its success.

"Yes, gentlemen. I am resigning effective the first of a year." A buzz of comments interrupted Quinn; he raised a hand for silence. "Next month will see a new administration in Washington and a new era in law enforcement. And about time. I have always abhorred politics, but given this new climate, I am persuaded I can be a more vital contributor to law and order by entering the lists of public life. Mindful of the district attorney's policy that his assistants should remain outside the political realm, I have tendered my resignation, and he has graciously accepted it, albeit expressing his reluctance to do so, although not by half my own in offering it.

"The district attorney has not yet reached a decision as to my successor. The chief assistant and the executive assistant have made their respective recommendations. Be assured that I will recommend a member of this bureau. Good night and good-bye, gentlemen."

The assistants proceeded to file out of Quinn's office.

"Reilly? May I have a word with you?"

"Yes, sir."

"Sit down, sit down. Now then, how is your investigation coming along? Have you collated all the available evidence?"

"Well, there are still some problems, sir."

"I thought it was an open-and-shut case." Quinn rocked in his chair.

"Not exactly. There were some statements made by a Robert Texidor which raised some questions I want to look into."

"Such as?" Quinn asked, his heavy eyebrows raised.

"That the deceased Tony Roman would never carry two guns, much less a .45. He implied it was a rub-out, an assassination."

"I see. Are you acquainted with the backgrounds of Texidor and Roman?" Quinn asked, his black eyes on Reilly.

"Yes, sir."

"Then you must be aware that they are two of the worst cutthroats in the city. They are also purveyors of narcotics. Liars and criminals of the most base variety."

"Yes, sir."

"And Lieutenant Brennan is one of the most able,

competent, and effective officers in the city. Albeit an aggressive one, of which we probably need more. I am surprised that someone with your experience on the streets can give much credence to the testimony of a Bobby Tex. The man is a scoundrel."

"I know that, sir. But I haven't had an opportunity to speak to the witness, Roger Montalvo."

"Roger Montalvo? Witness to what, Reilly?"

"Well, he's the informant that called Brennan and told him where Roman was. I have to speak to him to cover that area of the case."

Quinn shifted in his chair, exasperated. Elbow on desk, he pointed his finger. "A word of caution, Reilly. When you deal with the world of the informant, remember one thing. He always doubles back. He recants. Prepare for that contingency. Do not permit yourself to be pressed beyond the limits of good sense and reason. They are a guileful and deceitful lot. They have but one motivation—self-preservation. And they have no compunctions about turning on anyone, least of all a prosecutor."

"I appreciate that, sir."

"I want you to present this case as soon as possible to the grand jury—preferably before I leave."

"Yes, sir."

"Incidentally, I understand you had words with Jason Bradley."

"Well, not really. Just a discussion of conditions in the ghetto, Mr. Quinn."

"Those conditions antedate your arrival here and, rest assured, will prevail long after your departure."

"But there are things that can be helped, sir."

A slight smile came to Quinn's lips. "Reilly, the fact is, I find it charming that an Irish cop from a ghetto precinct should harbor such sentiments."

"I learned the hard way."

"The slot for house liberal will be vacant when Leon Blumenfeld retires. I suggest you apply."

"I could do worse. I have a lot of respect for Chief Blumenfeld."

Quinn vaulted to his feet, startling Reilly, and leaned forward, his hands on his desk.

"Stop right there. I picked you because I saw potential. Do not allow yourself to be shuffled back into the pack because of some misguided search for a mentor or a surrogate father. Blumenfeld has shot his bolt in this office. You are to have nothing to do with him. And you are expressly forbidden to ever discuss the business of this bureau with him. Is that understood?"

"Yes, sir."

"Let me tell you a few tales out of school so that later you will not plead ignorance. Blumenfeld affects a down-home, self-effacing facade which should immediately alert you to keep your hand on your wallet. He formulates his opinions, juridical and otherwise, in accordance with Max Lerner's column of the day. He has the morals of a tomcat, his office being conveniently located on the ninth floor, opposite the secretarial pool, where he can letch ad nauseam. And he is an alcoholic, tolerated here only at the sufferance of the district attorney himself."

"I see."

"You have been told. Guide yourself accordingly. Now, this Roger Montalvo business. Is that what is holding everything up?"

"Yes."

"All right. Lean on Valentin and Chapman to wind this up. When the whereabouts of this Montalvo are ascertained, you will come to me immediately and report. Clear?"

"Yes, sir."

Quinn sat heavily and spun his chair, his sharp-boned features in profile to Reilly. He adjusted his tie and jacket, bent down to dust off the cuffs of his pants.

Reilly stood up. "Is that all, Chief?"

"Reilly, there are not too many of us left in this city. But there is still room for a select few. The Jews cannot have it all. Modesty aside, you would do better to emulate me."

"I'll do my best."

"Your best." Quinn examined his fingernails. "In common with many of our race there is a discernible indecision about you. We are, I realize, to varying degrees, victims of a thousand years of popery and Thomistic claptrap. But we can, and will, rise above that. The will, Mr. Reilly. Steel the will, and there is nothing you cannot accomplish."

Reilly nodded blankly, confused.

"Good night, Reilly."

"Good night, sir."

•

It was 5:30 P.M. Most of the staff had left for the weekend. Reilly reclined in his chair. The door to his office was closed. He was not looking forward to a weekend in his cheerless apartment. He slumped deeper into the chair and fought his melancholy, shunting his thoughts to another corner of the city and another time.

Nancy had lived with her parents in a third-floor apartment, above the Weekend Bar. The building sagged like a pug who had taken too many head shots, but the apartment was clean, the accent on plaster saints, palm leaves, plastic covers, and multiple locks on the door and window gates. Reilly commented on how neat everything was.

"Before anything else, I'm getting my folks out of here," she said, shaking her head in that way that she had of turning off a subject.

Maria Bosch, her mother, was a tall, fair-skinned woman, with light eyes and hair pulled back in a long braid. She spoke no English and was either intimidated by Reilly's presence or shy, as she would only say, "permiso," and go into the bedroom. The living room was adorned with photographs of Nancy: an infant on a pinto pony on some Harlem street, kneeling on the perennial photo studio prie-dieu at first communion, a high school graduation photograph taken the year before. She was always beautiful. An only child, it was plain she was the center of life for Maria and Vicente Bosch in apartment 3A front.

Behind the sofa there was an old tinted photograph of Maria with Nancy's father, Vicente. A garden in Puerto Rico, Maria in a long dress, sitting on some kind of hammock. The father, with Nancy's features, stood alongside in a white suit. He seemed dark, very dark. A merchant seaman, he was expected home for the Christmas holidays.

Marriage was not discussed. It was understood. How could it have been otherwise? It was at the time of the Thanksgiving recess that they had conspired their prenuptial honeymoon plot. Nancy was to persuade Maria that they were going to visit Maria's sister, Antonia, in Puerto Rico. After all, it was high time that their relatives in Jayuya, their hometown, should meet Nancy's pretendiente. As Nancy spoke, her hands gesturing, Reilly sat on the sofa, wishing he could wrap its plastic cover around him. Legs and wrists crossed, Reilly assumed an expression he hoped would denote respect, placidity, and best of all, ignorance. After all, he did not comprende. Maria's shy, benign eyes widened as she turned and clasped them on his now disquieted face. "Uh-o!"

But Maria Bosch only said, "Que Dios los bendiga," with a shrug of resignation and retreated to the bedroom. Reilly felt that they had been pronounced man and wife.

They left for a week in Puerto Rico.

Awakening under blue snow-soft skies trailing white wisps, he traced his fingers over her half-moon breasts, which rose visibly to the touch. Her voice calling his name with every thrust of his body into hers, the color rising in her face as she swayed from side to side.

The cabana by the sea the morning she stood naked, brushing her hair, in front of the bathroom mirror. He slid out of bed, crawling serpentlike, intent on frightening her. But within touching distance, there on his stomach on the cold tiles, he stopped, fascinated, as the water beads snaked their way down the curves of her browned back, paused on her lighter-shaded buttocks, then downward again, gently sprinkling his outstretched hands. He thought of a Gauguin print he had seen. Only the flower was missing. She stepped backward, over his head, her legs spread apart, straddling him.

"I knew you were there," she said as she knelt down on top of him, her breasts and wet hair in his face. The sum of it was that she, the novice, had consumed him, brought him, literally, to tears. He had never come to that with a woman.

They rented a car and drove into the mountains to her mother's village. The aunt, Toñita, could not do enough for Nancy and her gringo. It seemed half of the village turned out for the dinner she gave them. The generosity, the warmth, the openness of the people seemed so natural in the setting of those cool mountains and green valleys.

The next day they drove south to Ponce in the rented convertible, then along the shore to the east coast of the island, where they turned north. There were stretches of beaches all along the way; often they were the only bathers. They would stop at small inns and guesthouses. By evening the day's sun had browned her skin to a copper gloss.

At dinner they sat across from each other, the table lamp shooting glints of light into her dark eyes. They held hands, deep in conversation.

"Do you understand my point, Al?"

"What? Of course, definitely."

He would laugh; yet his delight in probing her mind was genuine. She was surprisingly self-motivated. Books, she told him, had been her haven from the rancid slum streets. With enthusiasm and gentle prodding she encouraged his return to school.

Reilly, the hard-nose, found himself searching the heavens for some sign of divine intervention. But mostly that week they had fun.

He remembered her laughing, till the tears flowed, at his pseudo-Cockney rendition of "Gunga Din." They had been diving from a reef off a deserted cove. Reilly, high-spirited, tramped around in flippers and snorkel as she lay on the white sand. "For it's 'Din, Din, Din,' " he yelled, waving a spear gun, as she laughed and applauded.

That was the afternoon they swam in the waters of a lagoon that shimmered, silver-coated.

" 'Que tarde aquella la de aguel gran diá, que dia aguel el de la tarde aquella,' " she said.

Reilly was lost, of course, but he knew she spoke of love.

"Arco iris, a rainbow!" she gasped.

"I've never seen such colors, Nancy."

"That's why we come in so many colors, Al. We are a rainbow people."

They were by the water's edge, where the sand was cooler, side by side, on their backs, the sea rising and receding under their spread-eagled bodies.

"Tell me something, Nancy. Tell me what you feel."

She spoke softly. " 'Tell me, Captain, you who know the waters of this sea. After the storm, will there, over the calm, be a void between my arms, or perhaps, a heart broken in pieces?' "

"You expect that?"

"No. It's just a song that was going through my mind." She sat up. "Let's take our bathing suits off. We'll go in the water. Adán y Eva. Amor mío."

Rising to her feet, laughing, she unfastened her bra, which fell on him; then running to the water, she tumbled backward, breaking the calm, sun-streaked surface. He watched her submerge, then burst, almost full body, to the surface in a spray of water, the lighter hues of her naked breasts startling against the brownness of her upstretched arms. She sank slowly into the water, the sun making spangles of the drops in the midnight of her hair.

Sunset found them in a darkened room, locked in a naked embrace.

She intoned softly, "Did you not see me today come to you from out of the green water, drawn by phosphorescent sea horses through rows of gold coral?"

"From you I believe it. You've already got me crazy."

They laughed, rocking back and forth on the bed.

Then, only half in jest, she said, "I will make you crazy. And when I am gone, you will never forget me."

"Never. La morto first," Reilly said.

"La muerte, silly," she said, giggling as she fell asleep on his chest.

The plane had arrived back in New York after midnight. Kennedy was cold and dark. Huddled together in the taxi, they rode in silence toward Manhattan.

Finally she said, "How will I sleep tonight without you?"

Later they stood in the hallway by her door like two teen-agers. People kept going up and down the stairwell; loud music blared from an open apartment below; doors kept banging. No matter. They could not let go of one another. Five times he started down the stairs.

"I can't go inside, Al. I want to stay with you. Take me with you."

He reached past her, knocked on the door, and went down the stairs quickly, pausing on the second floor to call up that he would phone her as soon as he got home.

They spoke on the phone almost to daybreak.

The following month she told him she was pregnant. Reilly was elated. Nothing could ever take her away. She was his now.

"What do you want me to do, Al? I'll do whatever you want me to. I know you want to go back to school."

"The hell with school. We'll get married after the holidays."

He had picked her up in his arms and spun her around until he remembered the baby. He would be named Francis, Frank, like his father. Aunt Flo would like that. It was a kind of madness. He indulged himself. Liberation. He would answer to no one. He was beyond the world's reproaches and censure. There was a newness within him, great ambitions. The leopard had shed its spots.

Then came Christmas Eve, dank and drizzly. It was early afternoon. Mullins had stopped the patrol car in front of Nancy's building.

"Wait here, Jimmy. I got this for her mother. I'll run upstairs. Won't be a minute."

Reilly stepped out of the car. Nancy turned the corner, holding the arm of a tall, dark man. Reilly could see Mullins lowering the window. Nancy rushed forward when she saw Reilly, pulling the man by the arm. He wore a hat, but Reilly could see their faces were almost identical—except he was black.

"Al, I want you to meet my father. He's home for the holidays. What a treat for us. Pápi, this is Al Reilly, el policía that Mámi wrote to you about."

Vicente Bosch was long and thin, almost cadaverous. His small features were tightly drawn over his face, the muscles like rope. They shook hands, and Mr. Bosch smiled, his fine teeth white against his brown skin.

"I have a pleasure to meet you, Mr. Reilly."

"The pleasure is mine, Mr. Bosch. This is my partner, Officer Mullins." He could see the light coat of a sneer on Mullins' fat face. "Well, look—ah—we're on duty. This package is for your mother. I'll call you tonight. Nice meeting you, Mr. Bosch."

He'd put the box in her hands. His own hands were unsteady. He had to get out of there, go somewhere, sort things out. Jesus.

Reilly got back into the patrol car. Mullins drove north, then west, and came to a halt. There was no way Mullins was going to keep his mouth shut. He shifted to the right, placing his knee on the seat, corkscrewing his rump until he was comfortable. Then he said, "He's a nigger, Al. Face it."

"Jesus Christ, Jimmy."

"This ain't no phony Hindu or Hawaiian. This is a regular nigger."

"Will you shut up? Jesus. Mother of Jesus."

"Okay. I won't say nothin'."

Mullins faced forward again. The silence was broken only by the sound of the windshield wipers. Reilly lowered his window; a light rain sprayed his face. He felt a feverish ring of heat around his coat collar, which chafed as he rubbed his fingers against the heavy wool.

"What am I going to do, Jimmy? What am I going to do?"

"You're gonna close it out. That's what you're gonna do. We had this same shit during the war. Guys would bring their Jap broads home. It don't work. Blood is thicker than water. White guys like you and me, wadda you think we're doin' here? We're the army of occupation, that's what we are. So you get a little bit here, and you get a little bit there. But, 'ey, don't get involved. That's crazy. You won't make it, especially you. I can tell."

He gave Reilly the old-pro routine, complete with the waving of the hands and winding up with his finger jabbing Reilly's chest. But Reilly had focused on Mullins's cigar-stained lower denture, which was bobbing up and down, and felt nauseous.

"Move the fucking vehicle," Reilly said.

Mullins started to laugh. "I saw the whole thing in the movies, with Hattie McDaniel." Then he looked at Reilly's face and sobered a little. "C'mon, Al, you take everything so serious."

Reilly was at a cops' bar on 104th Street when he called her at home that evening. She picked up the phone on the first ring. He knew he was in trouble.

"Nancy—"

"You should have seen your face and the smirk on your partner—"

"Nancy—"

"Don't interrupt me, goddamn it. Listen, and listen good. It's over. Gone. Whatever I had for you was finished today, right on my stoop. My father is the most wonderful man in the world. Working on his stinking ships, away from my mother and me. And I had to look at your face today when you met him. You never gave him a chance. Do you know what he's been through? Do you know how he has worked and sacrificed? Even when he's been sick? You never gave him a chance. He's black—step back. I guess you can't help the way you are, the way you were brought up. It's my fault for starting up with a gringo. But you needn't worry. I will take care of everything, you hear, everything. It won't cost you a cent."

"Nancy."

"One promise. You will never see me again as long as you live. Good-bye. Para siempre."

"Nancy, give me time. Let me think this out. I mean, he's a black man. My Aunt Florence, my Uncle Brian, my cousins, the wedding. I want things right for us. You're always so positive about what's right, Nancy. I'm not as quick. Give me time. Jesus."

Reilly sat in the phone booth for ten minutes after she had hung up.

Somebody pushed the door of the booth. Stokes, a black detective.

"You okay, Al? Little too much Christmas spirit, eh?"

Reilly stayed at the bar all night with Stokes and the officers from the four-to-twelve shift. He went on sick call for three days. Even his Uncle Brian, an alcoholic, was worried about his being on a toot for three days.

The fourth morning he cleaned himself up and went over the Triboro Bridge at seventy miles an hour. He chased up the stairs to her apartment, two steps at a time.

The eye at the peephole belonged to Maria Bosch. "Qué quieres?"

"Mrs. Bosch, please, por favor, let me speak to Nancy."

"Ella no está aquí, se marchó."

"No comprendo, Mrs. Bosch. Where's Nancy?"

He heard the turning of locks. The door opened, and there stood the gaunt figure of Vicente Bosch.

"Mr. Reilly, Nancy no home. Go far away. Don't come back."

"Where, Mr. Bosch. Where did she go, in the name of God?"

"No say. She just go away. Sorry. Good-bye, Mr. Reilly. Y que Díos lo perdone."

The door closed. One, two, three locks, then the chain sliding across. Reilly stood there. A quiet settled into the hallway, as if the worn, crayon-scrawled walls sensed the finality of his undoing.

He walked down the steps very slowly, his hand gripping the sticky wooden banister mounted on twisted iron rungs. The hall lights were nearly all out. The first floor was in total darkness. He lit a match but a draft of cold air quickly blew it out.

She was unrelenting in her promise. She vanished. And Reilly commenced his purgatory, walking the streets in search of her. He saw bits, parts, flashes of her everywhere, of course. But never Nancy.

"You gotta pull yourself together, or I'm not going to work in the car with you no more. I'm tellin' you, Al."

"Go fuck yourself—Moon!"

"What did you call me? Jesus fuckin' Christ, all this fuckin' aggravation over some spic twat. I mean, what's the matter with you, Al?"

"You degenerate scumbag, you open your mouth again, and I'll blow your fuckin' brains out."

That was the end of the team. They never worked the sector together again.

His letters were all returned. Spring arrived early that year, with the profusion of colors that follow a hard winter, colors that brightened the trees, the skies, and ultimately, Reilly's pallid spirits. Reilly was surprised. He thought he had interred his soul with the winter snows, yet he had endured.

He enrolled at Brooklyn Law School. After three years, two summer sessions, and the failure of his first examination, he was at last admitted to the bar.

●

The telephone on Reilly's desk rang. He picked it up.

"Hello, Al Reilly?" It was Valentin.

"Yes, speaking."

"Al, Johnny here. Johnny Valentin. We tried to get you earlier, but they told us you were tied up. Listen, we gotta talk to you, me and Chappie."

"Can't it wait till Monday? I was just leaving."

"Can't wait. Gotta see you."

"Bad?"

"If it gets any worse, I'm goin' back to the La Salle School of Cafeteria Management."

"All right, I'll meet you guys someplace. I don't want to stay here. Where do we meet?"

"What about across the park there—Giambone's?"

"Okay, what time?" He looked at his watch.

"Give us an hour or so, say . . . six thirty."

"Roger."

"Don't say that word."

"What?"

"See you in an hour."

Reilly rolled down his sleeves and linked the cuffs, then put on his jacket and picked up his overcoat from the other chair as he left. He took the elevator to the ninth floor and pushed open the door to the Indictment Bureau. A cleaning lady stepped aside as he walked into Leon Blumenfeld's back office.

"What can I do for you, Al? I got a lotta work here."

"I got a problem with a case," Reilly said as he shut Blumenfeld's door.

"Guido Brennan."

"Yeah, all kinds of bad vibes in the air. I'm worried about it."

"Nothing to worry about. Play it straight down the middle. Ass on the table. You do your job, you can't get hurt. That's the way the boss runs this office. Don't give a shit who it is. Could be a patrolman; could be an inspector. Makes no difference. If he's wrong, he goes. Don't get screwed up with departmental loyalty and all that shit, Al. You're an assistant district attorney now. You're a lawyer. Don't forget that."

"I won't."

"If things get out of hand, go straight to Quinn or, better yet, come to me, and we'll go straight to the district attorney himself."

"Okay, Leon. Thanks a lot. I'll see you later."

9 Chapman and Reilly sat at a table against the wall opposite the bar and listened to Valentin's order.

"I want the clams oreganata. Minestrone soup, veal cutlet parmagiana with spaghetti. Give me a nice salad, plenty of anchovies. Don't give me no bread. Gotta watch my diet. Oh, give me a schooner of beer," Valentin added as he stuffed a large napkin into the collar of his shirt.

"How can you eat like that at a time like this?" Chapman asked, disgust on his face.

"In times of crisis, all great men scarf. Good for the brain, Chappie," Valentin said, holding knife and fork upright on the white tablecloth.

"That's brain food?"

"Of course."

"You eat like a man with two assholes."

"What is this shit about crisis?" Reilly interjected. "Don't keep me in suspense."

"You guys order first," said Valentin.

"Just bring me the chicken cacciatore and some wine —Verdicchio. A little salad," Reilly said as the waiter wrote.

"Just bring me a Scotch on the rocks," said Chapman. "I can't eat. That's all, waiter."

"The situation is approaching ground critical, ceiling zero," Valentin said, waving his knife for emphasis. "Someone's tilting the machine. Guido Brennan."

"I knew it," Reilly said, nodding.

"My investigation has revealed that he tried to put the fix on me. For ten large—"

"What?"

"And I don't mean capicollo."

"You told him no?" Reilly asked.

"Think I'm crazy in the belfry? I told him yes. Think I want to get washed in my own house? He also said you were a queer."

"That cock sucker."

Chapman tossed his napkin on the table. "You gotta throw that in, right, Honey Dripper?"

"Well, he said it."

Reilly banged his hand down. "That son of a bitch. I'll fix his ass. This Brennan is a maniac. He iced Julio Sierra; then he zonks Tony Roman and puts the gun on him. And now he calls me a fag."

"Wait a second," Chapman interrupted. "Let's not go off the deep end here. Let's check everything out before we jump to conclusions."

"Chappie, he's going. He is going. He doesn't have a mortgage on you, does he? I mean, you guys ain't been settlin' cases out of court?"

"You got some fuckin' nerve tellin' me that, Reilly. You ridin' with that fuckin' Jimmy Mullins, walkin' around with his Santa Claus bag."

Chapman and Reilly glared at each other across the table.

Reilly said, "You're full of shit. I never took a dime. I hated the son of a bitch."

"You stood by, right? You never gave him up, right? So you're on the pad by proxy."

"What the fuck was I supposed to do? Be Joe Hero? Louse myself up?"

Valentin raised his hands, palms out. "Gentlemen, gentlemen. Take it easy. First things first. The food is here. Ummmm, have a clam, Chap."

"Don't want nothin'."

"C'mon, you guys gotta get together. Al, you gotta understand. Brennan saved Chappie's ass. He owes the guy. This thing is torturin' him."

They sat quiet for a few seconds. Reilly rubbed his eyes. "You're right. I know. Chappie, I'm sorry I blew up. I didn't mean to insult you. I'm all fouled up. I'm sorry I ever left the job and came into this office. I'm sorry I ever came into this fucking case."

"No, Al. You did the right thing. I'm sorry I got off on you. I been close to Guido. This is the worst hassle I been in since I come to the department."

Valentin signaled the waiter. "Bring me some bread. What the hell, you only live once. Put the plates down here, boy. Look at that, madonna."

"Tell me about Roger Montalvo," Reilly said.

"Uh, how can I enjoy my veal cutlet while I talk about Roger the faggot? I hate that mother fucker."

" 'Cause he's a fag?"

"Nah, I got nothin' against the gay fruits element as long as they don't try to give me the mano morta. I have nothin' but respect for the faggot people so long as they don't try to do the rim job on Detective John Valentin of the NYPD."

"Who would want to trim yo' rim?" Chapman asked.

"Shit, are you kiddin'? Everywhere I go, there's a faggeta. If I get on the subway, there's bound to be one in the car. IND, BMT, you name it. They're gonna find me. If I'm in a movie by myself, there they come. If I could score with the broads like I do with the queers, I'd be all right."

"Roger's a bad guy?" Reilly asked.

"He's done everythin'. Even done time for homicide. Did a pound. He told me about it. He was cookin' dinner for his boyfriend at the time. Roger was dressed in his baby doll outfit 'n high heels. Ugh! What a sight. So, anyway, he's cookin' up a storm of rice and beans 'n pork chops for the boyfriend. The boyfriend gets mad and throws all the food on the floor. This was too much for Roger. Roger stuck him with the kitchen knife. 'The only man I've ever loved,' says Roger. Guy used to be the super in Roger's building. Cornhole artist."

"Did five?" Chapman asked, spinning the ice in his glass.

"Did three out of the five. But that's nothin'. Since then he's come up big—sellin' heavy junk. Then turns around and fingers everybody. Plants shit in people's apartments, cars. If he don't go for you, he'll set you up. I don't know how he stays alive. Guess people in the street are afraid of him. Then he's got the feds in his corner and maybe somebody else."

"Like Brennan?" Reilly asked.

Chapman said, "No way. Guido hates fags. Can't stand them."

"You mean violent?" Reilly asked, looking up at Chapman.

"Well, no. But he's hard on them. Hey, but just 'cause a guy is hard on fags, don't mean he's a fag. Gui was a pug, a rough cat."

Valentin shrugged. "Don't mean nothin'. I seen fags

look like the Creeper. But don't get caught in no re-volvin' door with him."

"Have you seen Brennan act up on a fag, Chappie?" Reilly asked.

Chapman nodded. "One time in particular—because it stuck in my mind. Worst thing I'd seen since we found the human dick near the west wall in the Ramble."

Valentin clutched his stomach. "Ugh! Be careful. I'm eatin'!"

"Me and Guido went to this pad on the West Side. DOA in the bathroom. Had been there for days. You know the smell."

"Jesus Christ!" Valentin threw down his fork.

"Craziest thing I ever saw. The guy was sittin' on the toilet, naked, with nylon stockings on. He'd set up a pulley system where he could hoist himself up and down on the bowl. Then he'd put like a big metal tube on it so he could slide it up and down his ass."

Valentin sneered. "Maldita sea la madre. You ruined my dinner."

"But it seemed like the pulley broke and the tube went all the way up and killed him."

"Aagh. I can't stand it!" Valentin stood up, his hands on his buttocks.

"Jesus Christ!" Reilly exclaimed.

"You know what Guido did? He kicked the corpse, kicked him hard. 'Fuckin' fag,' he said. It was terrible."

Valentin sat down again. "How am I gonna eat my dessert now? Anyway, I heard that story already," Valentin said in a matter-of-fact tone.

"You heard about it?" Chapman mimicked.

"Sure. Why I can't hear what you hear?"

"Fulla shit you heard about it. 'Cause I never told nobody that story," Chapman said.

"Well, I heard one like it. Only this fag would stand on top of the dresser, see"—Valentin stood up, leaning forward, his arms extended backward, as if about to take a racing dive—"with a rope tied around his waist—"

"Don't wanna hear it," Chapman said, waving Valentin off. Then he pointed to Valentin's chair. Valentin sat down, grinning and looking innocent.

"We gotta find Roger," Reilly reminded them.

"Don't worry," said Chapman. "We'll find him. Or, actually, Bobby Tex will do it for us. But it's too early. Time for cockballs, right, John?"

"He's right, Al. Waiter, do the thing. Meanwhile, what's the story on Nancy Bosch and Al Reilly? When it comes to affairs of the core, I am Emily Post and Dr. Kinsey combined. I knew it as soon as that Nancy walked into your office and put the lamps on you. I said, 'Aquí hay algo.' When it comes to women, right away I got the feeling. Never miss. And when we left the room, you and Nancy went into a heavy clinch, right?"

"Not exactly. She told me to get lost," Reilly said.

Valentin shook his head. "Don't believe it. That broad is yours to demand. I have seen that look in the eye before. That is the look of love."

"Don't start singin' now," Chapman said, smiling.

"These fuckin' married guys ain't got no romance in them," Valentin said.

"You're not married?" asked Reilly.

"Sure, but that don't mean I can't have emotions elsewhere, too. There's only one of John Valentin, but there's plenty of broads. They're all gonna walk by and I ain't gonna do nothin'?"

"I don't fool around no more," said Chapman. "I learned my lesson."

"Neither do I, unless I love the broad. Then there's no holes barred, and I go crazy."

"Don't listen to him, Al."

"Bullshit. I am here to declare that the Latina is in love with you. I know the women of my race. And a faint heart never won no broad. Especially a broad with Bobby Tex. But let me tell you somethin'. If it gets down to the biff-bams, you can do him up. He can't fight for shit."

"Why don't you put a contract on him, John?" Chapman asked.

"Do that, too. Shit," Valentin answered, indignant.

"No. It's hopeless. I blew it," Reilly said, discouraged.

"Beautiful, Al. Beautiful. I love shit like that," Valentin said, his elbow on the table, his head leaning on his hand, a blissful look on his face.

"John, you're a meatball," Chapman said.

"You got no romance in you, Chappie," Valentin shot back.

"Well, I don't go too much for that intermarriage number. Marriage has enough problems without starting with built-in troubles," Chapman said.

"Oh, you ain't gonna go for no white broad nohow, right?"

"I didn't say that."

"You gonna take Moms Mabley over Raquel Welch, right?"

"That ain't what I mean, John."

Valentin turned to Reilly again, "Al, don't worry about it. I'm in the same bag now. I got a misgeneration problem myself."

"Miscegenation," Chapman corrected.

"Yeah," Valentin said, indifferent.

"With your wife?" Reilly asked.

"Nah, with my girl friend, Samia. She's Jewish, and a belly dancer. I'm Puerto Rican and Pentecostal. You don't see me worried. Drives my partner, Nat Zucker, crazy. He's Jewish."

"Waiter, give us another round. Al, here's to your brother-in-law, John Valentin."

"Did you rap to her Wednesday, Al? We kept them out awhile," Valentin said.

"She hates me. If only I could talk to her—half an hour, fifteen minutes."

"You want to see her? You're gonna see her," Valentin announced and slapped the table.

"What are we gonna do? Go to Sutton Place, knock on Bobby Tex's door, and say Reilly wants to talk to his old lady?" Chapman asked.

"How come I made gold shield in eight years and those other jerks with me in the academy are still handin' out parkin' tickets? Because Johnny Valentin uses the old cerebro and knows what's goin' on in this town. Tonight is Friday night, Viernes social. Every PR is out partyin'. And if they got bread, there's only two places midtown: El Liborio and the Chateau Madrid. Take your pick. You can bet yo' ass against a hamburger that Bobby Tex and company is in one of them. Believe me, I know my people."

"I don't know, Johnny," Reilly hesitated. "It's getting late, and I don't have a clean shirt on."

"Are you kiddin'? I got a haberdashery in the trunk of my car. Cologne, aftershave, you name it. I gotta change everythin' before I get home. My old lady got a nose like an anteater."

"Let's have another drink," Chapman suggested.

"What do you think, Chappie?" Reilly asked.

"I think this PR is a Matteawan case, but what the

hell. You might as well give it a try. We've gotta check out Texidor anyway."

"Yeah, fuck it. Give us another drink. You're on, John," Reilly said.

Valentin patted Reilly on the shoulder. "Attaboy, Al. Let's blow this joint. Moov-out!"

10 They pulled up at the Chateau Madrid, on East 48th Street, and the doorman took their car. They entered and descended the thick-carpeted stairs to the main room of the club. Reilly quickly took in the action. Tables were arranged in circular fashion around a large stage jammed with musicians; there was an upper tier, with a metal railing, that circled the room. A short flight of steps led down to the nightclub floor itself. The immense room was crowded with several hundred patrons, mostly non-Latin. Dancers had overflowed into the aisles and bobbed among the tables on both upper and lower tiers.

"Wow! Qué party!" Valentin exclaimed happily, rubbing his hands together.

Reilly was unaccountably nervous at the loud music, the congestion. "Why don't we go to the bar, guys?"

Valentin shook his head, "The bar is in another room. She's in here. Don't get cold feets. Chappie, give the maître d' a twenty. We demand a ringside table."

"Twenty! Are you crazy?"

"I'm a little short on bread. I'll give it to you later. We're on a case, shit."

"I got money," Reilly said.

"Don't put your hand in your pocket. Me and Chappie got you covered."

The maître d' walked over to them. "Table, gentlemen?"

"Yeah, we want a table, ringside, right on the floor in front," Valentin said, pointing toward the stage.

"We can't do that, sir," the maître d' apologized. "All the tables are taken."

"Ten," Valentin announced.

"It's impossible, sir."

"Fifteen."

"I wish I could accommodate you."

"Twenty."

"I'll see what I can arrange."

The maître d' had a table placed to the left of the stage, up front.

Valentin beamed. "There they are. I told you. That long table to the right of the stage. Whole mob. All right, I'm gonna orchestrate this number. We stash in cool, sit Reilly facin' their table. Then we go by ear. Let's go. Hot damn!"

The dance floor had emptied in anticipation of the stage show. The three men strode, single file, across the middle of the floor to the table, eyes straight ahead. They sat down. Valentin broke out cigars.

"I don't like cigars," Reilly said.

Valentin was insistent. "Smoke a cigar. The broads go for a cigar. Shows you got class."

The waiter approached. "Gentlemen, are you going to eat?"

"Nah," said Valentin, "bring us a bottle of Chivas Regal, thirty-five years old."

"Uh, I don't think we have that. Maybe twenty-five years."

"Never mind. Bring a Johnny Walker Black. Don't

look over there, Al. Just puff on your cigar. Show plenty of cuff link there, like Dean Martin. There's gonna be two shows here tonight, the club's and ours."

The curtain went up, and a line of flamenco dancers leaped from the stage onto the dance floor. Valentin called out loudly, "Cho time already!" The company went into a fierce fandango to the accompaniment of guitars and vigorous clapping. Valentin joined in and shouted, "olé" and "sa, sa, sa," whenever a particularly rigorous step was executed.

Reilly was captivated by the beauty of the girls in the troupe. I must have a weakness for Latin women, he thought. His eyes strayed, almost involuntarily, to Nancy. She was seated with a dozen people at the ringside end of a long table. There were flowers and a large cake on the table and buckets of champagne. Reilly stared, beguiled.

She was dressed in a black gown. Through the smoke haze and dim light he could see the shimmer of her white jewelry. Earrings, bracelet, rings. Diamonds. She looked almost regal, but Reilly sensed a melancholy air about her. This is not Nancy, he thought. She's doing a bit. I will get to her, even if I have to kill this fucking Tex.

Texidor sat opposite Nancy, resplendent in a dark maroon, brocaded tuxedo. He sat with legs crossed, black pumps gleaming.

"Lookit, the Count of Monte Cristo," Valentin sneered, "or maybe the pimp of Mount Morris Park."

"Who said crime don't pay?" Chapman asked.

"I used to see that mother fucker in the poolroom in sneakers," Valentin sighed.

Reilly sat stiffly; the slight high he had brought with him had quickly dissipated. "She looks like a queen. I think I'll slash my wrists."

"Be cool." Valentin counseled. "The show's just beginning. Happy birthday, Bobby Tex. There's probably a bomb in that cake. Hey, that's Larry Pesh and his flunky, Bruno, at Tex's table. And who's them other two guys on Tex's side of the table? Them is gumbas. Chappie, you make them?"

"Yeah. The older guy is Enrico Mastrangelo. Hank, they call him. I don't know the other guy. Must be his lobby boy. Hank is Larry Pesh's boss. Larry is a mopery next to Hank."

"The bosses must think a whole lot of Bobby Tex to be seen in public with him," Valentin observed.

"Maybe they got no choice. I'm thinkin' maybe Larry Pesh can't control Tex. You saw what happened Wednesday morning at the office when Bobby Tex blew up," Chapman said.

"Yeah, so Larry brings his boss to talk turkey to this turkey. I always said, sooner or later the wops are gonna whack out Bobby Tex."

"The sooner the better," Reilly muttered.

Valentin looked at Reilly, his head slanted sideways. "Counselor, I'm surprised. Wait a minute. Look on Nancy's end. See those two blond kids? Them's the Segal brothers from Miami."

"Wadda they got, a shoe store?" Chapman asked.

"Shoes shit! Stone assassins. Cuban Jews from Miami. Terrible kids. No sooner they're in town, somebody gets buried. There's only two left. The other brother got taken out last year. Russian roulette, they said. Ha! Gentlemen, the fiesta is about to begin."

"Who these kids with?" Chapman asked, leaning forward.

"Got to be with Bobby Tex. They don't even speak English. Armandito and Alfonsito Segal. Dig it."

"Tex is runnin' scared," Chapman announced.

"Sure, gonna get permanated. The last of the Mohicans, the last of the Sinners. Unless he gets off first," Valentin agreed.

"On Brennan?" Reilly asked.

"Who else?" Valentin said.

"What the fuck is goin' on with these people?" Chapman asked, rubbing his head, troubled. "What kind of mess is Guido in?"

"Like Tex said, that's for him to know and us to find out." Valentin chuckled.

"Tex is the key," said Reilly.

Valentin whistled. "Will you look at the lovelies at their table, and the champagne. Somebody ought to report this Bobby Tex to the police."

"Don't worry," Chapman said. "His bill is due. Gui is heavy dues."

The show was over. The band promptly went into "Happy Birthday." Bobby Tex got up and waved. His exuberance was infectious, and people at nearby tables toasted him. Texidor walked over to the bandstand and spoke with the leader. The leader took the microphone and announced the engagement of "Miss Nancy Bosch to Mr. Robert Texidor" as Texidor strode back to his table, picked up a glass of champagne, then turned and faced Reilly's table. He raised his glass and gave Reilly a mock salute, the smile never leaving his face.

"You and your bright ideas, Honey Dripper," Chapman said.

Valentin was beaming. "It's gonna get better. The evening is young. She's lookin' right at you, Al. She feels bad. You're the underdog. She's in the bag."

Chapman whistled low. "Look at this. Larry's giving Tex a watch. Looks like one of them coin watches."

"Yeah. They use twenty-dollar gold pieces," Valentin said.

"That watch will go for two or three thou, easy. And you with your fuckin' Timex," said Chapman, smiling.

"I'm not a man for joolery. Just give me that blonde at the other end of their party."

The hilarity at Texidor's table was rising to a crescendo. Six or seven women in varying degrees of décolletage were cavorting about the table, and there was much singing and pouring of champagne. The Segal brothers were banging the table in rhythm with the mambo the band was playing and shouted for another rendition of "Guantanamera." Throughout, Texidor was laughing, offering toasts, and strutting around his guests.

•

Larry Pesh leaned over toward Enrico Mastrangelo. Hank Mastrangelo was one rung above Larry Pesh in the pecking order of the East Harlem mob, although he was only forty-two. His early career in the Red Hook section of Brooklyn had been distinguished by daring and innovative bank and armored car robberies.

Larry Pesh concentrated on the right tone of voice. "Hank, Bobby Tex gives a great party, don't he? Take your pick of any one of these cunts. You, too, Zack." Pesh motioned toward the women, his obese body sprawled over his chair, both arms stretched out over the backs of the chairs flanking him, his right hand holding a large white handkerchief. He took up a lot of room. He wore a powder-blue mohair suit, the sides of his jacket flapping over the seat, a navy-blue shirt opened halfway down his chest, with a silver silk tie hanging loose around his neck. His stubby left hand, with its large star sapphire ring, was curled around a champagne glass. Hank Mastrangelo, a gentle smile on his finely boned face, turned to a companion seated at his right, Frank Zaccarelli.

Frankie Zack, of the dark complexion, with an even darker scowl behind his round, steel-rimmed glasses, was a lifelong associate of Mastrangelo, his executive officer and mob enforcer when problems of discipline arose. Their approach, tried and true, was one of rose and thorn. Mastrangelo scented his arguments with deference. Once matters were in Zaccarelli's hand, they were beyond mediation.

Pesh appealed to Mastrangelo again. "C'mon, Hank. Meeng! You work too hard. You gotta relax. You pick the broad. Ya think I'm kiddin'?"

Mastrangelo, still smiling, said, "Nah, Larry. You know I'm a family man. Maybe Zack is interested."

Zaccarelli shook his head. "No. I'm not crazy about this place. Let's take care of business and get back where we belong." He sat on the edge of his chair, his shoulders hunched forward.

"Relax, Zack." Mastrangelo said, his voice soft. "It's Bobby's birthday. Let him enjoy himself."

Pesh waved his handkerchief. "He's a good kid. Very grateful. Did ya see the watch I brung him? He loves joolery. Spanish guy. They like that."

Zaccarelli, his glasses beaming into Pesh's eyes, said, "Keep looking at me, Larry. Who are these two white guys on the other side of Tex?"

"Them ain't white guys. They're Cubans. Don't worry. They don't even speak English. They're supposed to be tough kids."

Zaccarelli straightened up in his seat. "They're coked to the gills. These are two shooters. This is no good for you, Hank. Andiamo."

Hank Mastrangelo nodded. "Me and Zack are going to the bar. Have Bobby join us for a drink. Tell him to come alone. I don't want these two coke heads near me. Capisce, Larry?"

"Hey, Bobby Tex is okay. I mean he's done all right by us."

"You've made a lot of money with Bobby, huh?" Mastrangelo said, his eyes bristling through his smile.

Larry Pesh wiped his neck with his handkerchief. "I don't mean that. I mean he's not a bad kid. He's just scared."

"Do you know what's going on?" Mastrangelo asked, leaning closer to Pesh over the table.

"Well, no."

"Then mind your fucking business."

Mastrangelo and Zaccarelli rose from the table and walked out of the room.

Bobby Texidor slid over beside Pesh. "Where's Hank going?"

"Bobby, do me a favor. Go to the bar. He wants to have a drink with you."

"Okay. Mandito, Alfonsito." The Cubans stood up.

"Leave the kids here. Hank don't want them around. Will you do me a favor and go have a drink with the man? What do you think he came all the way up here for? Afangul, I'm tryin' to help you, Bobby."

"Okay, Larry. Esperen aquí." The two Cubans sat down again. Texidor went to the bar alone.

●

Reilly said, "Chappie, see where they're going? Something is on. Did you see the puss on Bobby Tex?"

Chapman got up and made his way through the crowd to the stairs. The band began to play a merengue. Nancy motioned to Alfonsito Segal. They got up to dance. Reilly could see them laughing and making rapid turns. Then he realized they were making their way to his table.

Valentin said, "I knew it. I can talk to him, to Fonsito. The rest is up to you. Arriba, chico."

As the couple danced past their table, Valentin sprang up and said in Spanish, "Alfonsito, it's me, Johnny Valentin, from the Twenty-third squad."

Alfonsito Segal stopped in the middle of a turn. He released Nancy Bosch and faced the detective. His blue eyes searched Valentin up and down. "You were there that night on 86th Street. Is that not correct?"

"The guy never wanted to press the charges. You were lucky."

"It was all a misunderstanding, Señor Valentin."

"Listen, the federales and immigration were over to the squad asking about you and your brother."

"What—?"

Alfonsito was stunned. Nancy Bosch stood motionless, her face in profile to Reilly.

"Why did you cut your hair?" Reilly spoke in a deliberate, subdued voice.

"Felt like it. Got tired of it." Her tone was hasty, petulant.

"Do you love him?"

"I don't think that's any of your business. He's been good to me. He paid my father's hospital bill. He got my mother a house. That calls for love."

"Junk money. Even if you want nothing to do with me, get away from this. He'll have you carrying his pistol and snorting and maybe hauling a suitcase for him."

"What makes you think I haven't done these things already—and worse?"

"Why do you want to hurt me this way?"

She turned full face, her eyes on his. "Because you hurt me. Because I gave myself to you and you destroyed me—almost."

Reilly got halfway up and bent across the table. "Nancy, it's not too late. Let me meet you somewhere. Anywhere."

She hesitated, then, more restrained, she answered, "We never got to the Riviera, Al, and we never will. We're on different roads. Let it alone."

Armandito Segal made his way through the dancers to her side. The transparent light of his narrowed eyes fixed on Reilly.

"Qué pasa?" Armandito inquired of his brother.

"Mandito, you remember Detective Valentin from the time we had the problem on 86th Street. He is a gentleman. Very considerate. Would it embarrass you to accept a bucket of champagne from us, Detective Valentin?"

"No thanks, Alfonsito. We're drinking Scotch. Some other time. Buena suerte, muchachos."

The Segals bowed. "Encantado."

•

Texidor, Hank Mastrangelo, and Frank Zaccarelli were seated at a small table in the lounge.

Mastrangelo, raising his glass, said, "Bobby, I want to propose a toast to your coming marriage to a beautiful girl. May you have molti figli. A man needs a family to stabilize him. I been telling that to Zack here."

"Yeah," Zaccarelli said. "Why don't we get down to business?"

Mastrangelo's face clouded. "I decide when we get down to business. That's the trouble with you. You don't know when to relax. This is a special occasion for Bobby Tex, and I want to share it with him." Mastrangelo stared at Zaccarelli, who nodded, then looked away.

"Thanks, Hank. I appreciate your coming. I'm honored."

"Bobby, you been with us quite a few years, and we look out for our own. Haven't we always looked out for you, taken care of business?"

"Always."

"You've had a minimum of static in the street, right?"

"Yeah, Hank."

"And no wops have ever interfered with you or any of your people, right?"

"No, never."

"And you get first crack, and the price has always been right, right?"

"Right. And I've always done the right thing by Larry."

Mastrangelo spread his hands and smiled broadly. "Beautiful. Molto bene. Let's keep it that way, Bobby. Now here's a piece of straight business. These things, these matters of ours, can't function unless we have help, cooperation, from people in certain places. Now, these people can't be disturbed. They're too important."

"Brennan," Texidor said, his voice flat. There it was.

Zaccarelli removed his glasses. "You know better than to be using people's names."

"That's all right, Zack. Bobby's a little upset about it. I can understand that. But what you did at the DA's office was not smart, Bobby, not smart."

"I didn't say anything hardly."

"You pulled a thread out, a long thread. A whole suit can go that way, Bobby."

"He's going to kill me."

"Now, you see, you're upset."

"He killed Julio, then Tony. Now he's after me. Maybe he's one of them death squad nuts. But I'm not going to sit still and get whacked out."

"You *don't* go to the DA."

"He's a lieutenant of police. What am I supposed to do? Hit him myself?"

"Go away," Hank Mastrangelo said softly. "Take a vacation. Let things cool off. We'll straighten this out. But don't try to hurt that person. No way. Under no circumstances."

"Am I supposed to keep my hands in my pockets while this fucker is tracking me?"

Zaccarelli pointed at Texidor. "Listen. You've had a good thing going. You don't want to wind up a busted valise. You stay away from this guy."

"You been told," Mastrangelo added, standing up.

"I'll get the coats," Zaccarelli said as he pushed away from the table.

Mastrangelo and Zaccarelli left.

Bobby Texidor remained seated. He plucked my wings. Now he's trying to muzzle my beak. Brennan's isolating me. He's cutting me off from all my bases. So when he jumps from the tree, I'll be a grounded sparrow hopping on one leg. No contest. That's what these wops want. Don't be a stool; be a clay pigeon. Kiss my ass.

He returned to the party table. The frivolity of the group dampened by degrees as the various guests observed their somber host. The party was clearly over.

"You straighten everything out?" Larry Pesh asked. "C'mon. It ain't like that. Just lay low somewhere for a while. It'll blow over. Me and a couple of the girls are goin' to Patsy's to eat. You wanna come?"

"No, go ahead. I'm tired. I'll take care of this."

"There's no tab. Hank took care of everything. Like an engagement present," said Pesh with a sweep of his hands.

"He really made my night."

"He's a real sweetheart. I'll see you around, Bobby. Bruno, get the coats. I'll bring the broads."

•

Chapman rejoined Reilly and Valentin. "Mastrangelo put Tex on notice. I don't know about what, but Texidor was hurtin'. Wound him up tighter'n a clam's ass."

Valentin looked past Chapman. "Party's breakin' up. Let's get our tab. We'll go to the Brasserie for breakfast. They got this omelet pipérade—"

"For Christ's sake, the human Puerto Rican tapeworm. Okay, let's go," Chapman said. "Get the tab."

Reilly, his face set, said, "I'm glad I came. At least I got it out of my system. She belongs to him. Maybe I'll stop making a fool of myself."

Valentin disagreed. "Poppycocks. Where's your psychology, Al? Do you think a barrio kitty like Nancy Bosch can't see through this dude's silk underwear? You think she's blinded by his *Student Prince* jacket? He can play that Errol Flynn shit with some out-of-town broad, but Nancy knows the street. She knows where he's comin' off of. And she knows by heart that these street stars burn out quick, and she don't wanna get splashed. Bobby Tex is overdrawn now. He's a cohete quema'o."

"A what?" Chapman said.

"Cohete quema'o. Like a burned out comet," Valentin said.

Reilly finished his drink. "If this guy was right for her, I wouldn't even bother her."

"Don't worry about it," said Valentin. "This broad goes for you. Every sharp broad goes through one of these mother fuckers. It's like a stage. Don't mean nothin'. My fiancée, Samia, used to go with a grease-ball. He told her he was a boss, caporegime. Used to beat her ass—some ass. Took her money, the dumb broad. I checked him out. He was the capo in charge of robbin' hubcaps. I told him to take a walk. Later he walked off a pier in Brooklyn."

"Homicide?" Reilly asked.

"Nah, he was wearin' concrete drawers. Went for a swim. So you see, Reilly, these guys are temporary conditions. Flash in the pants. You will pick up all the marbles. Mark my words."

"God forbid," Chapman said.

Valentin scowled. "I don't see you comin' up with any great suggestions. The man is a lovelorn. We gotta help him."

"Don't think I don't appreciate it, fellas," Reilly said.

"Don't worry. We do. Let's go," Chapman said.

Valentin motioned to the maître d'. "Tell the waiter to bring us the check."

"There is no check. The heavyset gentleman that was at the large table across the way took care of it, including all gratuities."

"El Italiano gordo?"

"Sí, señor," the maître d' said.

"Well, guys, Larry put us on the pad, whether we like it or not. Shall I report it in my D.D. 5, Chappie?"

"Fuck you, John. You can always tell a rogue cop, Al. They write every little shit down, makin' brownie points for camouflage on the big score. Right, Puerto Rico?"

"This Ne-gro incinerates worse than a fuckin' janitor. Let's blow this joint."

The three men walked to the steps leading to the upper landing. As they reached the stairway out, Reilly turned full around. Bobby Tex and the two Cubans were in a deep huddle at the table. Nancy, sitting upright, stared straight at him. He stood in her glare. Exasperated, arms up and then, with fingertips bunched, he shook his hand at her, as if to say, "What are you doing to us?" Then he turned and walked out.

•

Bobby Tex said, "The man is a high-ranking police officer. Mandito, we have to be careful."

Armandito Segal was not impressed. "Roberto, this is not the first time Alfonsito and I deal with bandido cops. You know where we are from. We ourselves were police with Batista. We are not impressed by uniforms."

Alfonsito Segal said, "This man will bleed like everyone else. Our brother, may he rest in peace, used to say, 'Since the invention of lead there are no more tough guys.' "

"I know that you are men of arms and always ready to step forward. But my friends have cautioned me to be discreet," Texidor said.

"Italianos?" Armandito Segal asked.

"Yes."

Armandito said, "Roberto, we are young, but we have experience with these people in La Habana and Tampa. Treachery is their pastime."

Alfonsito nodded in agreement. "Our late brother taught us when you have a problem, seek out your man immediately, go to his face. That way the time and place are of your choosing, and you are ready. When you delay, not only must you suffer the problem, but the hour and the terrain may be his when there is the collision. Did not Bernardo teach us that, Mandito?"

"Surer than death," Armandito agreed.

"I need time to think. I want you by my side at all times. Is that understood?"

"Even in your soup," said Armandito, looking serious, as Alfonsito nodded.

At that moment a slender young man appeared at the steps to the dance floor, dressed in a black velvet suit and a white silk shirt opened almost to the waist.

Fernando Malpica, known also as La Malpagada, the ill-paid one. He had undergone electrolysis and silicone treatments and worked as a female impersonator at the 82 Club in lower Manhattan. A heavy cocaine user, he was dependent on Roger Montalvo, his lover and confidant, for his supply. It was Roger who gave Fernando the name, La Malpagada, as in the Mexican film in which the beautiful heroine is exploited by rapacious and evil men. La Malpagada was twenty-five. He came toward them.

"Fernando Malpica, your servant," he said, bowing from his slender waist.

"La Malpagada, eh?" Texidor said.

"That is what I am called, Mr. Texidor."

"Just call me Bobby. This is my wife, Nancy, and my friends, Mandito and Fonsito. Sit down. Give him some champagne, Fonsito."

La Malpagada took a seat next to Texidor. "You're very gracious. That's a beautiful jacket you're wearing."

"Not as beautiful as the one you're wearing."

"I design all the clothes for Roger and my—"

"What did you want to see me about?" Texidor interrupted.

"Well, eh—" La Malpagada's eyes shifted across the table to the Cubans.

"These people are of my confidence. Speak."

"Roger. He would speak to you."

"Thank God. When?"

"Right now."

"Where?"

"You live at 53d Street, Sutton Place South?"

"Yes, but how?"

"He's downstairs waiting since two o'clock. He sent me to find you."

"Mandito, the tab. Wait a minute. There's no tab. Let's go."

Alfonsito Segal said, "Roberto, this could be a setup."

"What do I have you guys for? Let's go."

The Cubans flanked La Malpagada and walked out first. Nancy and Bobby Texidor followed them out to the car.

11 They drove north on Third Avenue to 54th Street, then cut east toward Sutton Place.

"There's Roger on the corner," Malpica said, pointing.

Rogelio Montalvo. Roger was thirty-six, a multiple-felony offender. Homicide, narcotics, sodomy, impairing the morals of a minor, larceny—he had been up on everything at one time or another. Paid federal narcotics informer for at least four years, heavy cocaine user, always on the move between Miami, Puerto Rico, and New York.

Texidor hesitated. "Alfonsito, you go and bring Roger over. Search him first. We'll cover you from here. Malpagada, if anything happens, I'll blow your brains out right here, okay?"

"Nothing is going to happen. Roger wouldn't do that to me."

Alfonsito Segal got out on the passenger side. He removed his hat and placed it over his right hand and the .38 Police Special he held cocked. Then he advanced on Roger, who stood shivering on the corner.

Roger Montalvo had his hands in the pockets of his trenchcoat, his collar turned up. Legs astride, he kept shifting his weight from one foot to the other. Coming closer, Segal saw that he had a thick crop of multi-colored hair, the result of the home tints he and La Malpagada experimented with. This dense mass tapered down to a thin, almost cheekless face and a long Cordoban nose. The plucked eyebrows rose almost vertically over his large, filmy eyes, which looked like those of a drowning man the third time up. He was shook. Alfonsito could see that plainly.

"Roger, Bobby's in the Buick with La Malpagada. Take your hands out of your pockets, slow. Open your coat. . . . All right, walk to the car. I'm directly behind you."

Alfonsito Segal followed Montalvo to the car. Montalvo got into the front seat, Alfonsito next to him. The car shot forward, down to 53d Street, made a right turn, and rolled west.

"Go to Third Avenue, then come back to my house, Mandito," Texidor said.

"Fernando, I've been so cold waiting there," Montalvo complained to his lover.

"I had to go to a few places before I could find Mr. Texidor."

"Call me Bobby," said Texidor, his voice friendly.

Roger Montalvo put his hand over his eyes. "Bobby, you don't know what I've been through."

"Roger, two things. First, talk English only, and let's wait till we get upstairs. Then you and me can speak in private, okay?"

Montalvo turned to look at Texidor. "I thought these were your boys?"

"They are, but if they knew what you do for a sideline, maybe even I couldn't stop them. So let's keep it between you and me."

"Whatever you say, Bobby. My life is in your hands." Montalvo put his hand back over his eyes.

"Yeah," Texidor said.

They came east on 54th Street to Sutton Place, then south a block and into a garage.

"Send La Malpagada home, Roger," ordered Texidor as they all got out.

"Bobby, please. I'm very upset. I want her with me," Montalvo pleaded, his voice cracking.

"Send her, him—send it home."

"Fernando, go straight home," Montalvo scolded. "I'll call you later. If I find out you went to Dirty Dick's, I'll cut your fanny again."

"Roger, please. I'm not even dressed or anything. I'll wait for your call."

They kissed on the lips. The two Cubans looked away. La Malpagada walked up the ramp to the street. Texidor ushered the rest toward the elevator.

●

The apartment overlooked the East River. It was luxurious and tastefully decorated.

Montalvo's head turned in all directions as he exclaimed, "Oh, this is gorgeous. I wish Fernando could see this. Look at those drapes, that table. Mrs. Texidor, you have such taste."

"We had help from a decorator."

"No, no, this is you. I can tell. This is you. I've been trying—"

"Roger," Texidor interrupted, "before you get carried away, what would you like to drink?"

"Drink? Can't I have something else?"

Nancy said, "Bobby, I'm tired. I'm going to bed. You don't mind? Buenas noches, muchachos."

The Cubans stood up and bowed, "Buenas noches, señora."

"Fonsito, Mandito. Roger wants some candy," Texidor said.

Armandito Segal said, "Perico for the perico, eh? Fonsito, a snort for the gentlemen."

Alfonsito had the cocaine wrapped in a hundred-dollar bill. All four of the men inhaled the powder.

The brothers went to the far end of the room by the window and began playing cards. Texidor and Montalvo settled on the sofa.

"He's going to kill me, Bobby."

"I know."

"He's going to kill you, too."

"He's gonna try. I don't have these two assassins around for nothin'."

"He will crush them into wine. Listen, I am gay. I don't deny it, but I ain't no punk. I have backfired on a lot of people on the street who thought, because I was a maricón, they could abuse me. But this Brennan scares me. It's his eyes. I've seen it before. He's a fag killer."

"What's that got to do with me?"

"You are business. He *has* to kill you."

"Suppose we start at the beginning. Take your time; relax. That's it. Now, how did he get a line on you, and don't bullshit me."

"From the feds, four years ago."

"You fuckin' stool pigeon."

"Bobby, I'm a three-time loser, and I was in love with Fernando. I couldn't do any more time. I was desperate."

"All right, so you've been feeding Brennan for four years. Hey, this gorilla is not a fag, is he?"

"He's gay. He don't know it, but he's gay."

"He ever put hands on you or someone you know?"

"No. Maybe he only gets off once every ten years, but he's gay."

"Okay. So he's in the closet. How did my people get in his way?"

"Last year, late, he tracked me down again. I'm always hiding from him. I know if he ever gets me while he's drinking, he'll kill me. Anyway, he had these names of people he said he was checking out, said they were in some kind of conspiracy. I was terrified of the guy. So I went around finding out who these people were. Then I realized they were the old jitterbug gang from 103d Street, the Sinners."

"That was my club," Texidor said. "But shit, kids' stuff. We split up twenty years ago. What the fuck kind of conspiracy is that? Only me, Tony, and Julio stayed together. The other four got wasted one way or another, long gone."

Roger Montalvo turned pale. "I can tell you their names and what happened to them. Enrique Narvaez, 'Quique,' he got stabbed outside the poolroom on 108th Street. Ruben Vallejo, 'Pelle,' he got killed pulling a stickup near Canal Street. Jaime Cordoba, 'Cheyenne,' he O.D.'d on a roof on 117th Street. And Francisco Salazar, 'Paco,' he got killed in a car crash in Florida."

"You ran them down good for him, didn't you, Roger?"

"I swear"—Montalvo kissed the polished nail of his thumb—"I swear by Fernando, which is the only thing I love, that I didn't know what Brennan was up to. What would be in it for me? He hates gay people."

"You said he was a fag."

"That's why he hates them."

"So go ahead."

"Next thing I know, Julio Sierra got hit. Then Brennan comes to me with the idea that Tony Roman had hit Julio. I found that hard to believe. But he's a police lieutenant; I figure he knows what he's talking about. So last Thursday he picks me up. He tracks me through Fernando all the time. It's close to midnight; he drags me uptown to Harlem, which I hate. I got a lotta enemies there. He tells me that Tony Roman is in Mauricio's club in the basement on 107th Street. So I don't know from nothing. He tells me he don't want to go down into the club because Tony will run and he don't want to have to shoot him. All I had to tell Tony was that Julio Sierra's wife was outside and had to talk to him. And I was to leave right away and let Brennan talk to Tony. I swear I didn't know he was going to put him on ice. You think I am so stupid that I would have stuck my face in that club if I knew? I know you saw me."

"Go ahead."

"Well, I came out with Tony, into the alleyway outside the club. Then Brennan grabbed Tony. I heard two shots. I ran down the alley to the steps, got to the sidewalk, ran to Madison Avenue. Then I jumped in a cab."

"In other words, you didn't see anything. Right?"

"Not exactly." Montalvo struggled to light a cigarette with a shaky match.

"You faggot mother fucker. You saw him blow Tony's brains out and put the gun in his hand."

"I didn't see the actual shooting, Bobby. I was running. But I turned once. I saw Brennan squatting, putting the gun in Tony's hand. But I'll say it any way you want me to, Bobby."

"You make a liar out of Brennan twice. He says he came down alone to the club. We all know that's a lie. We saw you there. He can't shake you on that. And you saw him put the gun in Tony's hand. The cops have been saying that's the same gun that killed Julio."

"He's murdering everybody. He's crazy."

"He knows what he's doing. These are hits. He didn't plan to kill Tony there. He was going to take him for a ride and bury you with him. But Tony forced a move ahead of schedule, and you got away."

"Me?"

"You, you stupe. Do you think you can live in the same world with Brennan now? He's going to pull your tongue out with his bare hands and jam it in your ass."

Montalvo jumped up, horrified. "Please, Bobby. I'll kill myself. I swear. If it weren't for Fernando, I would kill myself."

The Segals glanced up from their game.

"No you won't, you rat weasel. You'll finagle your way out. You'll rat Brennan out to the DA; then you'll set me up for the feds. You'll do all right, Roger. You're a stool. You douche bag, I oughta throw you out the window. You can sell dope, commit murder, and still get police protection."

"Police? They'll set me up for Brennan. They're looking all over for me. They'll kill me. You're the only person that can save me. He's going to kill us both. But you have the money, the connections. You can stop him."

"You're the leverage, Roger?"

"I'm your witness."

"I can have this Brennan washed, you know. What do I need you for?"

Montalvo exhaled a cloud of smoke. "You're not going to kill a lieutenant. Everybody knows Tony was your ace. You'd get the electric chair for killing a cop. You need me. You have to protect me. I'm your weapon against him."

"I don't want to team up with no stool pigeon faggot."

"You think I wanted to come here? I had no choice. You're in with the wops; you have the connections. Together we can stop him."

"All right. Quiet. Let me think this out."

"Can I have a little snort?"

"Fonsito, give Roger a páse."

Montalvo was handed the cocaine, and he took a heavy snort.

Alfonsito, smiling, said, "I can see you are a heavy cornet player, Roger."

"I have snuffed a fortune through my nose. When I hit the right note, I feel there—"

Texidor shot to his feet, fists clenched. "Coño! Goddamn it, I should have pieced this together long ago."

"What is wrong, Roberto?" Alfonsito Segal called from across the room.

"Fonsito, Mandito. Puerto Rico. We go first thing in the morning. Nancy, Roger—all of us. We go to my boat in San Juan, at Boca de Cangrejos. Take it to Saint Thomas. We'll anchor and leave Roger on the boat at the yacht basin. No one knows him there. Then we'll return to San Juan by plane. This business will be settled once and for all. I know what to do now."

"Can I call Fernando to tell him where I'm going? He'll worry," Montalvo said.

"La Malpagada?" Texidor shook his head. "Are you crazy? That's the last person. Forget about that queer. I'll call up right now and make the reservations."

"Bobby, I hate boats. I get sick," Montalvo pleaded.

"The boat will be moored right at the dock. You'll have all the candy you want and a baby-sitter. Let me call the airport right away. We gotta get out of town. Don't worry, Roger. Everything is gonna work out."

12 Reilly awoke around noon. He knew it was the weekend; Columbus Avenue was quiet. He found his way into the cramped kitchen, opened the refrigerator, and carefully bent over to reach for the milk. Then, holding the cold container against his forehead, he poured out some cornflakes. The noise was murder.

Reilly took his bowl of cereal to the living room and sat down in the one piece of furniture in the room, a reclining armchair. He sat, the bowl in his lap, gazing out of the dusty window onto the avenue. It was drizzling. But over the gloom of the afternoon and his hangover there hovered a happy though vague memory of something, and suddenly he realized he had been dreaming about her.

The telephone rang in the bedroom. "Shit." He trudged over and picked it up on the fourth ring.

"Hello."

"Al, this is Chappie. Did I wake you?"

"Nah, I'm a little hoarse from last night is all. Been up for hours. What's up?"

"Listen, I know it's your day off, but Guido's with me. He asked me to call you. Wants to speak to you."

"Put him on."

"He wants to speak to you in person."

"Right now?"

"Yeah. We can be there in fifteen minutes. Corner house, 75th and Columbus, right?"

"That's right. You just dropped me off. Okay, come on over."

Reilly plodded back to the kitchen. He took a tray-less rack of ice cubes out of the refrigerator and cracked them into an empty bowl on the table. Then he took down a bottle of Dewar's White Label from a shelf above the frig. The doorbell rang. He took a deep breath and went to answer it.

"Jesus, you guys must have been waiting downstairs. Hiya, Chappie. Lieutenant."

Reilly led the way into the tiny kitchen and gestured toward the small table against the wall and the three wooden chairs.

"Just call me Guido, will ya. Chappie says you guys really tied one on last night."

Reilly nodded.

"We sure did. We hit all the Latin joints with that crazy Johnny Valentin," Chapman said, smiling widely.

Brennan chuckled. "The Honey Dripper, eh? He better not act too flush. He was in Narco for eight years, you know."

"C'mon. Johnny's all right," Chapman said.

"I'm not saying he's not. It's just you can't be too careful these days. Shoofly all over."

"Let's have a drink, fellas," Reilly suggested as they sat down around the table.

"Okay, just one," Chapman said.

"No thanks, I don't drink." Brennan waved off the offer. "You go ahead."

"You guys gotta sit here in the kitchen. I don't have

my furniture yet," Reilly apologized as he poured out two drinks.

Brennan looked around the room. "Bachelor like me, eh? Watch out they don't say you're a fag. Lotta them around here. Chappie can tell you. He was over the wall into the Ramble every night. Or he'd grab them under the balls of Teddy Roosevelt's horse by the museum. Ha!"

Chapman shrugged. "I never understood that fuckin' DC-8 law. If a guy wants to get cornholed, that's his business."

Brennan sat up. "Are you crazy? These sick cock suckers would be coming out of the woodwork. Walk along that park wall at night. It's a meat rack. You get sick. Ruining the city, they are. Come from all over. This is Faggot City. Remember that guy they had in the Two-Two that night? Guy had just come off the plane from Sweden, straight to the Ramble, knew just where to go. We gotta chase them."

"You live around here, Guido?" Reilly asked.

"Not me. I don't stay in one place too long. Got no old lady, so it makes no difference to me. Police work is my life. I never stop. I would never expect any woman to put up with my kind of life. Don't get me wrong. I'll pop a broad in a minute, but nothing to get tied down to, right, Chappie?"

"Ol' wisp-o'-the-will Guido." Chapman smiled casually at Reilly, but his eyes were dancing.

"Yeah—okay, what can I do for you gentlemen?" Reilly asked.

Brennan pulled his chair in close to the table. "Ah, I asked Chappie to bring me here to impose upon you 'cause I think you got the wrong slant about me. I want you to know who I am so you can evaluate better all the shit you're liable to hear from my enemies in the street. See, I believe in kicking ass, and I have kicked ass in the Two-Three, the Two-Five, the Three-Two, the Three-Oh—you name it. But I'm respected, and I get results. My first night on post on 111th Street and Madison, I told all the cutthroats there, 'I don't know what goes on in the other tours, but when I'm on the post, the baddest mother fucker here is me.' And I proved it. They could throw garbage cans full of bricks all night. I still kicked ass. And when they gave me that 'you got the stick and gun' shit, I'd take them off and rack up the bastards. How many times you see me go in the alley and deck a son of a bitch, Chappie?"

Chapman nodded. "The man was bad," he said.

But Brennan had already turned back toward Reilly. "And I didn't give a fuck who he was. Could be a spade seven feet tall or a guinea button from Pleasant Avenue. I didn't give a fuck." Brennan sat up in his chair, his small gray eyes right on Reilly's face.

Reilly nodded. "I know you were a hell of a cop."

Brennan waved it aside. "You been on the job. You know how it is. They try to set you up. They frame you—anything to get rid of you. But they can't get Guido Brennan out of their hair. I'm on the job twenty-four hours a day. First one through the door, first one through the window: Guido Brennan." He glanced at Chapman. "Am I telling any lies?"

"Just tellin' it like it is, Guido."

"They hate me, Al, out there I mean. They're trying to set me up. This fucking Bobby Tex—show you the kind of guy he is. A couple of months ago, Tex boxed this kid, Wolfie's, car in—you know, double-parked. When Tex came out, Wolfie complained. Tex shot him right in the mouth. Bullet hit him smack in the teeth.

When we got there, Wolfie was on his back on the sidewalk, arms and legs kicking in the air."

"Did he die?" Reilly asked.

"No. He swished it around his mouth and spit the bullet out like it was mouthwash. But he wouldn't finger Bobby Tex. See what we gotta put up with? It's scumbags like Tex that are trying to set me up. I might expect that from shoofly, but not from you, Al. I know you're a regular guy."

"Brennan, I promise you a fair deal. Soon as I talk to this Roger Montalvo—"

"That stool pigeon." Brennan's eyes disappeared into a tight squint that bared his teeth. "He'll say anything, whatever they tell him to say. They'll use him to sandbag me."

"Why should Roger Montalvo want to hurt you? Wasn't he passing you information?" Reilly asked calmly.

"Are you kidding? All a stool knows is what are you doing for me lately, who do I fuck today, and who do I put in to get myself out?"

"You have to be careful with them kind of people," Chapman added.

Brennan nodded. Then leaning toward Reilly, he said, "Let me give you an example. You rode in a car with Jimmy Mullins, right?"

Reilly's eyes locked on Brennan. "What the hell does that have to do with this?"

"I'm just trying to give you an example. Let's say Jimmy Mullins were to get popped by the shoofly. Some smart-ass DA in the Rackets Bureau might say to Jimmy, 'Who'd you ride with?' Your name would come up. You're still within the five-year statute of limitations. You're bigger fish than Jimmy Mullins. You know Jimmy is a dog. He would never stand up. So first he'd say nonfeasance—you were there, but you didn't take any money. But that wouldn't be good enough. 'Too bad, Jimmy. You gotta go into the joint with all them guys you locked up.' How long before Jimmy would say, 'Reilly took money'? Then he'd say you were his boss. Then he'd say you were the bag man for the whole fucking borough."

"What kind of shit are you trying to pull?" Reilly pushed his glass across the Formica table as he stood up.

Brennan remained seated. "I'm just trying to give you an example. Don't get excited."

Reilly glared at Chapman. "This your idea, Chappie?"

Chapman shrugged. "He just told me he wanted to talk to you."

Reilly walked to the counter near the doorway and leaned against it with both hands. "Get him out of my house."

Brennan nodded and rose to his feet. "I'm clean on this thing. But if I'm smeared, everybody else is, too. I'm gonna fight fire with fire, Reilly. Y'hear?"

Chapman leaped between them, his hands outstretched. "Al, he's very upset about this thing. He don't mean no harm."

Reilly pointed at Brennan. "If you're clean, I would be the last person to hurt a cop. But if you're not, dig up all the Mason jars you got buried in your backyard. Get all your money out 'cause you're going."

Brennan brushed past Reilly. "Let's get out of here, Chappie."

"Sorry about this, Al." Chapman whispered as he walked past. "I'll talk to you Monday."

Chapman and Brennan left the apartment. Reilly

poured himself a double. Ho-ly shit, he thought. Mullins, my ghost.

Communion breakfasts, Emerald Society shindigs, PBA meetings. Mullins was standout, and consistent. "The fuckin' Hebes are taking over. Deputy inspectors, shoofly. What's the department coming to? Wops in the Detective Bureau, and a white man like me is still in uniform. I ain't saying we don't make a stitch if we have to, but the guineas will be taking even junk money! And niggers—*niggers*—even in plain clothes. How you suppose to know who to shoot?"

Deputy bag for everybody—sergeants, lieutenants, captains, borough, division—but always a short count. Days off he would privateer in the South Bronx tenements, shaking down the action people or, gun in hand, kicking down some Cuban dope peddler's door. A staunch Catholic, he'd rip a gold crucifix off a headboard or somebody's chest.

Moon. That was the code name on the tapes the DA and the PC had in their vaults. But the stool pigeon backtracked on them, and Moon wriggled off the hook. To call him that was to risk getting shot.

Who could touch him? He had survived departmental trials, grand jury investigations, civilian complaints, the rubber gun squad, Alcoholics Anonymous, Gamblers Anonymous. The Hibernian mafia watched over him like a wayward child. One of the boys.

What was I supposed to do? Wire myself up? Frank Reilly's boy—scumbag PC hero, stooling on his own kind. I couldn't have stood up to that. But Mullins was always a dog.

"Jimmy, I told you. I don't play. I don't want to know your business. Don't tell me nothing."

Mullins scoffed through his nose and pressed down on the gas pedal, jerking the patrol car forward.

"Al, me boy. You wouldn't be having a wire on ya, would ya?"

"Go fuck yourself."

He went into his Arthur Shields brogue. "Saints be praised. Lookit the Irish blushing yer checks, me boy, just like yer father, Frank Reilly, may he rest in peace, *pride* of the men in blue."

"Cut the bullshit. You never worked with my father."

"Your father? What's so great about working with your father? What, he pissed holy water? I mean I'm sorry he got killed by some niggers. But I've been out here twenty years fighting crime in the ghett-o." Mullins laughed, loud.

"That's very good, Jim. Talk into the mike, self-serving declarations. The commissioner's office will be duly impressed at your fifth departmental."

The banter stopped cold. Mullins sucked in his round, hairless cheeks, sat up, and adjusted his cap. They rode on in silence. He glanced at Reilly, then turned back to his driving.

"Ya gotta have balls, Al. Your father tried to be a boy scout, a Jesus Christ. What did it get 'im, huh? I'll tell you. Crucified. Left you an orphan, right? With your aunt, right? So what was your inheritance, a nightstick? Where's the fuckin' money? In other words, we're supposed to be out here twenty years in this shithouse with these fuckin' Virginia hams and these fuckin' spics shootin', cuttin', maimin' us, and we ain't gonna make no money? Get outta here!"

"Jimmy. For the last time, I'm not here to reform you or anybody else. I just want to stay out of trouble, put my time in, get through school, and get out. So you go your way. I'll go mine."

"Lawyer, huh? Big fuckin' deal. I put more contracts with lawyers—and judges, too. Ha. Sure. Had one old bandit downtown. I'd go right in his chambers at night court. 'Judge, I got a toss-out, but all the defendant has is fifty dollars.' 'Wadda you insulting me?' He threw me outta his chamber. Case is called. He pulls me over to the bench. 'Give me the fifty.' 'Right here?' 'Where else, dummy?' I'd slip him the fifty behind the bench, on the side. Case dismissed. Meanwhile I already had four hundred and fifty in my pockets on accounta I had glommed it earlier from the yom. Neat, right? That's what's happening all over. Wake up, Reilly. This is a zoo. Look out your fuckin' window at the animals. You gotta get paid for that."

He had both hands off the steering wheel and was waving wildly in all directions. "Look around you, Al. Lookit that quiff over there with high heels and pocketbook. Right? He'll crack your spine with one hand. And lookit this one, the pretty one. She's fifteen. She's had two overdoses. Lookit that mob ahead, standing in the water, like cutthroats on a pirate ship."

"I think you've got battle fatigue, Jimmy. Pull up. I'll close the pump."

The car stopped in front of the gushing fire hydrant. The water was shooting into the air through a milk crate mounted on the hydrant. The street was flooded. They stood in a six-inch pool of water, dozens of them, wet, pants rolled up.

They were quiet when Reilly stepped out of the car, a lug wrench in his hand. He kicked the milk crate off, and it went skidding across the street. He got wet in the process, and the sidewalk crowd became hysterical. They could barely stand up from laughing and slapping palms. Reilly clamped the wrench on and shut off the water. Now they got ugly. "Boo! Boo! Fockin' moder focka."

This was clearly his show; Mullins was not about to

get his shoes wet. Mullins used to play at laying back on him. "To test balls," he'd say. "If you don't steal, it's 'cause you ain't got no balls. Then what good are you on the street?"

Reilly pointed to the biggest young black, who stood there bare-chested, his shirt wrapped around his head and trailing down his neck like the burnoose of a Sudanese warrior.

"You, you fucking jadroney. One more word out of you and I'm bringing you in. Anybody interfere, I'll blow a hole in him. Open the pump on the next tour."

It was bluff, but it was all he had going for him. More jeers, but nobody threw a hatchet. Reilly slid back into the squad car.

The hatchet was not far off. Just a few blocks north they came on two men locked in battle. Their hands clasped around the handle of a fire ax, the pair lurched clumsily around a garbage-littered lot. They staggered back and forth in a drunken dance, muscles knotted, sweating from their violent embrace. The spectators were the usual amorphous mass, surging, receding, stumbling over the refuse as they followed the fight. But they were unusually quiet. The steel of the bladehead had them awed. Like a canefield machete. Then, slowly, the struggling men raised the ax, jointly, as if by accord. The quivering metal glanced sunlight into the eyes of the crowd. A loud gasp arose.

Mullins shoved through the onlookers and circled the two men. Then, from a crouch, he leapt forward and grabbed the handle, yelling, "Let go. The two of you. I got it."

The fighters released their grips and fell down among the broken bottles and dog shit, exhausted. Mullins waddled back to the car and threw the hatchet on the

seat. He was fat, but he could move. Reilly and Mullins
got back in the car. Somebody said, "Mullins got plenty
cojones." Reilly knew some Spanish by then and
nodded, but mostly to himself, as Mullins had already
pulled out. He was humming to himself: "Hi, hi, hee, in
the field artill-ery-y." Smiling, he turned to Reilly.
"Even in the army you get extra pay for hazardous duty.
Sure, combat pay. That's all it is, Al, me boy."

What could you do with a man like that: write him
up, rat him out, louse yourself up in the process? What
a lousy fucking job.

They looped in and out—106th Street, 107th Street,
108th Street—working their way north. Lexington,
Park, Madison. It was wino and junkie hot. By 116th
Street, they had seen a dozen derelicts hopping and
jumping around, insane with the heat and the poison
streaming through their insides.

Al Reilly, you're going to have to kill one of these
people one of these days, sure as shit. No doubt, after a
thousand provocations, he would pick the wrong time
and the wrong guy and get racked up by the department. Did it to avenge his father. Trigger-happy. Racist
cop. Suspension. Grand jury. There went law school
and his dreams of getting out of the bag. That was his
nightmare. And from the fear grew a hatred of the
street and the swarm clinging to the decaying walls.
Babies, unattended, sitting on fifth-story windowsills; a
hundred mattresses burning with people still sleeping
on them; whole staircases collapsing. Harlem seemed
like a broken-down, hand-operated carousel an old Italian would bring around for the kids to ride, only he'd
see it spinning faster and faster, out of control, a crazy
top, with people flying off, crashing, smashing themselves. Sometimes he felt close to jumping out of the

squad car and screaming, "Get out of here. Go home. Go somewhere. You can't make it. They're hacking you to pieces. You can't—"

Sometimes. But most of the time he would think of his day off and his own quiet street in Elmhurst and his aunt's concrete backyard, where he would snooze under a corrugated metal awning. But they were out in Queens, too. The dam had collapsed. They were downstream, the water rushing past, rising fast. And who's hauling the sandbags, manning the barricades, shooting the looters? The Irish, the harps. Who else. We need that, on top of the priests and the booze. Bigots we're supposed to be. Sure there's a Mullins. What about all the blacks I've carried down five flights of stairs? Or the Puerto Rican wedding with the carving knives and me trying not to shoot anybody? Who gives a shit about us?

Back cruising Fifth Avenue near 110th Street, Reilly saw a bald-headed man in shorts and house slippers, a leather belt in his hand, chasing a woman in a bra and half-slip. They ran out of one building and into another. Reilly yelled to Mullins to stop. Mullins kept on driving.

"That's Pelao and his old lady. That's their pre-fuck play." Mullins looked over. "They ain't people, Reilly. They just ain't people."

13 Brennan studied the strange little guy.

Nicola Petrone listed visibly to his left when in motion, his rib cage having been torn outward in a grapple hook fight in Hoboken, New Jersey, in 1928, shortly after his arrival in the United States. The subsequent manslaughter conviction plagued him for many years afterward, but he successfully frustrated all efforts to deport him.

Nicola Petrone, also known as Nicky Peters. Aged sixty. Capo. Overlord of the East Harlem mob. He began operations in the West Village in the thirties, his sotto capi, lieutenants, and soldati were now active as far north as the West Bronx, south to the Lower East Side, and west all the way to Newark. His funeral director dress, snow-white hair, and diminutive stature deceived no one, particularly the overly ambitious or refractory underbosses whom he would assault on the street in the presence of soldiers. American pavements, European cobblestones, it made no difference to Nicky "Peters" Petrone. Where he trod, he was the boss.

The house was a small, modest New Jersey home, with leonine figures displayed both in the house and on the grounds outside. A full suit of medieval armor and chain mail stood guard at the entrance to the den. Brennan considered momentarily the smallness of all the men of that era as he sat down. Besides Petrone, present also were Mastrangelo and Zaccarelli, and three button men, unknown to Brennan, who moved inconspicuously around the room. Their flinty looks annoyed Brennan. "Do we need these three spitters around, Mr. Petrone?"

"They get nervous when I'm alone with people. I am responsible for them. You can talk," Petrone said.

"I have a problem. A spic uptown—Robert Texidor, Bobby Tex—is trying to set me up because I killed Tony Roman."

"Who is Tony Roman?" Petrone asked, looking at Mastrangelo.

"A lapo," Zaccarelli volunteered, "for Bobby Tex." Mastrangelo nodded.

Brennan smirked. "Yeah, his flunky. He pulled a gun on me, and I blew him away. So now this Tex is out to get me."

Petrone was startled. "Get you? A lieutenant of police?"

"He went to the DA and ratted, said I sly-zapped Tony and planted a gun on him. Larry Pesh knows about it. He was there."

Petrone turned again to Mastrangelo. "The DA? Hank, what's going on?"

Mastrangelo said, "Larry spoke to us about it. We pulled the kid's coattail a little bit, Nicky. He was upset, but he got the message. Tex is all right, Nicky. We talked nice to him. He's moved a lot of furniture for Larry. The count has always been right. We can't find too many guys like him among those people. We need him."

Brennan's dusky face paled with rage. "Need him? A

Puerto Rican skag peddler?" He rose, his legs spread out. "All right. I'm gonna take the scabs off the sores for everybody right here and now. Six years I been with you wops. I've saved your guys from big junk collars. I've traced lost stuff for you. I've fingered stools for you, any one of which would have set up a forty-man conspiracy. I've even gone on special assignments for you, Nick. And you're going to tell me you need Bobby Tex?"

Mastrangelo bunched his fingertips together and shook both his hands at Brennan. "Why don't we wait awhile and see if we can straighten this out, ey?"

Brennan took a step backward. "*If?* If you had a square asshole, you'd shit bricks! I don't wanna hear that shit!"

Mastrangelo stood up. "Watch your mouth."

Brennan opened his suit jacket. "What? You're gonna put on your Al Capone face? Right? I'm ready to step out, here and now. You want it with guns right here? You wanna go in the kitchen with the knives? You're talkin' to *me*. I chew on wise guys and spit out faggots. Y'hear!"

Mastrangelo, Zaccarelli, and the three soldati stood rigid, congealed.

Petrone put his hands on his chest. "C'mon, Guido." His cheeks were on fire, but his voice was conciliatory. "We're all wops here. You've made money with us. What's to get excited about?"

"I'm wop only by half, and you guys would be the first to remind me. I know where I stand. I know that treachery is catechism here. I know you guys would crawl over your dying mother to fuck your sister. Okay. If I go down on this Tex thing, then everybody goes, every greaseball in the crew. And if you get ideas about having me taken out, there's papers in my locker that say everybody goes anyway. My head is very bad. Nick, you know that."

Petrone said, "Guido is right. Everybody sit down. Guido is right. This Tex is a stool pigeon, disgraziato. We're not gonna lose a man like Guido for a fuckin' scungeel of a spic. Afangul'. Bury him. Hank, you get Larry Pesh to set it up. He's the closest to him."

Mastrangelo puffed out his cheeks. "Larry likes Tex. He's made a lot of money with him, Nicky."

His lips tightening, Petrone said, "Larry will do this thing, or I will personally go to 116th Street with a fungo bat I got in my car and splatter his brains all over Pleasant Avenue. That fuckin' cafone."

Brennan nodded, slightly appeased. "Yeah. Larry owes me for the Indian rope trick he pulled on Trentino."

"We'll go to Harlem tonight, Nicky," Mastrangelo said, suddenly enthusiastic.

Petrone said, "Guido, I want to apologize to you for this misunderstanding. Ya know, I gotta do everything myself. These kids I got with me. Supposed to be smart. Cavallo, stupido. We will take care of this thing for you, Guido. You did right to come to us. That way you're clean when this Tex gets hit. If you need anything—don't care how much—you see Hank. Y'hear, Hank? This man has carte blank with us, capisce?"

"All the way, Nicky," Mastrangelo agreed. "Sorry about the misunderstanding, Guido. It's clear now that this Texidor is a threat to us all."

Zaccarelli said, "Yeah, Guido. We'll get on it right away."

"I gotta go," said Brennan. "Maybe one of your guys can start my car for me. It's a rented car. I been having trouble with the ignition."

Petrone smiled. "Very good. Un uomo intelligente.

But if there was gonna be a scene, it would have been as soon as you came over the bridge, not in my house. You are a guest in my house, Guido."

"Yeah, I know. See ya."

Brennan was shown out.

"What's this shit about Trentino and the rope what?" Petrone asked.

Mastrangelo took a gold lighter from his pocket. "That's from the time Tony Trent turned stool and was making a case for Brennan. Somebody put a rope around Trent's neck, and Brennan got written up as negligent. Brennan blamed Larry for the job. He went bananas. Everytime he caught Larry in the street, he'd throw a rope around his neck. If it wasn't for that nigger that goes around with Brennan, he'd have choked Larry for sure."

Petrone shook his head, frowning. "His brain is gone. He can be trouble for us. Too bad. He was very good for us."

"Right away, Nicky?" Mastrangelo asked.

"No. Tex first. That will calm Guido. Then you check out this locker business. Probably bullshit. But check it out. Use any amount of money. Then Guido is taken out. But he must disappear. His body must never be found, capisce?"

"He killed another one of Tex's kids before Tony Roman," Mastrangelo said. "Bananas, I guess."

"It's a shame. But he lasted longer than I expected. I mean, a rogue cop is more dangerous than a stool. Maybe it's better this way. Clean out the pipes. Set up a new operation uptown."

"We'll go see Larry tonight and make the arrangements. Ciao, Nicky."

"Ciao."

14 Stanley Lubin shuffled into Reilly's office carrying a transcript and slumped into a chair across from Reilly. Lubin appeared tired.

"Hi, Mr. Lubin. Whatcha got for me this beautiful Monday morning?" Reilly asked.

"What do I got for you? I got the Q and A from that huge guy that don't fit in a chair—Lieutenant Brennan." He handed Reilly the transcript.

Reilly leaned back in his chair. "Big stoop, ain't he, Stanley?"

"Big? Like an Abe Simon he's big. Many times I have seen him in the precincts. He scares me. He scares the defendants."

"What do you mean?"

"I have seen a defendant tell the assistant DA 'fuck you' for half an hour. Then Brennan will talk to the man, and we get a full Q and A."

"He must be a persuasive talker."

"His eyes, they're very bad. The muzzle of his gun inside the mouth or ear helps."

"You've seen him do that, Stanley?"

Lubin chuckled. "I have not. After twenty-five years taking statements in the bureau, I see and hear only what is necessary. I take long blinks with the eyes and sometimes wax in the ears."

"You've been here that long?"

"I seen them come, I seen them go, but old Lubin is still here. And I have caught all the big ones. When Lubin is catching, the big ones break. Ask the boys in the steno pool."

"You've worked with Mr. Quinn on a lot of cases, huh, Stanley?"

"The chief goes out on all the big ones, and Lubin is right there."

"He's an able guy, isn't he?"

"Brilliant lawyer. The jury is a Stradivarius with twelve strings, and he is three Heifetzes. Up is down; black is white. He stuns them. I have seen him many times take a shit case and bury the defendant. God forbid the defendant should take the stand; better he should be in the dental chair and have four molars extracted."

"Suppose to be a great cross-examiner."

"Quinn is the best. He has never had even a hung jury. His memory is total. He will sum up three hours without a note. If a witness says eight thirty A.M. on page one of the transcript, he better not say eight forty-five A.M. five hundred pages later. He is inhuman. You can learn a lot from this man. He seems to like you."

"What kind of guy is he, Stanley?"

"What?"

"I mean, what do you think of him as a person? What's inside him?"

Lubin turned to look toward the door, then faced Reilly again. "With all due respect, he's a shtonk," Lubin said, his puffy eyes expanding into a stare.

"A what?"

"N.F.G., with the oak leaf clusters. Cold man. When they sat Saturnino Burgos in the electric chair up in Ossining, they had to drag him by the heels. When this was discussed in front of Quinn, who got the conviction, you know what he said? 'I *hope* he was guilty.' He is an ice man."

"Well, I guess he's like the nurses in the emergency ward. They develop a crust. Otherwise they can't function."

"None of the DAs wanna go up to Sing Sing when they're giving someone the jolts. Quinn used to go all the time. Like he was watching a recital."

"Well, he's going into politics now."

"He is going to will himself to power. He believes in the will. I have seen him in front of the mirror in his office, hypeing himself up before a summation. 'I *will*' this; 'I *will*' that. Crazy. He can will dead men from the grave. He can will a verdict from a jury. Crazy."

"I guess that's what distinguishes great trial lawyers, that edge they have."

"He's a racist. An anti-Semite."

"Well. I don't know."

"You're an Irisher, Al. But I know. Believe me, I know. Ask Leon Blumenfeld. Listen, you want I should bend your ear all morning? Let me get back to my typewriter." Lubin labored to his feet.

"Stanley, I appreciate your being frank with me."

"He'll be gone in a few days. So why pretend, right? Al, I'll see ya," Lubin said, walking out.

"Okay, Stanley."

Reilly remained at his desk studying Brennan's statement taken the previous Monday, December 9. He was chagrined at reading the clumsy phrasing of his questions.

The telephone rang.

"Reilly. Quinn here."

"Yes, sir."

"Would you step into my office for a minute, please? Bring the Roman folder with you."

"Be right there, sir."

Reilly gathered all the U.F. 61s and D.D. 5s on the Anthony Roman homicide, placed them in the folder, and walked to Quinn's office.

"Good morning, Chief."

Quinn got up from his desk and came around to shake Reilly's hand. He seemed expansive as he motioned Reilly to sit down while he himself stood leaning against his desk, his arms crossed. Reilly scanned the charcoal gray single-breasted suit and subtly black-flecked gray tie. Quinn's crossed legs rode the perfectly creased pants up a little, revealing tightly fitted black socks.

Probably uses garters. Never see him with droopy socks, thought Reilly, trying to hide his own.

"Reilly. A pleasure to see you. Winding matters up here. I'm leaving in two weeks, you know."

"I know, sir."

"Can't say I'm sorry. My wife, Pamela, has been trying to convince me to undertake a political career for a long time. I have scoffed at the idea, but this national election last month is clear indicia that changes are imminent. The winds are shifting, and I feel duty-bound to stand up and be counted. The lunacy of the Warren court has to be curtailed. Insipid doctrines, such as propounded in *Miranda* versus *Arizona*, can't be allowed to stand. A more infernal decision has never been handed down unless it's the abolition of capital punishment. Wait until you have to dismiss a case against a man who has murdered his wife and five children because the confession is imperfect under the *Miranda* rules, thereby—as the esteemed Supreme

Court put it—'tainting all evidence as fruit of the poisoned tree.' Sophistry of the most convoluted variety."

"I know, Chief. We had to walk around with the *Miranda* rules pasted inside our hats."

"Indeed. The law has emasculated law enforcement. We must change the law. It's as simple as that. Unfortunately that requires giving up the work here. I shall miss it, but I am prepared to make that sacrifice."

Reilly thought he should say something but couldn't frame anything fast enough.

Quinn stepped away from his desk and stood straight. "When I am in the right, there is little I cannot accomplish. The means cannot be subject to inquiry under the present circumstances."

"But a Christian society can't—"

"Reilly, please. Spare me your twaddle. It is this same woolly-headed quibbling and nit-picking have brought us to our present state of judicial bankruptcy. Please, spare me."

"Yes, sir," Reilly said, drawing back.

"Forgive me. I did not wish to sound arbitrary. It's just that I have gone into this subject. . . . Well, no matter. Let us dwell on more pleasant topics."

Quinn walked around the desk, returned to his high-backed leather chair, and rocked slowly from side to side. "All right, Pamela and I are having a little cocktail party at my house tonight, around eight or nine o'clock. A few friends of mine are coming by. But solid people—of substance—people who want to get this country back on the right track. I want you there."

"I'm flattered, Chief."

"These are the people to whom you have to expose yourself early. Do not wait twenty years. Now is the time to make your alliances. I wish someone had so advised me fifteen years ago."

"I appreciate it, Mr. Quinn."

Quinn waved away the gratitude. "I have taken to you because I consider you a veteran of the streets"— smiling then—"notwithstanding a few chinks and fissures. Be at my apartment around eight. Number Eleven, Fifth Avenue. Now back to your work, young man."

"Yes, sir." Reilly started to rise.

"Oh, I am getting absentminded. What new developments in the Roman case?"

"We are going ahead with the investigation, Chief."

Quinn looked amused. "Come now. Don't dance about. There isn't the time. Answer my question directly."

"Well, we still haven't found Roger Montalvo, but that shouldn't take too long."

"You have developed an animosity toward Lieutenant Brennan, have you not, Reilly?"

"No. He's just a little rough."

"I would prefer to characterize him as zealous myself. I am astounded at your lack of perspective in this case. No matter. Close it out at the earliest moment possible. Get a date for the grand jury. Present this piece of trash, and have done with it. Understood?"

"Yes, sir."

"There will be a few of my wife's young friends at the affair this evening. Might prove to be fun for you."

"I'm looking forward to it."

"All right, Reilly. Leave the folder, please. I want to check a few things. I will have it placed on your desk."

Reilly left the room. He returned to his office and sat down with his elbows on the desk, his hands propped under his chin. I'm being set up, he thought. Jesus H. Christ. I got off the job to get away from all the shit. But this tingle in my balls don't make mistakes. They're trying to hump me. Well, like Leon said, play it straight. That's all I'm gonna do. Devil hump the hindmost. In the meantime, there's lunch.

Reilly took the elevator to the lobby of the Criminal Court Building and headed for the lunchroom. As he walked past the rotunda, he ran into Preston Pearlstein.

"How you doing?" Reilly smiled.

"Terrible, horrible. I just lost another client to the Legal Aid. They're wipin' us out," Pearlstein lamented.

"You'll always make a buck."

"Are you kidding? The private bar is being cannibalized by our own kind in the fuckin' legislature. It ain't bad enough with the Legal Aid. Now they're gonna have appellate division assignments where the state pays the lawyer. All on account of that fuckin' *Gideon* versus *Wainwright*. We're gonna have subsidized crime."

"Well, you can take assignments, Preston."

"Never. I'll starve first. Where's the attorney-client relationship? There's no respect. The lawyer is on the dole, too. What is this, fuckin' communism?"

"Guess you'll have to move to other areas."

"What other areas? This no-fault law is coming, sure as shit. Then you're gonna have do-it-yourself kits for the divorce cases. They're doing a genocide on the private practitioner worse than the Germans. Bunch of fuckin' pinkos."

"That's progress for you."

"Progress! You call that progress? Where are the great lawyers gonna come from? The Edelbaums, the Kriegers, the Di Renzos—they're not coming out of no welfare agencies. I'm gonna have to open an abortion clinic with my brother, Dr. Keith Pearlstein."

"Yeah, I heard about him. Makes a fortune."

"Oh, you heard about him? That's right. Makes a

bundle. You never know. I might end my career as a medical man, Al."

"I'm going to eat, Preston. Be good."

"I'd join you, but I'm waiting since twelve o'clock for a client."

"It's one o'clock."

"For money I wait. Take care."

"Good luck."

Reilly walked into the lunchroom and took a stool in the corner near the griddle. "Just give me a cheeseburger 'n a vanilla malted. And that piece of coconut custard there, the small one."

The harried waitress looked at him, then proceeded to take another customer's order.

Pearlstein walked in and sat down on the next stool. "Give me a cup of coffee, Miss," he said with the face of a man in pain.

"You give up, Preston?"

"Cock suckin' rat bastard. That's the second time he beats me outta my fee."

"Don't you get your fee in front?"

"It don't work that way. You know the guy. He's crying, 'Mr. Pearlstein, you gotta save me. I'm being framed. I got your money next week. But my wife is pregnant. My mother needs an ingrown toenail operation. Don't worry, I got your fee. I swear on the grave of my father. I got your fee.' Shit. They suck you in. Then when you want your fee: 'Oh, you're a greedy bastard. All you think about is money. What about my civil rights?' Rotten rat bastards. The client is the mortal enemy of the lawyer."

"Can't live with them. Can't live without them."

"When am I gonna learn? Once you're in the case and you ain't been paid, why should they pay you? If you lose, you did a bum job or sold out to the DA, so why should they pay you? If you win, they're off the hook, so why should they pay you? Heads you're humped, and tails you're pogued. Filthy, scurvy—" Pearlstein slapped his palm down on the counter.

"I heard you the first time," the waitress yelled. "I only got two hands."

"Take it easy, Preston. You're going to make yourself sick."

Pearlstein glared at the waitress, unconsoled. "Look at that. I gotta take lip from everybody. Wait until you get into private practice, Al. You'll find out."

"If I ever get started here. I need trial experience. I want to get into a courtroom. I want to be a trial lawyer, not an investigator."

"If you got it to try cases, you'll know it right away. It's a natural thing. Like Joe DiMaggio going out in center field for a fly ball. You got it? You got it. But if you ain't, that doesn't mean you can't make money. Look at me. I don't claim to be a Choate or a Louie Brandeis, but I've done okay. Plenty of big ghees have been my clients, guys like Larry. They know I deliver. And I can try a case if I gotta. I can sell ten pounds of shit in a two-pound bag. I got the ol' regular-guy, man-in-the-street rappaport with the jury. But I lose money doing that. I'm better off jockeying around, drumming up new cases. I've hired plenty of sharp kids, even former DAs, to try cases for me. But they can't talk to a client. They can't sell themselves to a client. That's the art. Sitting on a barstool or talking in the tank in the Tombs, you got to sell yourself to your client. 'So what you got three murders. So what you got twenty pounds of junk in your closet. Don't worry about it. I got everything under control.' Salesmanship. That's the key."

"You have to bullshit your clients?"

"What bullshit? That's what they wanna hear, Al. How many guys come to me complaining about another lawyer. 'He don't give me no hope.' It's a crazy business. Talking about crazy business, how are you doing with your Brennan case?"

"You know Brennan?"

"I know him all right. And you got your hands full."

"Crazy guy, eh?"

"Don't quote me. He's one of a few, and he ain't the first. But he's the worst."

"Listen, Preston, if you got together thirty thousand bishops or rabbis, you'd still have some bad guys."

"Yeah. But they don't walk around with a badge and a gun. I've seen such cops before. Can spot them a mile off. I had one right here on the fourth floor. Right on the stand he went nuts. He was a landlord, too. Every time a tenant would ask for heat, he'd give the tenant a beating and lock him up for assault. He locked up my client. I had him on the stand. He started screaming about his father being a lawyer and he shouldn't take this abuse. The DA threw the case out. Everybody knew this cop was crazy. Nobody said anything. Next thing I know, he got locked up as a burglar."

"That's the problem. Nobody wants to stool on a brother officer."

"I can see that, sure. But sometimes they let it go too far. You had another nut job there a few years ago. Wouldn't talk to anyone in the precinct. Used to pull his gun regularly in the locker room. Always in church. Nobody said anything. Then on his day off, he went to a midtown bar and shot four people in the head—all dead."

Reilly nodded sympathetically. "Nightmares. You don't know the wringer a cop is put through."

"I wouldn't take the job for anything."

"You think Brennan is over the deep end, Preston?"

"I'm not saying anything, Al. Don't quote me. But if he continues his, ey,"—Preston seesawed his hand—"interrogations, then I'm going to run out of clients."

"There's Gentleman Jack Bradley. Why is he still around?" Reilly exclaimed, looking over Pearlstein's shoulder toward the door.

"That putz. He'll run and tell Quinn that I tried to bribe you with a hamburger."

"Fuck him."

"A fortiori. He tried to wire up one of my own clients against me. I shoulda called up the bar association. Instead I called him up and told him I was gonna slap the shit outta him."

"What did he say?"

"He said he was gonna have me locked up for assault."

"Stand-up guy, eh?"

"You guys got a good office. There has to be a house prick or two. What the hell?"

"Preston, I gotta run. Be good." He motioned to the waitress.

Pearlstein leaped from his stool—"There goes my client."—and dashed out of the cafeteria.

•

Reilly rang the doorbell, feeling elegant in his dark blue pinstripe suit and new wing-tip shoes.

Quinn opened the door. "Reilly, how nice of you to come."

Reilly stepped into the foyer and was ushered on into the living room. Grace, symmetry, everything understated, thought Reilly. That's true of their clothes, their cars, their furniture, even their women. A tall woman, close in height to Reilly's six feet, made her way through the large gathering in the room.

"Al, this is my wife, Pamela. Pamela, this is the young man I have been speaking to you about, Aloysius Reilly."

"Welcome to our home, Mr. Reilly. I've been hearing such nice things about you from Peter." The smile was direct and pleasant.

"Please call me Al, Mrs. Quinn. I'm honored to be here."

"Come in and meet some of the other guests," she said.

Reilly measured her a full two inches taller than Quinn. Long-limbed, slender, with a sharply structured face and a full head of soft, tawny-colored hair. A graceful lady, Pamela Quinn. Jesus, how do you get into bed with a woman like that, Reilly wondered as she took him by the arm into the center of the room and announced, "Ladies and gentlemen, this is Al Reilly, a dashing new assistant district attorney in my husband's bureau. Let's introduce ourselves and make him feel at home, shall we?"

A dazzling crowd. The names escaped Reilly, but the titles and affiliations were awesome: bank trustees, senior Wall Street lawyers, jurists, legislators. Al Reilly was in the big leagues. Farewell to Elmhurst, good-bye Brooklyn. Pop would have been proud. Poor Pop, blown away in an empty garbage lot two years from retirement. Well, I'm out of the streets, Pop. Like you said, lace curtains all the way. If they don't stick me in a shroud, too.

A dark-skinned man wearing a white waistcoat and carrying a metal tray approached Reilly. "What would you like to drink, sir?"

"Habla español, señor?" Reilly inquired.

"No, sir. Grik."

Reilly heard a titter coming from behind him. Jason Bradley. Son of a bitch. "Scotch and soda, please." Fuck you, Jack.

Bradley was settled smugly between two beautiful heads of streaked blonde hair. He was attired in a dark blue suit and his usual brown shoes.

"Mr. Reilly, I was just telling Kimberley and Vanessa about the deplorable conditions you had witnessed in the ghetto. They're *very* community-oriented and so much want to help. Ladies, Reilly spent years in the trenches uptown. But he overcame, 'ey Reilly?" Bradley slid into another group. It took Reilly a full half hour to extricate himself from the sociologically committed Kimberley and Vanessa, but not before he was peppered with the whole panoply: gut reactions, viable alternatives, political options, community action, Urban League. They got more Orientals in the Lindsay crew than they got in all of Asia, thought Reilly, as he fell into another cluster.

The drink and the discourse continued until close to midnight, Reilly growing less nervous with each drink. And Quinn was everywhere, moving smoothly from guest to guest, the right word for everyone.

Then the gathering began to disperse, and Reilly noticed Guido Brennan for the first time.

"Hi, Al. Just came by to pay my respects to the chief."

"How you doing, Lieutenant? You're looking real dapper."

"The chief wants us to stay awhile. A nightcap with some of his special friends," Brennan said.

"Special friends?"

"Some of the people that run this town. You have no idea the pull that Chief Quinn has. He's a winner, Al.

Everybody says so. He's got money, his wife has plenty of money, and with these people behind him, the sky's the limit."

"Like what?"

"Like mayor for starters. After that, who knows?"

"Holy shit. You think so?"

"Believe me, kid, you're in the right place."

•

The five special friends, all captains of their respective realms, sat on Quinn's large L-shaped couch. Diverse physical types, their common denominator was the distinct aura of cash that they exuded. Reilly, Brennan, and Bradley sat in chairs flanking them.

Quinn clasped his hands behind his back and addressed the group. "Gentlemen, a few minutes of your time. I take this, the eve of my departure from the district attorney's office, as an opportunity to speak with you. Politics. The very word is abhorrent to me. These are not, however, times to indulge one's personal desires or fancies. We all witnessed the recent spectacle at the convention in Chicago and our own local anarchists at play on Morningside Heights. The assassination of Senator Kennedy, the assassination of the Reverend Martin Luther King, the conflagration in our cities—the fire is not next time. It is now. Lawlessness must be vanquished, or all we know and hold dear will perish. I need not belabor the perils with which our society is being confronted.

"The criminal must be expunged. Only then can some semblance of normalcy be reestablished. The means we have discussed on numerous occasions, so I will not tax you with details now.

"Who anointed me as savior, gentlemen?" Someone

tittered, and then they all laughed heartily, right on cue. "I foresaw this era of lawlessness over a decade ago and stood by, as did you, with arms enfolded. The result: near anarchy. Therefore, I am prepared to abandon my safe perch. Given the proper authority, I can put a stop to this in the state of New York. I will not shrink from the most extreme measures, and I mean capital punishment if it is called for. I will not be dissuaded by the carping and catcalls of the bleeding hearts.

"These statements of mine may appear to you as commonplace utterances, platitudes. If you question the sincerity of my convictions, you need but to examine my record. I am a believer, and when I set course, there is nothing that will deter me. If you question that, inquire of those who have crossed my path. Make no mistake. I have the will to power. That is the ever sustaining force common to all leaders and captains throughout history.

"The cynical among you will say, Man is a predatory beast. The fatalist will say, the Hydra will reemerge, no matter how many heads are lopped off. That, gentlemen, I cannot accept. That is the road to nihilism and surrender. It is our duty, it has fallen upon us by virtue of our privileged stations, to cry, 'Halt. Enough.' There is yet time.

"You all know my record. There are no skeletons in my closet. You have met my wife; you have heard my views. I believe I have a role to play, and if I can enlist your aid, I can fulfill it. The restoration of law and order—the mandate is clear. The national elections last month mark the turning point. The train departs, my friends. Make haste, lest you be left behind. Thank you for your patience."

Jack Bradley started the applause. Then all followed suit. Quinn accepted their hearty congratulations and signaled for a fresh round of drinks.

Brennan whispered, "Jack and the fat cats will be leaving now. Stick around. The chief wants to talk to us, private."

"Jack handles the cue cards, eh? Campaign manager maybe?"

"You'd be smart to sign up yourself. Al, he's a great man."

"What's he going to make you, police commissioner?"

"Stranger things have happened."

When only Reilly and Brennan remained of the guests, Quinn approached, smiling. "Pamela went to bed. Let's go to my study. This room reeks of cigarettes."

He put his arms around their shoulders and led them into a room, the walls of which were covered with books from floor to ceiling, as was the large writing desk by the window.

"My workshop," Quinn said proudly, his arms extended. "The accoutrements of my trade. You want to be a trial lawyer, Reilly? Read the classics. When you're on your feet and the questions and answers fly in a cross-examination, lights and buzzers will go on and off, little compartments and drawers will slide open and close." Quinn smiled impishly.

Then the smile vanished. "There is more psychology in a Dostoevsky or a Shakespeare, a Dickens, even a James Joyce than can be found in the whole of psychiatry. The twin plagues of our time, Freudianism and Marxism. I have had to battle this army of mumbo-jumbo charlatans parading up and down the witness stands." Quinn held his nose, affecting a nasal sound. "Dr. Snozenberg, for instance: 'In the reality of the mind of this defendant, is this pistol a banana?' Charlatans!"

Reilly was unsettled by Quinn's outburst.

"You will, no doubt, report me to Blumenfeld," said Quinn.

"No, sir, not at all."

"Speaking of the Chosen, I understand you were having lunch this afternoon with Preston Pearlstein. Is that correct?"

"Well, not really. I just happened to run across him in the lunchroom."

"Your position as an assistant district attorney requires not only the reality of integrity but its appearance as well. Pearlstein is Texidor's lawyer, and Texidor has raised scandalous innuendos regarding Lieutenant Brennan. You have charge of this delicate matter, yet you see nothing wrong with socializing with this shyster."

"My conscience is clear, Mr. Quinn. I don't believe I've done anything wrong."

"Was your conscience as clear when you rode with one Patrolman James Mullins, of the poisoned-pup belly, late of the Twenty-third Precinct, a notorious thief and bagman?"

Reilly glared at Brennan, who had taken a chair in the corner. Brennan raised his narrow brow, feigning surprise.

"It was," Reilly answered. "And I'm a better man for it. My soul is my own. My drawers are clean. I'm not on any reformed-whore crusade. I'm just trying to play it straight down the middle. If I can't, then you can have my resignation first thing in the morning."

"Reilly, Reilly. Do *not* misunderstand. We admire your zeal. We have need of that quality in the office. But it must be properly directed, and that is my function in the short time left to me. So, let me attempt to enlighten you, for I fear you have lost your sense of priority and proportion in the Roman case. How well do you know Lieutenant Brennan, here, Reilly?"

"I know he has a hell of a reputation as a cop."

"I have known Lieutenant Brennan for close to fifteen years, and I represent to you that there is no finer or tougher police officer in the country. His heroic exploits in the department speak for themselves. That his reputation should be sullied by the likes of a Roberto— Robert—Texidor is intolerable. I won't have it, Reilly. Consider the effect on every rank-and-file police officer. It cannot be. This intransigence bodes ill for your future in the office and even beyond that. The elite of the city were here tonight. You witnessed the reception accorded me. I have resigned from the office; my path is clear. I am going to tame this city. After that, who knows? My base is being formed now. I want to include you, Reilly, on my team when we clean up this town. Can I count on you, sir?" Quinn put his hand on Reilly's shoulder.

"Yes, of course."

"All right. Shake hands with Lieutenant Brennan, and let us put an end to this prattle about Texidor and this Rogelio Montalvo."

Brennan approached, smiling. He thrust his right hand forward to Reilly, who accepted the handshake. Reilly, not on guard, was clasped around the knuckles. He thought his hand was broken.

"Atta boy, Al. I knew the chief would straighten us out," Brennan said.

Quinn put his hands on their shoulders. "I need two men such as you for the difficult days ahead. I feel a bond has been forged between us this evening. I propose a toast to the union, gentlemen."

They clinked glasses.

15 Pan American flight 209, New York to San Juan, was one hour out of Kennedy Airport, carrying Larry Pesh and two young men, Richard Buttofuco and Philip Sandrelli. They were seated in the last row of the plane, behind some elderly Puerto Rican women.

Pesh was frustrated. "Richie, get this fuckin' partner of yours to pay attention before I slap 'im in the mouth. Madon', you guys think you're still in Red Hook. Wake up, goddamn it."

Buttofuco and Sandrelli sat upright in their seats.

"We got it all worked out, Larry," Buttofuco protested.

"Never mind. This ain't no mopery operation. Meanwhile, they gotta send me two mopes. Listen up. One more time I'm gonna say this, and that's it. He's at a hotel called the Caribe Hilton. I'll be across the lagoon at a joint called the San Geronimo. You guys will be at La Concha. Stay in your fuckin' room until it's time. Rent a car right in the hotel. I'll be at the Swiss Chalet at nine o'clock sharp with Bobby Tex. You seen the photos; you know what he looks like. He'll be drivin', so come up from the driver's side. I'll get out quick, but let me get out of the way. Don't shoot me, abafongul!

Don't bring your car too close. Leave it a ways off. I'll get back on my own. What could be easier? Ey, don't lose the silencers if you can help it. They cost eight hundred bucks apiece."

"Yeah," Sandrelli said, "but suppose we can't find the joint by nine o'clock?"

"Cafone, stupido, you take a cab there. Swiss Chalet Restaurant. Condado section. Richie will follow in the car. Be there no later than eight o'clock. You wait for me."

"You sure he'll be alone, Larry?" Buttofuco asked.

"That's my job. I've had guys whacked out with my arm around their shoulder. Don't worry about it. Just do your job. In the head, all right?"

"Morto subito," Buttofuco promised.

●

Sandrelli got up to answer the door. Alfonsito Segal shot him in the center of the forehead. He reeled back, crashing into a dresser behind him. Alfonsito and Armandito rushed into the room. Buttofuco, naked except for a towel, dove across the bed toward his suitcase. Four muffled shots bore through his back. Then Armandito put a fifth bullet in the back of his head.

Thirty seconds later they put the Do Not Disturb sign on the outside knob as they left.

●

Robert Texidor and Nancy Bosch were reclining on hammocks in the afternoon sun of their solarium. The telephone rang. Texidor rolled out of his hammock and ran to pick it up. "Qué pasa?"

"Todo bien."

Texidor hung up and returned to his hammock.

"Who was it, Bobby?"

He reached for the piña colada next to him. "Wrong number."

A half hour later the telephone rang again in Texidor's suite.

"Tex, Larry here. Just got in."

"Come on over, Larry."

"Nah, don't want to be seen around these hotels too much. Let's go eat tonight. Just you and me, Tex. We'll go to the Swiss Chalet. I liked the food there last time I was here. Pick me up. I ain't got no car. Eight thirty sharp. I'll be in the lobby."

"Where you at, Larry?"

"Oh, the San Geronimo. I'll be waitin' in the lobby. I'm travelin' alone, so don't bring no people. I don't want to attract no attention."

"Solid."

●

Larry Pesh and Texidor pulled up in front of the restaurant. Pesh immediately sprang from the car and started walking rapidly away.

"Larry, where you going? The joint is this way." Texidor pointed at the spotlighted entrance.

They stood fifty feet apart, facing each other. Finally Pesh walked back to where Texidor was standing. He appeared distracted, shaking his head. "Jesus, Bobby, all this trouble in New York. I don't know whether I'm comin' or goin'. I'm gettin' agnesia. Forget everythin'."

"That's terrible. Look what happened to Willie Moore in Fort Lee for the same thing."

Larry eyed Texidor. "Well, it ain't *that* bad."

"Are we going to stand out here all night? Or are we going to eat, Larry?"

"We're gonna eat. We're gonna eat."

They went into the restaurant and took a table for two, Texidor with his back to the door, Pesh facing it.

Texidor was in an expansive mood and smiling broadly. "Eat anything you want. This is on me. That was some tab you picked up for me at the Chateau Madrid. That was class."

"We don't fuck around, Bobby."

"I know that. Tell you what. I'm the expert here. This is my island. Let me order for the two of us. We'll have caldo gallego, arroz con pollo, fried plantain, avocado. *Mangiamo*, Larry. There's no telling when you'll get a chance to eat like this again."

The food arrived in steaming plates. Texidor piled the food high in front of Larry, sorting and stirring it for him. "Nothing but the best for my compare," Texidor exulted.

Pesh ate sparingly as Texidor gorged. Pesh tried to restrain his eyes, but they kept wandering to the door. At ten o'clock, Alfonsito and Armandito Segal appeared in the foyer, dressed in white linen.

The food in Pesh's stomach rushed back up into his throat. "Puttana madre, I never thought you'd do this to me, Bobby."

Texidor looked up from his plate. "What's the matter, Larry? Your food's coming out of your mouth," he said in a surprised tone.

Armandito and Alfonsito pulled up chairs on either side of the table and sat down.

"How could you do this to me, Bobby, when all I came to do is to help you, to warn you that them people wanna hurt you? I can't believe this, Bobby, not after all I've done for you. The money you've made with me."

Texidor, his eyes constricted to slits, spoke in a whisper. "If you make it to the door, you're gonna take a message for me. That's *if* you make it to the door, Larry."

"I came here alone, to talk to you, man to man."

"That's enough, Larry. Your kids took off on you, left you holding the bag."

"What kids? I come alone."

"Okay, you come alone. If you make it back, here's the message. You tell the wops I'm going to bury Brennan—and I'm gonna do it legally—because I've got the proof that he's trying to whack me and my whole outfit out. But if they want to stay in his corner and fuck me, then you tell them that I got it arranged that if I meet with a sudden accident, then the U.S. attorney's office in New York gets all the addresses and names in Marseilles and Ajaccio, including Jean-Pierre's."

Pesh choked into his napkin. "I never gave you no fuckin' names."

"What do you think? I've been sucking my finger all these years we been dealin'?"

Pesh wiped his lips. "I don't know what you're talkin' about."

"Just deliver the message. Tell them to mind their own business. This is personal between me and Brennan. And he's a loser already. I got a witness."

"Do I leave now?"

"Why not? Your bill is paid."

"I ain't got nothin' against you, Bobby. I just take orders, like everybody else."

"I ain't mad at you, Larry. But I can't talk for the Cubans. They don't know from your being a boss."

Pesh stood up and casually tossed his napkin on the

table. "Do what you gotta do." He strode out without looking back.

Alfonsito leaned forward, his elbows on the table. "They had silencers in the room, Bobby."

"Of course. Once they split up from Larry, they gave it away. Do you think I arrived at my birthday last Friday by bein' a fool?"

"Mauricio and the boys want to know how much longer they have to stay at the airport," Armandito said.

"Tell them they stay there until I tell them. Do they think I'm going to let Brennan sneak in on me? Mauricio knows Brennan. He stays at the airport."

"Bobby, while we were at the hotel changing, Roger called on the phone," Alfonsito said.

"Phone? From where? He's not supposed to leave the boat for nothin'."

"He was calling from the phone booth on the dock. Said he was only a few yards from the *Nancy*."

"Maricón de Roger! Somebody'll spot him on the dock. I told him to stay put. He's got everything aboard: food, drink, even snort. He'll spoil everything."

"He said he hates the boat, that he is all alone, that he will go crazy without La Malpagada."

"It's just for a few days. I'll kill that—alone? What about Angel?"

"Angel's back. Roger did not want him on the boat," Alfonsito explained.

"Mauricio says the men will not stay on the boat with Roger, that he wants to bring boy-ass aboard, that he even abuses him. Roger is frightened; he has no money; he is going nowhere, Bobby," Armandito added.

"Cock sucker."

Alfonsito Segal shrugged.

"A maricón is a maricón."

"It has been said that he is also a chiba, an informer. My brother and I cannot be associated with such a man. Our reputation, Bobby," Armandito cautioned.

"Don't worry about Roger. That is my business. Your business is to protect me here from the big gringo policía when he comes to kill me. You are my banderillas. But Roger is the Toledo steel I will sink into the neck of the sons of whores in New York who are trying to kill me. Roger is my dagger."

Armandito nodded. "You have a reputation as a man who reasons. My brother and I will rely on that."

"Tonight matters will come to a head. I'm going to call New York. Where's Nancy?"

"She said she would be at the casino at the Flamboyan."

"Okay. Alfonsito, you go to the Flamboyan. Stay with her. Mandito, you will come in my car. We'll go to my room. I must make an important call to New York."

•

"Reilly, is this Assistant DA Reilly?"

"Yeah. Who's this?"

"Bobby Tex, Reilly."

"What's up?"

"You don't know how I got your home number, right?"

"I'm in the phone book. What's the big deal?"

"Oh. The big deal is that I'm at the Caribe Hilton in Puerto Rico and you gotta come over right away to talk to me."

"Are you crazy? Why the hell should I go down there? You got something to say, say it."

"I got Roger. . . . Yeah, I hear you suckin' wind from here. But just to crank you up, let me tell you that

Brennan is the least of it. We're gonna talk about Quinn . . . and me . . . and old times. Yeah, your boss. You want me to keep talking on the phone, Reilly?"

"No. No, I'll come, soon as I can get a plane out."

"Okay, now you listen to me, Reilly. If anybody else gets into the scene, then all bets are off and your office gets blown sky-high. Strictly confidential, okay?"

"Strictly confidential. I got it."

"And don't bring no wires on you. And no Chapman. That spook has been rattin' you out to Brennan."

"No Chapman. I'll get Valentin and somebody else."

"You be here first thing tomorrow. If you're not, then I know you went to your bosses, and I won't be here when you arrive and neither will Roger. Believe me, Reilly, you are over your head, so don't try to pull no shit. You were not put in this case for nothing."

"First thing tomorrow. Caribe Hilton Hotel."

"Yeah. Top floor. I'll be waiting."

Reilly dropped the receiver back into its cradle and got up from the bed. He walked to the kitchen and brought down his one bottle of Scotch.

"What the fuck am I doing?"

He put the bottle back on the shelf, walked to his bedroom, took his memorandum book from the dresser, and found Leon Blumenfeld's home number.

"Leon, Al Reilly. Did I wake you up?"

"No, of course not. Something wrong, Al?"

"I have to get to Puerto Rico right away, Leon. The eyewitness is there, but he says right away or never. It's that Roman homicide with Lieutenant Brennan. It's a double murder. Brennan is dirty. I'm afraid of this thing, Leon. It's a terrible mess."

"Did you call Quinn?"

"He's in this thing, Leon, in with Brennan. I'm sure of it. The witness, Texidor, he knows the whole story."

"My God, Quinn?"

"This is going to blow the office sky-high."

"All right. Don't panic, Al. You just play it straight. Nobody will get hurt who's not supposed to. Okay, you fly down in the morning and talk to this guy. Call up sick. You've reported to me; you've done the proper thing. I'll alert the DA immediately. Not a word of this to Quinn."

"You think I'm crazy?"

"I never knew Quinn to be friendly with Brennan."

"They're asshole tight. Brennan was at Quinn's house last night for a political rally. They've both been leaning on me since this investigation started. They're in, believe me."

"I'll handle it from this end. You go to Puerto Rico and come right back. The district attorney will have to come into this personally. Do you have money?"

"Yeah, I got enough to go. I'll put in for it when I get back."

"You got your cops?"

"I'll take two with me, Valentin and Zucker. I'm going to call right now."

"Careful what you say to them. This is a very delicate matter."

"Don't worry. Only what's necessary."

"Quinn. I can't believe it."

"Let me call my cops."

"Just keep playing it straight, Al. I'll talk to you tomorrow. Call me at my house."

16 Valentin cut the Plymouth across the Grand Central Parkway as they approached the overhead sign that read Kennedy Airport. Zucker, at his side, sat rigid, teeth clamped on a cigar, his head back, eyes fearful.

"Do you have to drive so crazy already? The plane's not leaving for an hour."

Valentin laughed. "Wasumadda fo' you, my frien'? We're going to Puerto Rico. *Move* out!" He gunned the car. "They're gonna give us a ticket, Nat? Don't we have a DA with us?"

Reilly, in the backseat, chuckled. "Don't count on me, Johnny. They had a ball-buster on the Triboro tried to give me a ticket when I was in the uniformed force."

"Nat says you were a gung ho guy in uniform, Al, always up in the squad room asking questions, y'know."

"He was the only detective that would talk to me, for Christ's sake. How long on the job now, Nat?"

"Twenty-four years. Most of it in the lousy Two-Three."

"Imagine that, a Jew on the job twenty-four years ago," Valentin said.

"They made me feel right at home. A great career I've had in this shit-house job."

"Talking about careers, what about Mullins?" Reilly asked.

"Did his twenty. They gave him a big send-off. He went to Fort Lauderdale. Fruit preserves he's going into; he's got all the jars," Zucker deadpanned.

"If this conversation is private," Valentin muttered.

"What private? I see guys in the war walk through a field of land mines. That's Jimmy Mullins. He wrote the manual. No checks, no refunds, no doubling back. On-the-spot deals only. Moon was the master. And he retired in one piece, laughing at the shoofly. There won't be any more like him," Zucker said.

Reilly nodded. "Amen. Now listen, let's get this straight. You guys are only my backup. I will conduct the interrogation. This is a very touchy situation."

"Sure, Al, we'll stretch it out till Monday," Valentin said.

"Are you crazy? We have to be back right away."

"Shit. I brought four suits."

"Put them all on at once, John," Zucker suggested.

"Fuck you. I won't even have time for the cocktail dansant at the El San Juan Hotel. I'll have to settle for Roger Montalvo."

"For shame, a married man fooling around with fairies," Zucker said.

"Don't put the knock on the gay freak squad. They got their appetites, and we got ours. Eat and let eat, as they say."

"Eat, eh?" Zucker snickered.

"Are you accusin' me of bein' a hair-pie man, Nathan?"

"There's been rumors."

"Well, unbeknownst to the truth, I been there—and back. And lived to tell about it. Ha!"

Zucker winced. "Ugh, a deviate. And with a Jewish wife. Johnny Honey Dripper, imagine!"

"I told you, don't call me that. Gets me in trouble. My wife thinks it has a sexual commutation," Valentin said, his tone serious.

"Meshugana," Zucker muttered. He lowered his window and flicked out cigar ashes.

"Jesus, it's freezin'," Valentin squeaked. "Close the fuckin' window, Nat."

"I don't feel good. Need a cup of coffee, a real cup, not that shit-house precinct coffee."

Reilly leaned back, smiling to himself.

Nat. Always with the coffee. Must have been around '62. Zucker used to wear suspenders and a belt. Carried an old long-nosed .38 instead of the detective snubs. Greater accuracy against roof snipers, he'd say. But he was a gentle person, liked to work with kids. He had been unable to make first grade. This he attributed to Irish prejudice in the Detective Bureau. Reilly had heard his chart read "lack of aggressiveness." A widower, childless, Zucker had one year to go for the full two bits and retirement. He dreaded it. He had told Reilly his dream: A sticky afternoon, his sand-filled shoes creaking him into an orange and yellow motel room. "I see it, Al: Hot shades are down, painted flowers on the wall. I'm in the kitchenette, on a vinyl chair —yellow, too— having a lemonade. Then I pitch forward on my face, my right eye looking up at the light bulb. It gets dimmer and dimmer."

Reilly liked him. Zucker had taken an interest, found time for him.

Reilly felt the wind sting his face as Zucker lowered the window again. Perspiration glistened on Zucker's bald head.

"Nat, remember the night Brennan shot up the squad room and we recovered the knife in the park?"

Zucker turned slowly around to face Reilly. "That's right, Al. You were there. You were worried about smudging prints. Twenty-four years on this lousy job and I never seen a fingerprint yet."

The three of them laughed.

"When was that, Nat?" Valentin asked. "I mean Brennan shooting up the precinct?"

"What, five or six years ago. Sure, shot holes in the floor. Prisoner named Covington. Got a statement."

Valentin whistled loudly. "Coño!"

"Fucking hotshot Brennan," Zucker continued. "If I'd known he was going to be in the precinct that night, I would've gone on sick call. Made me sick with his violence. He doesn't give you a chance to talk to people. That's not right. I mean, what'a we, cossacks? Last year I was talking nice to this guy, guy was holding onto the car door, but he would have gotten into the car, just a few minutes more. Enter Guido Brennan. 'What? Who?' Bang—the guy's laid out on the sidewalk, his head cracked. I had a near riot on my hands, Al." Zucker turned, facing forward again, his cigar back in his mouth.

"That's nothin'," Valentin said. "Chappie told me Brennan once threw a guy out the window in the Two-Five, broke his legs."

"I know about that," Zucker said.

Reilly leaned forward. "What guy was this, Johnny?"

"Some half-a-button guy. 'You can't print me. I'm a connected guy,' he says. And he kicked Brennan in the balls. Ave Maria! Through the screen, out the window, into the alley. That's right."

"Jesus."

"And the guy belonged to some downtown cheech. There was a hell of a row with the mob and with the department."

"Didn't bother Brennan none," Zucker said.

"Das a bad nigger," Valentin growled.

"The man's Irish, Italian, something—" Zucker waved his cigar vaguely.

"Still a bad nigger," Valentin insisted, shaking his head.

"See what I have to associate with in this lousy job, Al? Me, the rabbi's son, supposed to be a professional man. Comes the depression, then comes the war, and I end up in a shit-house precinct. You did right to get out in time."

"I heard your father was a pants presser," Valentin said.

"See what I mean, Al?"

•

Zucker slid the glass-panel door open and walked out onto the terrace. The Caribbean was emerald-clear. Sailboats lazed by in a soft breeze that seemed to purify the lungs. The sky was azure, cloudless.

"Beats the hell out of Brighton Beach," Zucker said, taking a deep breath.

"How can people trade this for that dung heap of New York?" Reilly shook his head.

"You can't eat sunny skies," Valentin said. "But P.R. is a beautiful island."

"I couldn't get through on the phone," Reilly said. "Let's take a cab over."

Reilly, Valentin, and Zucker rode down Ashford Avenue through the Condado section, past the row of modern hotels, then around the lagoon to the Caribe

Hilton. The lobby was open, vast, and swept by trade winds.

They stood at the corner of the bar, between the swimming pool and the beach.

Valentin motioned with his chin. "Alfonsito Segal. By that cabaña in the shade. Sleeping or making believe he's sleeping. No Tex around."

Reilly bit his lip. "I see her! She's on that beach chair, by the water."

"Oh, yeah. Look at that white bikini. Qué cuerpo! No wonder she got you mental."

"Stay here." Reilly walked toward the beach. She lay in a canvas chair facing the water. He sat down in the sand alongside.

She would not turn her head, her eyes on the white-caps breaking over the reef. The beads of seawater on her face and hair glistened in the sun. She closed her eyes. A solitary droplet made its way down her cheek.

"Nancy."

"Let it alone. Too many things have happened."

"It's just no good for me."

"Al, I was a child. You don't know me anymore. Let it be. We're not going to make it. Not now, not ever."

"Let me see your face. Tell me that you feel for this Tex what you felt for me. Tell me that, Nancy."

"You tore my insides out. I will not go that way again. Not for you, not for anyone."

"What about my insides? What do you think happened to me? Nancy, people change, grow up. I'm not a kid worried about who thinks what. Look at me. Do you think I would let anything come between us now? I'll quit my job. We can live here; we can take off. We'll go wherever you say. But don't, don't do this to us again."

Reilly's voice broke. He lowered his head, staring

into the sand, his eyes tearing. He became angry. "You with that fucking greasy pimp. How could you belong—"

She turned full face to him. "I don't belong to anyone. I belong to myself. I come and go as I please. That's the understanding I have with Bobby. When it no longer suits either of us, I walk."

"I'll bet."

"Believe what you will. He's been good to me and to my family. He's tried to change. I've never said a word, but he's tried. Now he's in trouble. Bad trouble."

"He'll never change." Resignation blunted Reilly's anger. He felt tired.

After a while she said, "That's true. It will run its course. When it's over, I'll go on to other things . . . other men."

Reilly bit his lip.

"I have not given of myself completely this time. The part I have reserved will see me through. That much I learned from you. Nadie se muere de amor." She rose from the chair. "Bobby will see you tonight. The penthouse suite. He expected you later. He had to see some people this afternoon."

She got up and walked into the water, then dove into a wave, swimming toward a raft.

Reilly returned to the bar.

"Struck out again, Al?" Valentin asked.

"Something like that."

"Where's Texidor?" Zucker asked.

"Tonight." Reilly pointed upward. "The penthouse."

●

At 10:00 P.M. Reilly, Valentin, and Zucker were at the door to Texidor's suite.

The door was opened by Armandito Segal, Alfonsito by his side.

"Ola, Mandito. Ola, Fonsito," Valentin said.

"Como está, Señor Valentin? Entre, por favor," Alfonsito invited.

The three men entered the room.

Armandito looked only at Valentin. "Bobby is on the terrace," he said in Spanish. "He will speak to Mr. Reilly alone. You two gentlemen can make yourselves comfortable in here. Anything you wish to eat or drink is available for you. Please sit down."

Alfonsito beckoned Reilly. Reilly nodded to his companions, then followed Alfonsito through the sumptuous living room and into the night air of the solarium. Then Alfonsito stepped back into the living room, sliding the glass door shut behind Reilly.

A cool wind was blowing south, dispersing the few clouds that were in the sky. The stars rose from the northern horizon of the sea and into a brilliant canopy overhead. Far below, the waves washed onto the shore, the breakers white under the artificial lights. The battlements of the medieval fortress, San Geronimo, were outlined in the darkness below.

"Takes your breath away, right?"

Texidor sat behind a small table in a white wicker chair. White suit, black silk shirt, opened wide at the neck, legs crossed above gold-buckled black Gucci loafers. Like a whiskey ad, thought Reilly. Fucking Puerto Rican.

"Mr. Texidor, I presume."

"Yes, Mr. Tracy, have a seat and take in some of my island's air."

Reilly sat down facing Texidor. On the table between them was a bottle of twenty-five-year-old Chivas Regal, a bottle of soda, a small pitcher of water, a bucket of ice cubes, and two glasses.

"You drink Scotch and soda, right? I take mine on the rocks. Let me do the honors."

There was a two-carat glint of light from Texidor's little finger as he handed Reilly a glass.

Drinks in hand, the two men regarded one another. Reilly felt pale in the glow of Texidor's Bain de Soleil face. Handsomer than me, in a greasy, pimpy kind of way.

"You hate guys like me, don't you? Me with six hundred dollars' worth of linen on my back and you with your Delancey Street original, right?"

"Tex, I didn't come fifteen hundred miles to examine our conflicting psyches. What difference does it make? I'm cops, you're robbers, remember?"

"That's it, Al. Except I want out. I want to get away from the rackets, from the wops, cops, from everything. I want to start a new life."

"You don't mean turning around?"

"What the fuck you talking about? You're talking to Bobby Tex, not Roger Montalvo. I mean I want to retire. Travel. Educate myself."

"Nancy?"

"You might say that. We're going to get married, do things together. She's got me reading books, Me, who never got past page four of the *Daily News*. I did Europe with her. Never did nothin' but hang out. She had me walking around Torremolinos, Biarritz, places like that. She's changed me. The way I've been living, I've just been marking time, waiting for a bullet in some after-hours joint. Like li'l Tony Roman. They pulled him out of a drawer. Had a fuckin' tag. I don't want that anymore. She can save me, Reilly."

"Nancy's going to salvage you?"

"Yeah."

"You're going to live happily ever after?"

"You might say that."

"Well, now that you're a good buy, who's going to save you from the bad guys?"

"That's what I want to talk to you about, Mr. Reilly."

"Are we going back on the record now?"

"Hey, you're not wired, are you?"

Reilly held his jacket open. "Search me if you want."

"Okay, okay. Nitty-gritty time. I got a story to tell you. But I ain't telling you no story as a stool. There ain't no witnesses here, and I would deny it."

"So why tell me?"

"Because I'm a citizen and my life is in danger from a crazy cop. You're an assistant DA, and it's your duty to protect me. Even if I have a record."

"Go ahead," Reilly said, leaning back and crossing his legs.

"So what we discuss here is strictly between you, me, and your boss, Quinn. Because if you rat out, then we all go—you, me, Quinn, and the whole fuckin' district attorney's office. You got the idea?"

Reilly nodded.

"Ordinarily, I wouldn't play it this way. I ain't no stool. But I can't put a hit on a lieutenant of police. And I want to get out of all the shit."

"And become a respectable citizen?"

"Right."

"I get the picture. Now tell me the story."

"Brennan is on a contract. I'm the last installment. I only pieced it together after I got to Roger."

"Where's Roger?"

"Me to know, you to find out. Think I'm crazy?"

"Go ahead."

"Gotta go back—way, way back. Right after the war, 1945, '46, around that time. There was a jitterbug gang in Spanish Harlem, around 103d Street and Madison Avenue. That was our hangout. The Sinners, me and six guys. We were a small crew, but we whaled the shit out of everybody, very tight, we were. Rumble with anybody."

"You were bad, I know. Go ahead."

"Yeah, so the thing is there was a stray kid. Skinny. From 99th Street off Madison Avenue. He was not a knock-around guy, more like a bluff. He wasn't in the gang, but when we had a rumble comin' down, I'd get in touch with him. He had a pistol, like a Luger. He used to work as a delivery boy at the A & P on 103d. The gangs had outside guys like that in them days, guys that liked to rumble. Some of them used to come from as far as Long Island, like ringers. Anyway, this kid was bad. I seen him standing in the middle of the street, bullets flying all around him and him shooting his pistol. Wouldn't take any cover. Didn't give a shit. But he was not into the boostin' and thievin' with us. That's why I was surprised when he came to see me about pullin' a job. There were some fancy houses around 102d Street and Fifth Avenue. Rich people. Just one block from the garbage cans."

"I know the area."

"Yeah. Seems there was a very rich old lady, a widow, who kept a big bundle and jewels around the house. He'd seen it himself on a delivery. I happen to mention it to Tony. Pretty soon we had the whole gang. All the Sinners wanted to go up to the pad. No good, of course, so they all stayed behind the wall in the park when me and the kid went up through the service entrance. We walked up a whole bunch of stairs. I knew how to use the picks. That's why he needed me. I spun the lock in no time, and we were in. I assumed there was no one home in the apartment and started looking. Right away I fell over cash and jewelry. It was stashed all over the place. Unbelievable. I didn't see the kid, so I went to the bedroom. He had his knee on his old lady's chest and an ironing cord around her neck. She was gone. I almost fainted. Jesus. An old lady. I got a mother, you know. I went crazy. 'What are you doing?' I asked him. He said the old lady recognized him. We grabbed the loot and split."

"Big score?"

"Biggest I ever had in a break-and-entry. I totaled fifteen thou for myself. I knew he got more. That was a fortune in those days. I gave the boys downstairs twenty bucks apiece. They were happy. They never knew."

"You mean the Sinners never found out what happened?"

"That's what makes this whole thing so ridiculous. Those guys didn't know from nothing."

"What about the newspapers?"

"Are you kiddin'? Those jerks never read the papers. But I read them. I read every goddamn newspaper. Found it in the *Daily Mirror* a few days later. A little squib. But it gave me diarrhea. A Mrs. Jean Delaney. I felt terrible."

"Yeah, I know. What happened to him?"

"Gone, disappeared. Musta blown town. Had a lotta money for a kid sixteen years old."

"What was his name?"

Texidor smiled. "I knew him as Petey, Petey Q."

"Peter Quinn. Are you telling me that was Peter Quinn?"

"Something like that," Texidor said, taking a sip from his drink.

"Jesus fucking Christ," Reilly said.

"I couldn't believe it either. Till around eleven or twelve years ago. The time of the Fuentes trial. I went down to general sessions, and there he was, trying the case as assistant DA. He looked different, talked different, but it was Petey."

"Did he see you?"

"No, I don't think so. Listen. Why would I want to hurt the guy? Been over twenty years, I never bothered him. I like to see a guy get ahead. He come up the hard way. His folks were lushes, the two of them. Shanty Irish. Petey even used to smell bad. I felt sorry for the kid."

"Maybe you were saving Quinn for a big one that no amount of money could help you with."

"Never. But maybe that's what he figured. So he got Brennan to chase all the Sinners down and whack 'em out, one by one. I mean the guys that were still around —Julio Sierra, li'l Tony Roman, and me. Maybe some others, too. I'm not sure."

"Why should Brennan jeopardize his life, everything, for Quinn?"

"That's for you to find out. You're the DA, not me."

"Why are you telling me all this? There's no statute of limitations on homicide, you know?"

"Where do you think Mandito and me been all day? I checked out my position with some heavy legal people. There's no notes, no minutes, no witnesses, and no *Miranda* on our conversation here. And I would deny it. I would say you're trying to mess me up because you're after my old lady. You already attacked me in your office. There's witnesses to that."

"You are a diabolical son of a bitch."

"I ain't the last of the Mohicans because I'm stupid. You just got out of school, Reilly. I been in the kicks-in-the-ass school all my life."

"Yeah, I know all about that university-of-life shit. Make your pitch."

"You talk to Quinn, private. Tell him to call off his gorilla. When in my life have I ever been a stool pigeon? When I get popped, I turn to stone. Everybody knows that. I will never hurt him. Besides, I'm techni-cally an accessory to that Delaney job. I'm not gonna jam myself. Tell him he got no alternative. I got Roger Montalvo for Brennan, and I got Mrs. Delaney for him. Tell him to call the war off. Call it a draw. I'll even vote for him."

"You obviously don't know Quinn. And you don't know me. What makes you think I would be a party to this game you're running? Before I get on your pad, I'll crawl under the covers in a bed of scorpions."

"You been on a pad all your life. Your father was a bull up in Harlem, wasn't he? Al Reilly senior. He was doing his thing up there."

The wicker chair screeched as Reilly bolted upright. "You leave my father out of this. I'm warning you."

"Don't play Snow White with me. I know the leg you limp on. I know you rode with Jimmy Mullins. He was the Lone Ranger, and you was Tonto, right? Never said a word, did you? Kept your mouth shut, right. Never made a wave, Kimo sabe, you was on the pad. You ain't no wave maker. You played it safe then, and you'll play it safe now. You ain't dealin' with no punks; you with the big boys now. C'mon, have another taste." Texidor picked up the bottle of Scotch.

"I'm tired of hearing that Mullins shit. I never had

anything to do with Mullins," Reilly said angrily.

Texidor brought the bottle down hard on the table. "What do you think this is, junior varsity competition? Fuckin' Roger would say in a minute, baby, that he seen you and Mullins takin' junk money, whore money, policy money. He'll make up the exact times and places for you. You in murky waters, Jack. And what's the big deal? Look out for the number one, Al Reilly. You got the hex on your boss now. He's going up in the world. You're going with him. Can't stop him, not with his balls. Hitch up. You got built-in insurance. The pad was here before you arrived; it'll be here long after you're dead and buried. Why do you think the wops turned against me? They got a junk pad with Brennan. There's big money here. They'll grind us to chalk dust if we don't jump off early."

"Now we're going to be partners?"

"Listen, Reilly. If you blow this up, you go, too. Quinn will splash your ass. You've done all right so far minding your own business. You ain't no hero. Don't change your style now. It could be fatal."

"You're going to retire, Tex? Get out of all the shit?"

Texidor spread his hands out wide, then brought his right hand to his mouth, kissing his thumbnail. "I swear by my mother, by Nancy, that I'm quittin' for life. Me and Nancy, we'll stay in Puerto Rico forever. Quinn will never see or hear of me again. My word is concrete —stone. Why do you think the wops singled me out?"

"I know your rep, Tex—stand-up. Everybody's got to look out for himself. You remember my father on the street, huh, Al senior?"

"Of course. He was no chump. He took care of business. Have a drink, for Christ's sake. We're talking like men now."

Texidor refilled Reilly's glass.

"I'll talk to Quinn," Reilly said and took a heavy gulp.

"Of course. He'll be expecting you. Why do you think he put you on this case? So he can keep tabs on you and protect Brennan. I'll bet Quinn's been circling you like a hawk. What stupid Brennan don't know is, once I'm knocked off, Quinn will put him on ice. Sure, that's the play. Petey Q. was never one to fuck around."

"I think I can talk to him."

"Just tell him Bobby Tex sends regards to Petey Q. and would he mind getting Brennan's teeth out of my ass."

"You're really something," said Reilly, glass in hand, elbows on his knees.

Texidor curled his index finger. "You gotta have balls in this world, Al. Gotta reach out, gotta push. If you make it, you got it made. If not, you know you gave it your best shot. So if you leave your balls hanging on the wire, you know they was on right when you started."

"Some guys got balls. They're just not hungry."

"Bullshit. We're all hungry. Look at those two jerks inside, Zucker and Valentin. You know the money they could make? Valentin always was jive. Who'd he ever bust? Rooftop junkies. Him with his little rubber ball in his elbow making like he's shootin' up. Undercover. Punk ass. Same with Zucker. Twenty years, he's never drawn his gun. The only cops with balls are the thieves, like Brennan."

Reilly put his glass down and stood up. "I'll go back to New York right away and speak to Quinn first thing. Maybe I'll go to his apartment and talk to him privately."

"Now we're dealin'. My boys will see to it that you guys get on the midnight flight back. I'll be waiting for your call. All you have to say is, 'The business is closed, and Petey sends regards.' Something like that. Roger will be all right; no problem there. If I don't hear from you by the weekend, then it's deuces wild."

"Don't worry about me."

Texidor got up from his chair. "I don't worry about you. I know you talked to my old lady today."

Reilly shrugged. "I was looking for you. You were in a big hurry, remember?"

"Don't blow your cool." Texidor waved his hand. "It's over, Reilly."

"It was over four years ago. But I just don't see the percentage for women in going around with guys like you."

"What?" Texidor laughed. "We're like buccaneers. Women love us. They wanna be near the action. Even the ugly guys. When you see a wise guy with an ugly broad? And me, a presentable guy like me, I been beatin' 'em off with a stick since I'm yea high."

"Even Nancy?"

"Nancy's special. Part of me. People even say we look alike. Did you notice?"

"Don't see it. Don't see it at all."

Texidor put his hands in his pockets. "We can't have no kids. She got messed up with you. Learn something else, too. Nancy was in bad company when I met her. That's right. Was with this jive crowd of artistes, right here in PR. Poets, painters. Weak on the art, but heavy on the dope. Was me pulled her up, was me held her up when you put her down."

"That's not true," Reilly blurted out.

"Forget her. It's over. I paid for the busted windows. We're even, awright? Everybody bleeds. Now go home and take care of business."

•

"You guys go downstairs and check out. I'm going to be a minute," Reilly said.

Valentin and Zucker left the room. Reilly sat on the bed and dialed Blumenfeld's home number in New York.

"Leon, it's Al."

"Al, I've been awaiting your call. What's up? Where are you?"

"I'm catching the plane to New York in an hour. It should get in around three A.M., so I can be in the office around four. I have to lay this out to you and the boss. This is a monster. Everything I told you and worse."

"Quinn?"

"All the way, Leon, all the way."

"Take it easy. Don't panic. The district attorney, the executive assistant, and the administrative assistant are all waiting for my call right now. We will be in Hennessey's office on the eighth floor at four A.M. Do not bring your cops upstairs. Don't talk to them about this."

"Four A.M. See you."

17 Lieutenant Guido Brennan sat behind the wheel of his car across the street from the 82 Club on East 4th Street. Just after 1:00 A.M. a group of young men, some wearing makeup, came out of the club. The group broke up. La Malpagada stood under a streetlight on the corner, trying to hail a cab. Brennan pulled up in front of him. He lowered his window, a hundred dollar bill in his left hand.

"Here it is, sweetie. One hundred dollars for a quickie front seat blow job."

La Malpagada looked tempted but wary. "How do I know you're not rough trade? Going to beat me up?"

"Here's the money. Put it in your pocket if you want. All I want is a little boy action. I'm tired of those syphilated skanks uptown."

"You got a dose?"

"Hell no. God forbid. I'm on my way back upstate to my family. I can't afford no sickness. A boy like you is more of a woman than any of those cunts walking the streets."

La Malpagada walked around to the passenger side of Brennan's car and opened the door. Then he hesitated. "You're not a cop?"

"Jumping jeepers, me a cop? I'm a salesman.

Where's my gun?" Brennan pulled open his overcoat and suit jacket.

La Malpagada got into the car and closed the door. "Okay, but only a quick Frenchie. Give me the hundred."

Brennan handed over the hundred dollar bill. The car pulled out. "Where's your place?" Brennan asked.

"What do you mean, my place? Just pull into the nearest parking lot."

Brennan reached under his seat and pulled out a long-muzzled revolver and pressed it against La Malpagada's ribs.

"Oh, my God, I'm going to be mugged."

"Fernando Malpica, you are under arrest for solicitation. That bill is marked and has paraffin on it."

"Oh, God, please. I can't spend another night in the Tombs. I can't. I'll do anything, please, officer."

"Whatcha got?"

"I got forty dollars."

"The fine has to be bigger than that."

"I got two hundred in my apartment."

"Where's that?"

"Twenty-third and Seventh."

"Okay. Let's go."

Brennan parked on Eighth Avenue, and they walked east on 23d Street to Fernando Malpica's apartment house. They took the elevator to the fourth floor and entered the apartment.

"Pretty messy for a fag pad, ain't it?" Brennan asked.

"Since my Roger's away, I just don't have the time. Let me get the money."

"There's no hurry, Fernando. Take your time."

"How do you know my name, officer?"

"Roger has been working with us for years, Fernando. We know all about you two."

"Then you weren't going to lock me up?"

"Of course not. Keep your money. As a matter of fact I was only looking for Roger to bawl him out. Tell him he is off the federal payroll. He's double-crossed us once too often. As a matter of fact I have five hundred in cash to give to Roger, his last payment as an agent."

Brennan held out five new hundred dollar bills, spread like cards.

"You can leave the money with me. I'll see to it he gets it. We're lovers."

"Looks to me like he left you flat. Our reports are that he's in Puerto Rico with Bobby Tex and having a high old time with some good-looking Cuban kids."

La Malpagada frowned. "Mentira! Lies. He's on a boat in Saint Thomas alone. He's going crazy without me. He called me long distance tonight."

"Sure. Okay, here's the five hundred dollars. You mail them to Roger right away. I don't want the feds to think I kept the money. You know how they are, Fernando."

"I'll mail it first thing in the morning."

"Wait a minute. You're not trying to pull a fast one? How can you send money to a boat?"

"Easy. Just wire it direct to the boat, the *Nancy*. Yacht Haven Basin, Saint Thomas. He's the only person on the thing."

"Roger must be crazy to leave a good-looking kid like you alone in this city."

"You don't know what I go through. All these creeps want to paw me. I don't mind turning a trick, but then they always want more, but they don't want to pay. You know, your voice fooled me. You don't have a cop's voice."

"I bet you got some shape."

"Everybody says I had the best body when I was at the club, especially my hips."

"I'd give anything to see you in panties and bra."

"Well, I still have your hundred dollars. If I can keep it, I'll give you a private little show. How about it?"

"You got a deal."

"I won't be a minute."

La Malpagada went into the bedroom. Brennan removed his overcoat and sat down in a chair.

La Malpagada pranced back out of the bedroom in panties, brassiere, and backless high-heeled pumps. He began to gyrate in front of Brennan. Clapping his hands and snapping his fingers to some imaginary tune, La Malpagada swayed and turned his back on Brennan, uplifting his buttocks as he bent forward. He felt a sudden wrenching of his spine. At the same time a hand cupped his mouth and snapped his neck back. Then La Malpagada felt his head unhinge as Brennan severed his windpipe. Malpica fell forward, knocking the glass-topped coffee table off its metal legs. He lay face down. The blood rushed from his throat to the carpet in torrents. He never uttered a sound. Brennan wiped the knife on La Malpagada's panties and quietly left the apartment. He cut notches into the outside lock to simulate the picks of a burglar, then went down the back stairs.

●

Reilly recognized the district attorney's official limousine parked in front of the Leonard Street entrance. The guard in the lobby informed Reilly that he was expected upstairs. He took the elevator to the eighth floor and walked down the corridor past all the photographs of former district attorneys. He had been in Hennessey's personal office only once before, when he was sworn in. He walked past the empty desks and into the room.

District Attorney Myles Hennessey was seated behind his huge desk, facing the door. His two top assistants, Dent and Parisi, sat at the sides of the desk. Blumenfeld was reclining on a leather couch. He got up to greet Reilly and introduced him to the other three men. The staff included over one hundred assistant DAs so reintroductions were in order.

"Well," the district attorney began, his voice even-keeled. "Leon tells us you had misgivings about this Roman homicide from the outset. We took the liberty of removing the folder from your files. We find no entry on your part denoting any irregularity, Al."

"That's true, sir. At the outset this was just a routine case of justifiable homicide. But last Wednesday one of the witnesses in the case, Robert Texidor, blurted out some information which cast doubt on the veracity of Lieutenant Brennan's statement as to the slaying of Anthony Roman. Since then his behavior has become almost irrational—I mean Brennan's. There is an eye witness, Roger Montalvo, who will contradict Brennan and thereby make him the murderer of not only Roman but of one Julio Sierra. Brennan is pursuing Montalvo relentlessly. I know he means to kill him. A few days later he offered my squad detective, Valentin, ten thousand dollars for Montalvo's whereabouts. Duly reported by Valentin to me. Then, Saturday, Brennan came to my apartment and made certain veiled threats to me personally."

"Are you vulnerable, Al, to threats from Lieutenant Brennan?" the district attorney asked.

"No, sir, I am not. When I'm right, I'll take on the whole world."

The DA glanced over his left shoulder at Blumenfeld, who nodded, then turned back to Reilly.

"What did you tell him?"

"I told him, sir, in effect, to go shit in his hat."

"That's my boy," Blumenfeld said.

"Continue, please," said Hennessey.

"Throughout all this, I'd like to add, I've been subjected to pressure from Mr. Quinn as to what a great cop Brennan is and how I'm to report to him as soon as Montalvo is located. I wasn't sure how to handle the situation. Who do I complain to? Mr. Quinn is my boss. Then I thought maybe I'm being overzealous or something. I was scared. I was all mixed up, sir."

"Al has been reporting to me, boss, but there was nothing concrete until the day before yesterday," Blumenfeld said.

"Yes, sir. Tuesday night I received a call from Robert Texidor in Puerto Rico. He told me that he had to talk to me about the Roman case, that it involved Brennan and Mr. Quinn. I reported to Chief Blumenfeld, here, called in sick, and flew to San Juan.

"Texidor's story is that Brennan murdered Julio Sierra and Anthony Roman. Texidor and these two men were the last three surviving members of a teen-age gang called the Sinners. Texidor states that Brennan is now out to kill him also—" Reilly swallowed, "—under orders from Peter Quinn." Reilly inhaled deeply and braced for the outburst.

"Go on."

"It seems that Mr. Quinn was in the gang or on the fringe of it as a teen-ager around 1946. He was known as Petey Q. then. The gang was around 103d Street in

Spanish Harlem. Texidor states that he and this Petey committed a burglary on Fifth Avenue around there and that Petey strangled an old lady by the name of Jean Delaney. It was written up in the *Daily Mirror* at the time."

"Yes. Go on."

"He told me he did not see Petey Q. again for many years. Then, ten or eleven years ago, he saw him trying a case here and recognized him. Defendant named Fuentes."

"I remember that case, boss, that was Maximino Fuentes. Quinn tried it, got a conviction," Blumenfeld said.

"Please continue, Reilly," said Hennessey.

"Texidor contends that Mr. Quinn is trying to destroy all links with his past and, in particular, the homicide of this lady, Delaney."

"How did Peter Quinn get Brennan to commit these other homicides?"

"Texidor doesn't know."

"This Texidor, isn't he concerned about his own complicity in the alleged homicide?"

"I guess he feels his legal position is strong. He would deny his statement to me, lack of corroboration, *Miranda*. Besides, his statement was to be relayed to Mr. Quinn to blackmail him into getting Brennan off his back. He also knows the whereabouts of Roger Montalvo."

"What makes Texidor think that you would be the purveyor of such a message to Peter, making yourself an accessory and coconspirator?"

"He cited many things, sir. My fear of being embroiled in such a mess, my allegiance to Mr. Quinn, the advantages in having a lien on Mr. Quinn's future career."

The district attorney rubbed his forehead.

"It's obvious, boss, that Texidor is terrified of Brennan," said Blumenfeld. "And the twenty-year-old homicide is the least of his worries, even if Al blew the whistle on him. He took the only shot he had—to try to get to Quinn through a young and inexperienced assistant."

"Were you ever tempted, Reilly?" the district attorney asked.

"No, sir. But he cemented his grave when he called my father a crook."

"Your father?"

"Yes, sir. My father was killed on duty as a police officer in the Thirty-second Precinct. His name was Frank Reilly. Texidor called him by my name—Al. Said he was a crook. I know how we lived. I know what my father left when he was killed. He was a hell of a cop, a hell of a man. Raised me after my mother died. I had to listen to this bastard slander my father."

"You did not react?"

"No, sir. As far as he's concerned, I'm in the bag. He gave me until the weekend to contact him. Otherwise he makes some other move."

"Like what?"

"I don't know. Maybe run away, sir."

The DA glanced at his two aides.

Dent looked pensive. "We'll have to move fast, boss. We'll have to reopen that Delaney case without Quinn knowing it. We'll have to check out Quinn's personal file, his school records, that A & P job he had as a kid. We'll need evidence to corroborate Texidor."

Parisi held his chin. "Then we have to lock him in with Brennan and the other homicides. What has Brennan done that Quinn can induce him to commit murder?"

District Attorney Hennessey stood. "We must work quickly. But in complete secrecy. Reilly, you will function as usual. We will conduct the investigation of Peter's background from this end. Your liaison will be Leon. We must exercise the *utmost* caution and secrecy. We have a lot of work to do. Reilly, go home and get some rest. You've earned it."

Blumenfeld shook his head. "I think Al should be at his desk bright and early. He was out sick yesterday. Two days in a row. You know Quinn better than I."

"You're right, Leon. Catch a couple of hours anyway, Al. Peter . . . I can't believe it."

Parisi frowned. "The truth is, some of us found Peter a little pompous, a poseur even, but this—this is incredible."

18 Guido Brennan arrived in Charlotte Amalie, Saint Thomas, Virgin Islands, on the 6:00 P.M. flight. He wore a dark suit with a gray fedora, his eighteen-inch collar and his thick-bridged nose jutting beyond its brim.

The small overnight bag he carried contained two thousand dollars in two packs, both wrapped in rubber bands. The bills were of small denominations except for the top and bottom bills of each pack, which were hundred dollar bills.

He took a taxi at the airport, instructing the driver to take him to Yacht Haven Basin. He paid the driver and proceeded on foot down the cement walk that led to the docks where the boats were anchored. He walked casually along the dockway, scanning the names on the boats tied sternward to the dock, his gloved hands under the overcoat that he carried slung over his forearms. Then he saw the name, *Nancy*, on a forty-seven-foot cabin cruiser. The *Nancy* was at the outermost end, two berths from the nearest boat.

Clutching a fishing chair, Brennan let himself down softly on the *Nancy*'s deck. The cabin doors were open. He made his way down the ladder, barely managing his large bulk through the narrow passageway. The cabin was empty. Brennan sat on a bunk. Where is this fag?

He stepped into the tiny bathroom forward of the bunk and placed his coat and bag on the deck. He held the door slightly ajar, enought to accommodate his left eye. Brennan waited close to fifteen minutes, then heard the thud of feet landing on the rear deck. Roger Montalvo. He was wearing sneakers, shorts, and a tank top shirt. Montalvo walked past the bathroom door into the forward quarter area of the boat. Brennan jumped into the passageway behind him. Montalvo was cut off, his eyes and mouth like rings.

"Roger, I'm not here to hurt you. Please believe me. Just relax. Let me explain." Brennan held up his gloved hands in a gesture of appeasement.

"Lieutenant, please," Montalvo whispered.

"Will you stop. I'm here on a business proposition. I want you to help me, Roger. That's all."

"Lieutenant."

"Roger, sit on the bunk, will you please. You don't look well."

Montalvo felt a hot liquid rushing through his veins into his head. He sat heavily on the bunk, his breath coming through his breastbone. "My chest hurts."

"Of course. You've got yourself all worked up for nothing, Roger. I got here just in time. We got a bug on Bobby Tex's wire. He's got some Cubans—from Miami, I think—on contract to kill me, then murder you. Two brothers, Fonso and Orlando—something like that.

"Alfonso and Armando?"

"That's them, Alfonsito and his brother. That Bobby Tex is a psycho. He has got me in trouble with the police department. I'm thinking of putting in my papers and taking off for Majorca or Marbella. Get out of all this shit. I got no ties."

"That takes a lot of money, Lieutenant."

"Forget about titles, will ya, Roger? Call me Guido, for Christ's sake. I brought ten thousand. It's in my bag in the bathroom. I'll show you." Brennan reached into the bathroom and pulled out his bag. He opened it and showed Roger the two neatly tied bundles of cash. Montalvo's breathing subsided. Brennan removed his gloves.

"That'll hold you awhile," Montalvo said.

"That is shit. I got an inside wire on the biggest score of my life. That's what I want to take away with me. And I'm going to take it from the scumbag who's trying to destroy us both—Bobby Texidor."

"Bobby?"

"In excess of four hundred thousand dollars, Roger."

"Four hundred?"

"Yeah. I found out where he keeps his cash in a safety-deposit box in San Juan. He carries the key and signature card on him. That's where you come in, Roger. I'm not Latin, but you could do it—grab the cash. Split it up between us."

"How could we ever get to Bobby with all his body-guards?"

"That's easy. We con him into coming to the boat alone. I grab him, hold him here. You go to San Juan, get the money. When you come back here, we'll decide what to do with Tex."

"I go to San Juan alone, Guido?"

"Sure, why not? You know better than to double-cross me."

"Oh, Guido. You know me better than that. It's that fucking Bobby Tex who forced me to come out here. He's got me a prisoner here. Without any money. And he's got four hundred thousand. That bitch."

"Half of that will be yours. As a matter of fact, just

to show you I mean business, you take that ten thousand in the bag and stash it somewhere safe on the boat. That's an advance on your two hundred thousand."

"You don't have to do that, Guido. After all—"

"Roger, I need your help, and I'm willing to pay for it."

Montalvo's large eyes flicked from the overnight bag to Brennan, then back. It was the best offer he had had all day. He sucked in his cheeks, "Okay, Guido." Montalvo jumped off the bunk and took the two bundles of cash out of the bag. Then he shoved them down the side of the bunk against the bulkhead. He raised his penciled eyebrows, "Wow, Guido. You're all right!"

"Now what's the best way to get Tex on this boat, alone, so we can grab the key to the box?"

"I know. I'll get hysterical on the phone. Like when I chased Angel."

"We gotta get Bobby Tex hysterical. What shakes him up the most, next to me?"

"The wops and the feds."

"That's it. You tell him that you just found out that the feds had set up a conspiracy involving him and the wops. Yeah. And that you been pegged as a stool. You found out the wops got a horde of hit men looking for you. You're gonna blow town, but you'll give him an hour to get here and bring you some money. Tell him you can't talk on the phone, but it's dynamite. He'll go crazy."

"Yeah, but he'll show up with the Segal boys."

"Tell him he must come alone. That you suspect his crew, all of it, especially the Cubans. They're gonna double-cross him. Tell him you won't be on the boat when he arrives at the airport. You'll spot him from outside, and if he brings people, he'll never see you again."

"He'll bring a gun."

"That's my department, Roger."

"Then I go to San Juan and get the money?"

"Sure, you'll just practice the signature on Texidor's card a few times. I know you have experience in that line."

"No problem, Guido."

"I brought you a little present, Roger."

Brennan removed a small tinfoil packet from his inner vest pocket. Montalvo clapped his hands with glee and snuffed the white contents of the packet in two breaths. He immediately gagged, almost throwing up.

"Roger, take it easy. This is good coke. You're off your habit. Don't be so greedy."

Montalvo's eyes and nose were running. "You're right. Must be some strong shit. But I need it."

"All right. Let's go make that phone call. Remember, you panic him about the feds. Then you panic about him not coming alone. The Cubans are out. Treachery. He has to come to the boat alone."

"I'm straight now. Let's go. We better take the money with us."

"Put it in my bag. You carry it, Roger."

Brennan stepped into the portside bathroom, where his coat was, and slipped his gloves into the left-hand pocket. He felt a wire in the pocket. He left the coat there, closing the door. They walked together to the motel near the dock to telephone San Juan. The connection was made at the poolside bar after Texidor was paged to the telephone.

Montalvo, in an agitated voice: "Bobby, I've been calling you all over. I've been double-crossed, ratted out, Tex. I'm running away. The feds and the wops will never get their hands on me. Good-bye."

"Hold it, you crazy faggot. Don't talk this shit on the phone. I'll come over and talk to you tomorrow in person," Texidor said.

"Never. I won't be here. You be here by eight o'clock, or our deal is off. Anything goes. I'm telling you, Bobby, they got you and me in a conspiracy with the wops. And the wops are gonna cowboy me on sight. Open contract."

"Don't talk this shit on the phone, Roger, maricón. I'll be right there. Give me an hour. I'll be on the boat with you. Don't do anything crazy. I'm expecting word from New York anytime now. Everything is gonna be okay."

"Eight o'clock. That's it. And God forbid you should bring those Cubans with you. They hate me. They probably got the contract already for both of us. I'll be watching you from outside the boat. If you got anybody with you, I'm gone. I might even kill myself. Don't fail me, Bobby. I'm desperate."

"I'm going right to the airport, Roger. I won't fail you."

•

Texidor put the telephone down and rejoined Nancy and the Segal brothers.

Armandito said, "Bobby, you have the look of pain that Roger brings to your face. Every call from that maricón clamps the pliers on our fingernails."

Alfonsito agreed: "Let us have done with that person, Bobby. Mandito has special faculties about people like that. He knows. Not to heed Mandito cost our brother, Bernardo, his life."

"Eh, it's just something that has come up. I have to get to the boat. Right away. I'm going upstairs to change. You guys call the airport for me. Seven thirty flight, one seat."

"You are going alone, Bobby?" Armandito asked.

"You heard me, one seat." Texidor stepped from the bar and walked quickly toward the elevators.

Armandito pivoted on his barstool and faced Nancy Bosch. "Nancy, you bear witness that Fonsito and I have cautioned Bobby about dealing with this Roger. Since childhood trouble has been our profession, but this is madness. We wash our hands, like Pontio Pilato."

"I know you have done your best. Since this problem with the police officer began, I cannot talk to him. Let it be as God wills," Nancy said, shrugging her shoulders.

"Así sea. So be it," Alfonsito added.

•

Brennan and Montalvo walked back to the boat.

"Guido, he will have a gun."

"Let me worry about that, Roger. But just in case anything happens, you won't be on the boat. We'll just go back for you to change clothes for the trip to San Juan. You have to look respectable when you walk into the bank tomorrow morning."

"You can count on me. I'll take the first plane back here."

"I know that, Roger. Okay, after you change clothes here, you stay around the dock but out of sight. I'll hide on the boat. When Tex comes aboard, I'll overpower him. Tie him up or something. Then I'll come out and give you the key and the card. You go to San Juan, and I'll wait here until tomorrow, when you come back, right?"

"Oh, you can count on me, Guido. First thing in the morning, bingo, in the bank and out."

"Looks like we teamed up again, Roger."

Montalvo led Brennan down the ladder into the cabin area of the *Nancy*. Brennan closed the doors behind them.

"I'm gonna take a piss, Roger. Count out a couple hundred dollars for expenses for your trip while I'm in the head."

Brennan stepped into the portside bathroom, closing the door behind him. He put on his gloves, took the wire, and coiled both ends tightly around his fists. Using his teeth and forearms, he draped his coat over his hands to hide the wire.

Holding the coat in front of him, he stepped from the bathroom. His caution was unnecessary. Roger Montalvo was in the forward area of the boat, where he had laid the money out on a bunk and was counting the bills. Roger never saw the wire coil around his neck. He felt only his head thrust backward and his spine pushed forward and up on Brennan's knee. The wire throttled him quickly, silently. The tens and twenties scattered across the bunk and deck.

Brennan picked up all the bills and put them in his bag. The wire he put back in his overcoat pocket, and he put the bag and the coat in the portside bathroom.

He dragged Montalvo's body into the starboard-side toilet, laying the corpse across the toilet seat, with one sneakered foot jutting out into the passageway. He took a .38 revolver from his leg holster and attached to the barrel a cylindrical tube that he took from his suit pocket. It's gonna be a quiet party, Tex, he thought. He opened the cabin door an inch to give himself a view of the dock.

Brennan rested his shoulder against the sliding door and kept vigil on the darkening dock area. This is the last one. After Tex I'm free.

He took a metal flask from his inner jacket pocket and downed a heavy swallow of whiskey. The flask was almost empty. He put it back in his pocket, his hand steady. Brennan's reflexes had never failed him. That's the edge I got on 'em, he thought. Booze or not, I see 'em all in freeze frame.

Alcohol and lack of sleep had flushed his dark face with a feverish redness, the lifeless eyes honed to pinpoints inside blue-circled sockets. He felt little discomfort, if any. Only alcohol, boring from within, could unsettle Brennan's nerves, drawing taut these strings after a week of drinking.

A rubber dinghy crossed Brennan's line of vision. Two boys—one black, the other, his blond hair bleached white by the sun—were paddling in circles, laughing and splashing. A Dane, thought Brennan. Irish don't tan like that. Irish. Pappa Brennan was Irish. Chased me and Mom all over the fuckin' house. I gotta laugh at this child-abuse shit. What I went through with that cock sucker. "C'mere ya little nigger. Yer a dago like yer ma." Drunk mother fucker.

Brennan's breathing became heavy. Sweat was trickling down his armpits. He could feel the rage within him mounting. He took the flask out again, finishing it.

Then the foster homes, out for a free dollar. Nobody gave a fuck. Saint Vincent's, with the lay brothers beating the shit outta ya. Running away at ten and bagged in the freight yard by them three skells.

Brennan grated his back teeth, as if they could be pulverized together with the thoughts that came to torment him. The sweat ran down the seam of his back as he held his breath.

Easy, Guido, easy. We got even. We got one in Shit City; we got one in Gitmo. We got a slew of them in New York. The best was Buddy. I had time with him. Must have plugged a whole pack of cigarettes up his ass. Fernando was no trouble, and Roger went out nice. It's just the booze. Gotta take it easy. Could wind up like the skells on Houston Street with the pint in the paper bag. I just gotta be careful, that's all. I'll be okay. I'll put in for my pension, three quarters. Plus what I got stashed. Maybe I'll go to one of them clinics in Switzerland like Quinn says. Bullshit. Nothing wrong with me as long as I stay away from the booze. I really haven't had any trouble since the fifties. Long as they stay away from me. What the hell could Tex and his Harlem punks have on Quinn? What's keeping you, Tex? Come aboard and shake hands with the devil.

•

Texidor was in a taxi en route to Yacht Haven Basin. The evening was darkening, and Texidor's mind became clouded with reservations. Maybe the wops set this up. Can't be. Not enough time since Larry left. Maybe Roger's been setting me up from before. A junk case. That's all I need. This Roger, he's an abscess. The Cubans are right. Got to be drained. Cubans, treacherous mother fuckers. Maybe they're gonna set me up. Mother hopper. Maybe I better turn around and go back to San Juan. No. I got to settle with this punk-ass Roger. Texidor felt the .32 automatic in his waistband under his blazer. There was a round in the chamber. He had a spare clip in his pocket. "Step on it, man."

•

Brennan could see a tall, slender man in a dark blazer and white pants approaching unhurriedly. Texidor, left hand tucked inside his jacket flap. I'll be on his left side, thought Brennan, as he made his way to the port bathroom. He saw Roger's foot protruding from the toilet opposite as he closed the door.

From the outer deck Texidor called out, "Roger. It's me. Come on out here."

The only sound was the gentle creaking of the *Nancy* on its ropes.

"Roger, you mother fucker. I'm alone. Come out here."

The sounds of steel drum music began to waft softly across the water from the motel on the shore.

Brennan heard Texidor coming down the ladder. The cabin doors slid open slowly. Brennan braced himself for the footsteps into the cabin proper. But nothing moved. He's standing at the door, Brennan thought. He's got a piece in his left hand. The foot, Roger's foot, will suck him in. Then Brennan heard rapid strides across the cabin deck. He's in.

Brennan had his left forearm across his chest as he smashed open the bathroom door, firing as he came. His first bullet struck Texidor's left elbow, pitching the arm upward and exposing his left side, against which Brennan pressed the silencer and squeezed off four more bullets. Texidor never got off a shot. He slumped into a sitting position against Brennan's leg, dead. The blood from his severed brachial artery was going through his clothes and staining the deck.

Brennan took stock. Overnight bag, hat, overcoat, gloves, wire, pistol, money. He closed the cabin doors behind him and walked toward the motel.

19 The telephone jarred Reilly awake. The illuminated face of the alarm clock read 2:00 A.M.

"Who's this?"

"Al, Al, wake up! The shit hit the fan! Me and Chappie are down here on 23d Street. We got a DOA here that is the well-known mother fucker. We got Fernando Malpica."

"Yeah."

"This is Roger's asshole buddy, La Malpagada. His throat's been cut. Been dead close to twenty-four hours. The phone here has been getting collect calls from Saint Thomas. Roger must be on Saint Thomas."

"Of course."

"Chappie wants to talk to you."

"Al, the weasel is down there in the rabbit hole. Malpica was seen to come in here last night with a trick, but the description was Guido. We called Command. They don't know where he is."

"He's in Saint Thomas or Puerto Rico or both. My God. Give me the phone number where you are now. Stay right there. I'll call Nancy in P.R. You guys alert the police in San Juan and Saint Thomas. I'll get right back to you." Reilly dialed Texidor's suite at the Hilton in San Juan.

A familiar sleepy voice answered.

"Nancy. It's me, Al. Leave the hotel immediately. Brennan, the lieutenant, he's there now. He's going to kill you all."

"What are you talking about? There's nobody here. It's two thirty in the morning."

"Nancy, for Christ's sake. I'm telling you Brennan murdered Roger's boyfriend, Fernando. Brennan's gone down there to kill Montalvo and Tex. Where's Bobby Tex?"

"He's on the boat with Roger."

"What boat?"

"The *Nancy*, at the Yacht Haven in Saint Thomas."

"Jesus, that's it! Don't move from there. Call the police. Tell them to go to the boat. I'll get right back to you, Nancy."

"Al. I'm scared."

"Don't worry. I'm coming for you myself. Stay there. I'll get right back to you."

Reilly dialed Valentin at the Malpica number on 23d Street. "Johnny, I got it straight now. Tex and Roger are on a boat in Saint Thomas. The *Nancy* at the Yacht Haven. Brennan must have got that information from the DOA. He must be there now. Call the Virgin Islands police, and tell them to get to the boat right away. Maybe they can grab Brennan."

"He's had twenty-four hours. He might have gone and come back tonight. Or maybe he's coming on the morning plane."

"I think you guys better get over to Kennedy and watch the flights from Saint Thomas and Puerto Rico. Get down there. Check all the schedules. Eastern, Pan Am. Bring extra guys. Call Saint Thomas first. I'll call my bosses. Call me when you get to the airport. Call me right here."

•

"This is like a fuckin' nightmare, John. How could this happen to Guido?"

"You want out, Chappie? Stay here with the phone. Me and Nat will go down to Kennedy with some of the boys. He might not even show up."

"Fuck you mean? I'm handlin' this. I'm the Homicide man here. Get Zucker and that guy McTague to go with us. I'll alert my bosses. Move, turkey."

"We're gonna have to kill him, Chappie."

"Listen, Drips. I'm gonna talk to you straight business. I'm directing this thing. I take full responsibility. Nobody's gonna kill Guido. I'll talk to him. He listens to me. Never mind your cowboy shit."

"That's cool for you. You his boon-coon. But what about me and Nat? He'll be on us like shit on a stick. With Brennan, if you're late, you're never. He will wash us in a mother fuckin' moment."

"You a cop, ain'tcha? You get paid to talk first. That's your fuckin' duty."

"I got a duty to get home to my wife and kids."

"Not to mention your girl friend."

"They got rights, too. Shit! I been here already, Chappie. I know what this man is capable of. Head-on collision on a rainy night. Don't need that."

"Just don't overreact."

"Overreact? With a guy that'll give you the coup d'etat right on the floor?"

Chapman shook his head. "Now listen, John. Don't go crazy. Give me a chance."

"All right. You talk to Brennan all you want, but I'm

hiding behind the furniture. When the match drops in the gas tank, I want room."

"It ain't gonna be like that. If you go in with that attitude, we're gonna have a shoot-out. Now we do this thing right, nobody gets hurt. Okay, let's set up."

•

Blumenfeld paced his office. Reilly watched him coming and going.

"Al, it's six o'clock. Dinnertime. Go home and wait for the call from Chapman and Nat. They're responsible men. Under no circumstances are you to go to the airport. That's an order, Al."

"Think I'm crazy, Leon?"

"They got all the flights covered?"

"Yeah. Brennan is in the bag. He'll march toward the sound of the guns. It's Quinn I'm wondering about."

"Please. Don't even talk about that. He didn't show up this morning, didn't call. First time in fifteen years. Just as well. Gives us time to figure out how to work this out, y'know, with the least damage to the office."

"Maybe he'll run, Leon."

"Not Quinn. He's a martinet. Running is panic. Quinn pisses ice water. He'll do something dramatic. Give it a grand finale."

"You think so?"

"Götterdämmerung. That's what the boss is afraid of. The scandal is going to be bad enough without Quinn grandstanding on top of the Empire State Building. But"—Blumenfeld yawned and stretched—"this too shall pass. You look terrible, Al. No sleep?"

"How can I sleep?"

"By the way, the boss likes the way you handled

yourself. You'll move in the bureau. You watch. Just be discreet about your private life."

"What's that supposed to mean?"

"What goes on that I don't know? Cops are worse than washerwomen. I know about you and Nancy Bosch."

"And?"

"Just be careful. You know I've always been on your side. But she was Bobby Texidor's girl, and you're an assistant DA. It could get complicated."

"You know, Leon, I've always tried to play it safe all my life. Close to the vest. Play the game. No-ripples Reilly, that's me."

"Best way to be."

"Except with this girl. Like I would have fought Tex right in my office on the sixth floor. Things like that surprise even me."

"Well, if your feelings run that deep—"

"Deep? I'm going to marry that girl. I'm not bullshitting, Leon."

"I believe you. And whatever you want to do, I'll do my best to help you."

"I appreciate that. It took me years to get here; my dad wanted me here. But if it means losing her again, then my first case was my last."

"We'll work it out. Jeez, Al." Blumenfeld smiled. "If she's going to melt the polar caps and stop the earth spinning, then I have to meet her."

'When this is over, I'm going to bring her back with me." Reilly rubbed his face. "Let me get back to my desk. I got the duty chart today. If anything breaks on Quinn, I'll call you right away, from here or from home."

"Do that."

The phone rang behind Reilly as he walked toward the door.

"Al, for you."

Reilly turned back and took the receiver held out to him.

"Reilly? Is this Assistant District Attorney Reilly?"

"Yes, sir, this is he."

"This is Quinn—Quinn, chief of the Homicide Bureau."

"Yes, sir."

"Are you catching tonight, Reilly?"

"Yes, sir."

"I have a Q and A for you on a homicide. I've already alerted the duty stenographer. He's on his way to my office, as am I. The interrogation will be limited to you, the stenographer, and myself. If you disobey my instructions and bring additional personnel, there will be no statement. Is that understood?"

"Yes, sir."

Reilly heard the telephone click.

"Leon. He's coming down to his office. He wants to give me a Q and A. But me alone and the steno."

"Okay. I'll call the boss right now. We'll be there. See what you can get out of him. We'll be outside. He's not going anywhere."

20

American Airlines flight 519 now boarding at Gate 12.

Chapman briefed Valentin, Nat Zucker, and Young Terence McTague. "I spoke with Stokes at the Pan Am terminal. They confirmed Tex and Roger on the boat in Saint Thomas. Homicides. There's a G. Ballard coming in on this next flight. Arrives at one thirty-five A.M. our time. Me and Guido once popped a Harold Ballard. I think this Ballard is Guido. McTague, get the airport people to call the plane. Give them Guido's description. If it matches the passenger in this Ballard's seat, we're home free. Tell them to tell the pilot to make sure the stewardess is cool. No static, y'hear? Now, let's run through it again. Uniformed force stays in the lobby and outside. Me and Nat will meet Guido as he comes through the gate. I will do the talking. You just stand by, Nat. There won't be any trouble. Guido won't hurt me. Johnny, you stay out of sight with McTague, on the ramp. He don't like you."

"I don't know why. I'm crazy about him."

Chapman ground out his cigarette with his shoe. "Me and Nat will take him into the bathroom here. You two guys wait outside while me and Nat toss him. Then all four of us take him outside. There will be no shooting. Nobody gets hurt, okay?"

"No sweat, Chappie," McTague said, his freckled face grinning. "If there's a beef, I'll handle it. Bing, bing, bing. Right, Johnny?"

Chapman flared. "You will, huh? Let me tell you something, McTague. Ever see a weasel eye a mouse? When Guido beams on you, your balls gonna turn into grapefruit pits and you gonna get lockjaw of the elbow. This ain't no pistol range, McTague. Just do what I say, or he'll waste you. Nat, call Reilly again. Tell him what's going on."

•

The door was locked. Reilly knocked. It was opened by Lubin.

Quinn was at his desk, his hands folded in front of him. He presented a crisp picture in a dark suit, white shirt, and gray tie, freshly shaved and cologned. But as Reilly entered the room and drew closer, Quinn's face reminded him of a freshly powdered corpse. Reilly detected an odor of alcohol.

"Ah, Reilly, I believe you know Lubin?"

"Yes, sir. Hello, Stanley," Reilly said as Lubin nodded and they both sat down.

Quinn pointed at Lubin. "Set up your machine. But you will commence taking the statement only when I tell you. Is that understood, Lubin? And have a care in the preparation of the transcript. More than once your ineptitude has made me out to be an illiterate."

"Yes, sir."

Quinn turned full face to Reilly. "Lieutenant Brennan. I understand he has been taken into custody."

"I believe so, Mr. Quinn. They're waiting for him at the airport."

"Let us get to the business at hand. First off, I must congratulate you on the Roman case. The ardor with which you pursued this investigation is commendable. Blumenfeld would say bulldog tenacity. An amusing couple, you and Blumenfeld. Telemachus in search of Bloom." Quinn paused and smiled, amused at the confusion on the face of his audience. "Now then, new matters have risen in the wake of the Roman case. My resignation from this office is in effect, but let it not be said that I left the bureau with a cluster of unresolved homicides. That would be most unfitting." Quinn looked up. "I understand you have that ragamuffin trio of Chapman, Valentin, and Zucker at the airport."

"Yes."

"The mighty being cut down by the wretches."

"They are good men."

"It is the prism through which we look that is determinative of good and evil. They are interchangeable."

"Yes. Can we discuss Brennan, on the record, sir?"

"By all means. It is altogether proper that you, Lubin, should be the chronicler. Ultimate mockery. Put your question, Mr. Reilly."

"What motivated Brennan to act in your behalf in the removal of witnesses, sir?"

"Twofold. First, his own conviction that the lawless element in our society must be extirpated summarily. That this refuse—Texidor, Roman, Sierra, people of that stripe—are not to be suffered above ground. Secondly, he was indebted to me as the keeper of his innermost secret—now rendered academic. Shall I elaborate?"

"Please."

"In the late fifties, thereabouts, a killer of homosexuals was loose in the city. The pattern: a large, burly man would frequent their enclaves, entice one out, repair to the rooms of the homosexual. Invariably, the victim would be found stripped, throat cut, and sometimes, lit cigarettes stuffed into the rectum. Rumor had it the perpetrator was a police officer. But there was never any corroboration of this. The homosexual colony refused to cooperate, and the murders went unresolved. Abruptly, they abated. We assumed that the perpetrator, if insane, had gone into remission or had gone away. I subsequently took a routine statement from a defendant who had murdered his lover in a spat over dinner. This was, of course, Roger Montalvo. I was in the squadroom with Montalvo when Brennan came in. Montalvo blanched. During a break, he whispered to me that Brennan was the so-called fag killer and that he had seen Brennan leave the Peppermint Lounge with a Buddy Price the night Price was murdered. Montalvo told me that he would never get involved in a case against a police officer and would deny his statement to me. But he begged me not to leave him alone with Brennan."

"That Price homicide is still on the books, sir?"

"Of course. There was not nearly enough to obtain an indictment against Brennan. But to my mind all the parts fit together convincingly, and so I privately confronted the lieutenant. I knew of his achievements as a police officer, and I felt the allegiance of such a man could be useful. He denied his complicity to me, but the bond was forged. He was my man. I knew, he understood, and the issue was closed, save for the debt outstanding between us."

"You never told him about Montalvo?"

"He was my collateral. Exposing him to Brennan would have signed his death warrant. I might add, parenthetically, that it was I who persuaded Brennan to seek psychiatric help and stop drinking, thus putting an end to this episode."

"At least until you revived it in the Roman and Sierra cases."

Quinn's eyes paused on Reilly. "Yes. The local professional peaks appeared minuscule in this, the golden age of the prosecutor. My successes of late had elevated me into more rarified climes. But mindful of the scrutiny public life can focus on a man's past, I determined to eradicate mine before embarking. Liquidations followed via the good offices of Lieutenant Brennan. Not to appear callous, but the likes of Texidor will not be sorely missed."

"And what was the link or bond between you and Texidor and the Sinners? That is unclear."

"Your interrogation is characterized by an attempt at subtlety that is both commonplace and pedestrian, Reilly. You know full well that the Delaney folder has been taken from the files and that the district attorney is at this very moment on the eighth floor. As, no doubt, must also be Blumenfeld, chief choreographer of this clumsy performance."

"Mr. Quinn, I'm only doing my job the best way I know how. I don't have your experience."

"Your air of diffidence is what endeared you to me initially. Here is malleable clay, I thought. Inarticulate, not too bright, and privy to the pockets of Patrolman Mullins of the Twenty-third Precinct. Be sure you get this down, Lubin."

"Yes, Mr. Quinn."

"Yes, Reilly, I assumed, erroneously it appears, that your obvious participation in the graft and plunder of your sector for seven years would assure your cooperation in my venture. I overestimated. Or perhaps underestimated your ambition and audacity. Irrespective of which, my miscalculation has proved fatal. Still, you may be sure that you will not emerge unscathed, Mr. Aloysius X. Reilly."

Reilly felt a bubble of gas running through his intestines. He swallowed hard and said, "Can we talk about Mrs. Jean Delaney?"

Quinn smiled, "Ah, yes, 1946. In the abyss. Ill-matched sots for parents. Poverty, crime, drugs. Not an unusual situation. The distinction being that Petey Quinn was conscious that he dwelt in a purgatory. The others were not. He would get out at all costs. Mrs. Delaney. I knew those pieces of paper and baubles she had scattered around her decaying body would do it."

•

Guido Brennan carried no luggage. He had dumped his overnight bag in a trash receptacle at the airport in Saint Thomas. The wire was thrown out the taxi window; the pistol, broken into pieces and flushed down several toilet bowls at the Saint Thomas airport. The cash was in his overcoat pockets, a loaded .38 on his left hip, tilted to accommodate a cross-body draw. His coat and suit jacket were open.

Brennan filed through the gate, his small eyes raking the terminal from wall to wall. He saw them. "Hi, Chappie, Nat. Why ya' hiding? Come on out."

"Guido," Chapman said.

"Quittin' time, eh?" Brennan smiled.

"They want to talk to you, Guido."

"Fuck them. You know I don't give a shit about them."

"The Association's got to get you a lawyer. You

don't have to make a statement, Guido. Maybe an insanity defense. You know I'm in your corner, Gui. Never have let you down. You know what I'm going through now. Don't let's go the hard road, not after what we have been through."

"Semper fidelis, eh, Chappie? Me and Chappie were in the corps, Nat." He smiled, his dead eyes gripping Zucker.

Zucker's hands began to shake, but he was afraid to put them in his pockets. "I know, Lieutenant. I know," Zucker said.

"All right," Brennan said. "Let's find out what it's all about."

The three men walked down the carpeted corridor. As they passed the men's room, Chappie said, "Let's stop in here a minute."

They stepped into the bathroom. There were mirrors, sinks, urinals, and booths.

"You guys want to toss me?" Brennan asked.

"Has to be done," said Chapman. "Maybe it's better that I do it. Right, Gui?"

"Can't be. My pistol is like my fuck-stick. Don't go nowhere without it."

"Lieutenant, we have to take your gun." Zucker swallowed. "You know that. This is an arrest."

"Shut your face. Don't say another word, Zucker. Nobody takes my gun, Chappie, not even you."

Chapman stepped toward Brennan. "Don't do this to me, Guido. Don't get beyond reach. I still got my hand out for you. We can't fight."

"This is as far as I'm going. I just made up my mind. Get out of here, Chappie. Get back to Claudia and your kids. This one I do alone. Just me and the police department."

Brennan stepped back against a sink. A mirrored wall behind him. Zucker's eyes flickered momentarily beyond Brennan to the mirrors.

"Don't blink, Nat. You'll never make Miami Beach. Get in the corner." Brennan motioned to his right.

"Do like he says, Nat," Chapman ordered.

Zucker walked to his left, stopping where the last toilet booth met the wall.

Chapman was rooted in the middle of the bathroom floor, facing Brennan, six feet away. Chapman had his back to the door but saw it open in the mirror. Valentin and McTague came in single file.

Brennan dropped into a crouch. "Freeze!"

"Guido, don't lose your head. They were worried about me," Chapman pleaded, his hands in front of him.

"Honey Dripper, you stool pigeon mother fucker. Ratted me out to Reilly. Look at my eyes, you faggots. Go ahead. I got nothin' in my hand yet. Go ahead, McTague, you pussy, Valentin, you cunt."

Chapman moved to his left, breaking up the single line he, Valentin, and McTague formed in front of Brennan.

Brennan said, "That's better, Chappie. Now we got a clearer field of fire. Now the dance begins. Honey Dripper, you drop to the ground first, giving McTague a clear shot. Only when you drop, you ain't getting up, comprende? You ought to see your faces. Look in the mirror. Two faggots—"

A shot rang out, a deafening *blang*. Brennan jackknifed forward, hit. His right hand sweeping up and out even as he dropped. Chapman pumped four bullets into his neck and back. Brennan fell on his face, revolver in hand. Chapman stamped on the hand.

"S'okay, Chappie. I'm paralyzed," Brennan said, coughing.

"Lay still, Guido. McTague, get a doctor. Don't *stand* there, goddamn it. Get a doctor," Chapman said, his voice rising.

Brennan's was wheezing. "Forget about it. Nat's shot blew my balls off. Fuckin' Nat, you finally . . . drew your gun." Brennan raised his head slightly. Spittle and blood began to flow down his chin.

Zucker stood over him. "Guido, I had to do it. You would have killed everybody. We'll get you a doctor. I had to do it. Everybody saw it, Chappie, Johnny." Zucker's face was drained of color, his left hand on his forehead, in his right a long-nosed revolver.

"Take it easy, Nat," Valentin said. "Of course. You saved all our lives. Just settle down." He lowered Zucker's gun hand. "Put it down."

Chapman got down on his knees beside Brennan, who lay spread-eagled on his stomach. "Gui, Gui. Why're you such a hardhead? Look what you made me do. Look what you made me do."

"Fuck it," Brennan said. "What's the difference?" His upper body contracted suddenly as he retched a glob of blood. "That's it," he said, "I'm getting real cold, Chappie. Like Chosin, forty below. The CO said burn all the coats."

"Yeah, Guido, you brought everybody back."

"Them were the best times, Chappie. The rest was a bunch of shit . . . in this scumbag town."

Valentin squatted down. "Guido, you ain't gonna make it. You want to tell us about Tex? I mean why?"

Brennan's voice was barely audible. "Lieutenant to you, you punk. You don't even know how to take a dying declaration. I come into this world a man. I'm

not gonna leave it as a stool. Go . . . fuck yourself."
Brennan's breathing grew fainter.

Chapman lowered his head closer to Brennan's.
"Guido, don't talk. The doctor's coming. You'll be all
right. Don't try to talk."

"I'm going out now, Chappie. Funny, I'm thinking
about the guys in the plastic bags. They were all green.
Remember, the black guys and the white guys? Betcha
I'm green already. I'm okay now, okay ol' buddy——"

"He's gone, Chappie," Valentin said. "Get up, you're
gettin' your clothes all full of blood."

Chapman stood up. Tears streaming down his cheeks,
he turned to Zucker. "Some fuckin' job, huh, Nat?"

•

"The gang or group known as the Sinners accom-
panied you or assisted you in the burglary of Mrs.
Delaney's apartment? Is that correct, Mr. Quinn?"

"In a peripheral sense."

"They shared in the proceeds, sir?"

"Yes, Mr. Reilly."

"Sir, how did you gain access to Mrs. Delaney's
apartment? Can you describe it?"

"Two questions in one. Your technique is gross.
More seasoning under my tutelage would have served
you well. You should not deluge the record with
burdensome demands for particulars. Superfluous,
Reilly. I know you went to Puerto Rico. I know Texidor has supplied you all the grisly details. In the absence of Texidor, you must extract an incriminatory
statement from me."

"It would clear matters up, sir."

"Amateurs." Quinn shook his head. "All of a sudden, I am bored with this whole nonsense. I will make no further admissions."

"You have already acknowledged, sir, that Petey Quinn and Peter Quinn are one and the same person."

"Your lack of imagination is staggering, Reilly."

"Could you give us the names of the Sinners?"

Quinn rose to his feet, smiling broadly. "All that remains, is the descent into the surrealistic, the Kafkaesque phase."

Quinn looked at Lubin. This last phrase had brought an expression of pain and bewilderment to Lubin's face. "*K-a-f-k-a-e-s-q-u-e*, you numbskull!"

"He's doing his best, Mr. Quinn."

"Men such as Lubin rob us all of our dignity. Had he been the waiter at the Last Supper, it would have been devoid of drama."

Lubin whitened, but his eyes never strayed from the machine in front of him.

"This Q and A is terminated. Lubin, close your damn machine," Quinn ordered.

Lubin looked at Reilly, who nodded.

"I have to report upstairs, sir."

"Of course. One more thing, Reilly. Tell me, have I taken on that attractiveness common to condemned men?"

"Guess so, Mr. Quinn," Reilly answered, staring at the leper-gray color of Quinn's face.

The telephone rang. Quinn picked it up automatically. "Quinn here." He began moving his head up and down, the receiver against his ear.

Lubin sat slouched, his eyes half closed, his hands resting on the keys of the stenotype machine. Reilly wondered if he was asleep. He heard Quinn say, "Yes, sir, right away," and hang up.

"Brennan is dead," Quinn whispered as he rose from

his chair slowly, his eyes downward, distracted. As he stood to full height, he suddenly lurched forward but managed to grab the sides of the desk. His waxen face began to moisten visibly, the perspiration on his dark jowls and upper lip glistening.

"I am ill," Quinn said, his voice cracking, almost falsetto.

Reilly felt a belch of acid in his throat. He turned to a wide-eyed Lubin, who was now half standing.

Quinn, swallowing deeply, recovered his voice. "Reilly, you are to remain here. The district attorney wishes to speak to Lubin and myself. Bring the machine, Lubin."

His posture rigid, Quinn marched stiffly toward the door. Lubin trailed cautiously, his pallor almost matching Quinn's.

Leon appeared in the doorway as they left.

"Beautiful, eh, Al?" Blumenfeld said as he closed the door. His thick gray hair was disheveled. He ran his hand through it as he crossed the room, his head lowered, and stood by the long leather couch. He removed his suit jacket and bow tie, threw them onto an empty chair, and stretched out on the couch in his shirt sleeves, hands behind his head, looking up at the ceiling. "Real fucking beautiful."

Reilly sat motionless, his eyes fixed on the prone figure of Leon Blumenfeld, chief of the Indictment Bureau.

"Gotta bury this thing, Al. No good for anybody," Blumenfeld said, his voice low, conversational.

Reilly emitted a low whistle and stood up. He removed his tie and jacket, hanging them over his chair, then sat on the armrest of the couch by Blumenfeld's feet.

"Leon, how they going to do that?"

"It's been done. Closed, finished. Next case."

"The Q and A?"

"The man was under the influence of drugs, maybe a poison, and certainly alcohol. Private ambulance is coming. That statement would never survive a Huntley hearing, believe me. And you got a *Miranda* problem, too."

"The tape?"

"Flawed. The tape piled, garbled. Bad key on the machine. Lubin will say Quinn was largely incoherent and he missed portions. The tape is in the safe by now. Forget about the tape."

"And Lubin?"

"He types mechanically. They all do. He has no independent recollection of what people say. Lubin is okay. Forget Lubin."

"Leon, I don't want to get involved."

Blumenfeld sat up quickly, rotating on his haunches, and placed his feet on the floor. His glasses were perched on the wings of his nose. "You schmuck, you are involved. Where do you think you are, the Cloisters? The real world is in here, too. That don't mean the boss hasn't run a clean shop. Thirty years this office has been clean. When he took over, this office was selling everything. He made it the best in the country. But he's an elected official, and the sabertooths are out there waiting for one slipup. A mess like this will destroy the place. And for what? Conviction here will never stand up. Brennan's dead. Tex is dead. Zilch is what you got. Bury it, Al. Only way."

"I don't want to get in trouble," Reilly said as he opened the top two buttons of his shirt and scratched his neck.

Blumenfeld rocked back and forth on the couch, exasperated. "Wadda you think you're gonna get, a medal?" He raised his voice almost to a shout. "I'll tell you what you'll get. A shit-house full of committees, hearings, inquiries, and *you* under the microscope. Maybe you don't come up so good."

Reilly's face reddened. "My nose is clean. I just did my job," he said, his jaw tightening as he glared at Blumenfeld.

Blumenfeld returned his stare, then slumped back on the cushion and looked up at the ceiling. He took a deep breath and exhaled in a loud rush. "Al, we're proud of you. You have a fine career ahead of you in this office," Blumenfeld paused. "That statement from Mullins is a piece of shit. The district attorney said so."

Reilly jumped to his feet. "The *what*?" he shouted, his mouth open.

Blumenfeld peered over his horn-rims. "Yeah, they got Moon down in Florida. Strike force. He's turned around." Reilly had to lean forward and strain to hear. "Throwing everybody in the pot. Gonna piss on everybody's head to save his ass."

Reilly reared back, his arms tensing at his sides. "A dog, always a dog," Reilly said and began to pace the room in a circle. He came to a halt in front of Blumenfeld. Reilly poked his own chest with his middle finger. "Me, Leon? He threw *me* in?"

"Piece of shit, the district attorney said. Throw it in the safe; forget about it. That's what he said."

Reilly stepped to the other end of the couch, sitting down heavily. Neither spoke for what seemed minutes.

Reilly whispered his capitulation. "Whatever you think best, Leon."

"If Quinn dies—God willing, the cock sucker—that's it. If he doesn't, he's already resigned. We keep it in the safe, under advisement, continuing investigation.

You walk away, go on with your career. You don't know from hunger."

"*Jesus.* Quinn's just going to walk out of this? I can't—"

"Al!"

"*What?*"

"Grow up." He exhaled. "Take two weeks off. When you come back, there'll be a new chief in the Homicide Bureau," said Blumenfeld, his face crinkling into his broken-nose smile.

"You?" Reilly asked.

"Could be. A couple years in the slot will put me on the bench. And without having to kiss district leader Murray Klotz's ass, the cock sucker. So when I leave, there's gotta be a new chief, right?"

Reilly nodded.

"Go get your girl. The boss says a man's choice of women is his own business. Don't worry about anything. You got our blessing."

Blumenfeld removed his eyeglasses, and rubbing the bridge of his nose, he laid his head back momentarily. Then he struggled to his feet, slowly, with deliberation. "Gotta get upstairs, Al," he said, walking toward the door. He made his way past Reilly.

"Can they do one this big, Leon?"

Blumenfeld continued toward the door. His hand was on the knob. Without turning, he said, "Bigger."

21 "Qué pasa?" Valentin asked.

"John, you sound tired," said Reilly.

"No, Al. I just left the precinct with Chappie. He went home. He's in terrible shape."

"Some mess, eh?" Reilly said.

"Sooner or later I knew the wops would bury Tex, but I never thought they'd send a cop."

"Yeah. Johnny. Listen, I can't get hold of Nancy down there. I've called twenty times. What about the Segal brothers? Have you heard anything?"

"Nothing, Al. But they'll probably come to New York before going back to Miami. Settle up with Mauricio. They didn't lose Tex; he lost himself. That's the word on the street already. Roger conned him back to the boat without the Cubans."

"I'll talk to you later about that. If you hear anything about Nancy or the Cubans, call me immediately—any hour, day or night. I'll be home all weekend if I'm not in the office, okay? I have to talk to her."

"If the Segals are in the city, I'll find them. Call you tomorrow."

•

Valentin and Nat Zucker pushed open the heavy glass door to Victor's Cafe and walked in. Alfonsito

Segal picked up the menu to hide his face. Armandito, with his back to them, took the hint and did the same.

"There they are. Nat, sit at the counter. I'll go over. They don't speak English."

Valentin walked to their table and pulled up a chair next to Armandito and facing Alfonsito. "Hola, muchachos."

"Hola, Señor Valentin," Armandito said. "Pull up a chair and join us."

"To what do we owe the honor of this unexpected visit, Señor Valentin?" Alfonsito asked.

"You guys are hard to find. Took me almost the whole evening."

"You were fortunate," Armandito said. "We are leaving for Miami right away."

Alfonsito said quietly, "Señor Valentin, it is always a pleasure to see you. But we are expecting a guest, and your presence might be misinterpreted. Our reputation, you understand?"

"Gonna settle up the fee, huh? Your rep went down a few notches when you lost Bobby Tex, huh, guys?"

Armandito colored. "You made a mistake. Bobby thrust his neck forward like a chicken. He was hysterical. He is now at rest."

"Mandito read him all the signs. Bobby would not heed the advice of cooler heads. A tragedy."

Valentin nodded, his tongue pressed against his cheek. "Couple of wal-yos got whacked out while you guys were in P.R. Hear about it?"

Alfonsito sighed. "Please, Señor Valentin, the loss of our friend has us shaken. No more talk of violence."

"Okay. Just tell me where's Nancy."

"Ah, the beautiful widow. You are on an errand of mercy, Señor Valentin, and here my brother, Mandito, and I thought you came to harass us. He is the al-cahuete for Señor Reilly, Mandito."

Valentin shook his head. "Where did you get that from, Alfonsito? I want to talk to her on official business."

"I have no English in my speech. But my ears and eyes master any language. I was at the Chateau Madrid and the beach at the hotel." Alfonsito turned to his brother. "It was like the novela on Channel 47, Mandito. All that was left was for Valentin and I to stroll by with the violins. Poor Bobby. I hope the casket was made to accommodate his horns."

The Segals both smiled.

Valentin frowned. "You said nothing to Bobby Tex?"

Alfonsito turned back to Valentin. "Do you take me for a fool? When you are contracted to assist a man from a problem, you handle only the problem. To interfere in a matter of the heart is madness. It is a knife with a double edge because the cuckold will never forgive your knowing and the woman will automatically say you are slandering her because she rejected *your* advances. She'll say she did not tell him before to avoid trouble but now, slandered, she has no choice. Well do we know the script, no es así, Mandito?"

"The truth, little brother."

"So you see, Señor Valentin, we gave your Señor Reilly carta blanca."

"Lucky is he who has luck."

"Where is she?"

"We have not seen her since yesterday morning. She is a lady. We wish her well. Good-bye, Señor Valentin."

"You owe me for that night on 86th Street. This is not police business. This is a matter of the heart. You may need another favor some day, muchachos."

The Cubans exchanged glances. Armandito nodded to his brother.

Alfonsito gathered up his coat. "A British island, Virgen Gorda. But only for a few days. After that we do not know, por Dios."

Valentin stood up and threw his arms out to Alfonsito. The two men embraced.

•

The flat-bottomed boat raced out to sea, then around the island toward Long Bay. Reilly stood alongside the pilot, oblivious to the spray. Twenty-five minutes later the boat turned toward land and made straight for the middle of a deep cove. Reilly was drenched.

The sun was blinding, but as the boat drew closer, he could make out a solitary umbrella on the white beach. Then he saw her, the brownness of her skin accentuated by her white bikini. She stood, with hands on hips, her darkness vivid against the dry, pulverized landscape.

The boat stopped close to the shore. Reilly jumped into the water, knee-deep, shoes and all. He waded ashore.

The pilot said, "Your attorney from New York, Miss Bosch. Is it all right?"

Nancy took in the bedraggled figure of Reilly. "Yes, thank you."

"Three o'clock, Miss Bosch?"

"Three o'clock," she answered.

The pilot turned the boat around, and it sped out toward the open sea.

Reilly's eyes scanned the inlet. On a rise behind Nancy, just above the sand, loomed a solitary tree, its drooping limbs parched gray by the sun. The bleached rocks and boulders added to the primeval desolation.

They stood wordless. A pelican appeared, dove down, and struck the water full force.

Reilly flung his jacket. "Goddamn it." He picked up a shell and threw it out into the water, his back to her. "What the hell are you doing out here in the middle of nowhere?"

He sat down on the sand and started flicking pebbles, hard, into the water. She walked over to a towel and sat down under the umbrella ten feet away. Reilly kept his back to her, kicking at the pebbles and shells around him.

"He saw it in a dream," she said.

"What?"

"Bobby. He saw himself on one of the racks at the morgue, like Tony Roman. He started getting the dreams after he went to Bellevue to identify Tony. He went to pieces."

"Is that what you're doing out here? Picking up the pieces?"

Nancy shook her head. "Not really. His relatives took care of everything. They're swarming all over San Juan, looking for the safety-deposit boxes."

"His mother?"

"His mother died when he was born. No, his ex-wife and a bunch of parasites. I had to get out." She hugged her knees. "He used to come here on the boat, his favorite place. This is kind of my last good-bye."

Reilly remained silent.

"He was trying to change, Al."

"You know better than that. What about you, Nancy? I want to know about you."

"I'll stay in Puerto Rico for a while. Maybe go back to school. I don't know. There is no bad luck to last a hundred years."

"Come home with me." Reilly turned to face her. She did not respond. He walked to the shade of the umbrella and squatted down on his haunches, his hands on his thighs. She ran her hand through her hair, brushing it from her face.

The dark, tapered eyes examined Reilly. "I lived with the man a long time."

"You were mine first."

She frowned, turning her gaze from his face. "We were kids. Funny, the gap seems even wider now. It just wouldn't work. Not here, not there. Everything's different, can't you see?"

"No."

"It's not your fault, but it's not mine either. Two people getting along is hard enough without—"

"I know," Reilly interrupted. "Without built-in problems. Nancy, I don't want to hear about worlds and cultures. I won't accept that. We're more alike than we're different. And if we're different, so what? Maybe that's what attracted us. If you tell me, 'Al, I don't feel anything for you as a man. I never will again' . . . worn out as I am, I'll accept that. And I'll walk away from here, and you'll never see me again. Is that what you want?" His arms crossed, he stared at her as she pressed her lips together, saying nothing.

"Nancy, it's been four years. I realize that. I'm not trying to relive the past. I don't expect you to cry in my arms or see phosphorescent sea horses again." She shook her head vehemently. "You don't want to remember that. Okay, maybe it was kid stuff. We can find something better. If not as intense, then steadier, for the long haul. I don't know. But who really knows the waters of the sea before them? Let's take a chance." His eyes searched her face.

She sat silently as Reilly waited. Finally she said,

"You still believe that *West Side Story* bullshit?"

Reilly drew back and stood up quickly. He reached down for his jacket, which lay crumpled on the sand. "Not really," he said as he brushed the sand from his jacket and pants.

"I know. I never used to talk this way before. That's what you're chasing, the befores. They're gone. They never existed. Go find your career, your house in Mineola—"

"Elmhurst."

"How would I know? I never saw it." She shaded her eyes with her hand. "Good-bye, Al Reilly."

Reilly draped the jacket over his arm. He pointed to a steep hill in the distance. "Is that the road back to the hotel?"

"It's a long walk."

"Maybe I'll hitch a ride. Good-bye, Nancy Bosch. I wish you the best."

Reilly made his way toward the hill and the road back.

"The most authentic inside story of the big-time cocaine traffic that has hit print."
Publishers Weekly

SNOW BLIND

ROBERT SABBAG

A BRIEF CAREER IN THE COCAINE TRADE

From Amagansett to Bogotá, from straight to scam to snafu then the slam, SNOWBLIND is an all-out, nonstop, mind-jolting journey through the chic and violent world of Zachary Swan, the real-life Madison Avenue executive who embarked on a fabulous, shortlived career in smuggling—bringing better living through chemistry from South American soil to New York nose.

"A MARVELOUS, CHEERFUL ADVENTURE OF MODERN TIMES . . . ONE PART RAYMOND CHANDLER TO ONE PART HUNTER THOMPSON." *Washington Star*

"A FLAT-OUT BALLBUSTER . . . SABBAG IS A WHIP-SONG WRITER." *Hunter Thompson*

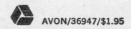 AVON/36947/$1.95